SILENCE AFTER DINNER

SILENCE AFTER DINNER

CLIFFORD WITTING

Murder is always a mistake.
One should never do anything that one cannot
talk about after dinner.
OSCAR WILDE

GALILEO PUBLISHERS
CAMBRIDGE

Galileo Publishers
16 Woodlands Road, Great Shelford, Cambridge
CB22 5LW UK
www.galileopublishing.co.uk

Distributed in the USA by SCB Distributors
15608 S. New Century Drive Gardena,
CA 90248-2129, USA

Australia: Peribo Pty Limited
58 Beaumont Road
Mount Kuring-Gai, NSW 2080
Australia

ISBN 978-1915530905

First published 1953 by Hodder & Stoughton

Series consultant Richard Reynolds

Cover painting by E. Prescott

EU Authorised Representative: Easy Access System Europe - Mustamäe
tee 50, 10621 Tallinn, Estonia, gpsr.requests@easproject.com
Printed in Poland

TO DIANA
OUR DAUGHTER

CONTENTS

PROLOGUE

1947

We paused—an ill-assorted trio—and looked down into the valley through which the Shanho meandered sluggishly eastward towards the distant Yellow Sea. Away to the left, far to the west of us, the jagged peaks of the great mountain range of Hantaiku cut saw-teeth in the upper hemisphere of the half-set sun. Below us, beyond the terraces and the cultivated fields, lay a village, its eight-storeyed pagoda dominating the cluster of little buildings.

"What village is that?" I asked Yi Cheng.

"Taochiaching, master."

"The last Communist outpost?"

My servant shot a glance at the man who stood with us—a soldier of the Communist Pa Lu Chun, the Eighth Route Army, who wore a patched, mud-coloured uniform and the traditional cloth slippers of the Chinese fighting man, whether he served under Chiang Kai-shek or Mao Tse-tung, and carried a rifle dating back to the First World War.

"Yes, master," said Yi Cheng at length.

I stroked my beard as I considered this.

"And where is Shungchow?"

Yi Cheng pointed across the river.

"Over the wooded hills, master—fifteen, sixteen li. *The town*

has not yet fallen to the Pa Lu."

From his resigned tone it was to be gathered that capitulation was only a matter of time. The soldier enlarged on this in a singsong shout, as if repeating a lesson to some stern teacher on the far bank of the Shanho:

"Soon all China will be liberated."

As if in oblique commentary on this statement, Yi Cheng said: "Already, outside the walls of Shungchow, there are ten thousand refugees who have fled across the river."

For a moment or two none of us spoke. It was the soldier who broke the silence.

"We must return to Haolaofen."

Yes, we must return to Haolaofen—to my two missionary companions, captives like myself in the hovel not far from the buildings of our former mission, which we had had to give up to the Pa Lu when Haolaofen had fallen into Communist hands. It was a prison without bars, but everywhere we went, one or more soldiers accompanied us.

It was due to my colleagues that I was now where I was, for it was they who had obtained permission from the mandarin for me to go to Tsinhotun, where the Christian Kio Mei had been reported at the point of death. I had arrived at Tsinhotun too late, for by then old Kio Mei was dead, and now I was on my way back to Haolaofen... and what besides?

Across the Shanho lay safety ... But my companions? What would happen to them if I did not go back? Would they pay the penalty for my default? Would they face torture ... death? I remembered what had happened, in similar circumstances, to the Catholic priests at Suihsien ... Shungchow might fall in a week or a month to the Communists, but now it was Nationalist-controlled. From there the railway ran to Nanking... I saw myself on a ship bound for England ... I saw myself on my beloved

10

South Downs, in the distance Spithead and the Solent, with the Isle of Wight beyond. . . . Then my mind went back to the half-ruined, lice-infested kennel that we shared with the rats at Haolaofen. . . .

Yi Cheng might almost have read my thoughts, for he said:

"The mandarin threatened to bury them alive if we are absent more than three days."

"That is too good for the foreign devils," said the soldier. "Come."

He made to go, but I stopped him.

"I am thirsty. I cannot walk further without a drink." Turning to the servant, I added: "Yi Cheng, go down into the village and fetch water."

"Yes, master."

His flat face was expressionless, but I knew that this Christian Chinese would have gone to his death for me—or would until he discovered the truth about lovely little Hsi-lo—Joy she would have been called in English...That, I admitted to myself, had been an indiscretion and was an added reason for my early departure from Red China. There was but one woman in Yi Cheng's life— Hsi-lo—and if he ever found out. . . But that was not yet.

"Yes, master," he said, and hurried off down the hill.

Under the trees, the soldier squatted down, his rifle between his knees, and began to eat peanuts. I remained standing, watching Yi Cheng as he made his way down the path towards the millet fields. No other living person was in sight; even Taochiaching seemed deserted.

The Shanho gleamed redly from the setting sun, which began to cast long shadows among the trees around us. . . . Yi Cheng reached the outskirts of the village; and acting on an impulse that I felt powerless to control, I swung round on the munching soldier, wrenched away his rifle and brought the stock down on his head.

His shaven skull cracked under his thin cap like an upturned earthenware pot.

The sun went down below the mountains and the red gleams on the Shanho faded. I made sure that the rifle was loaded, then, pressing through the brambles and thick-leaved persimmons, descended the hill, bearing away from Taochiaching and making for a point farther down the river. But before I had gone half a mile, Yi Cheng came running after me. It would be useless to argue with him, to explain my actions, so as he drew near with the pannikin of water—and a question as yet unspoken on his lips—I raised the rifle to my shoulder and shot him through the head.

Then I set off once more for the river, the rifle held ready to deal with anyone else unwise enough to bar my way to freedom.

Chapter One

THE PRODIGAL SON

SOME twelve hundred and thirty years ago, Wilfred, bishop of York, came south to evangelize those Teutonic intruders from overseas, the Jutes. Among his many good works was the founding of a number of churches, one of which was at Yateham, on the seaward side of the South Downs. Little is known about this early church, or how it came to be destroyed or damaged, but one thing is beyond question: after the Norman Conquest it was rebuilt or extensively repaired by one of the lesser barons of that period, and so exists to this day, with its square, squat tower, two circular windows in each side, its little porch, and its shallow-buttressed walls. Right up to the porch are the gravestones of long-dead folk of Yateham, and in a sculptured tomb in the sanctuary lies Sir William Chatthume, who gave his life in the Royalist cause in the last desperate and futile engagement of part one of the Civil War.

One of the several tablets on the chapel walls is to Thomas Micheldever, who was rector for fifty-five years in the eighteenth century. On his death other incumbents came and went until, in 1920, a direct descendant of his was appointed to the living.

This was Andrew Micheldever, who held office for nearly three decades.

Andrew Micheldever was not an ambitious man. In this

little parish in Downshire, some miles westward of the busy town of Lulverton—home of Boyson's Rubber Heels (They Never Wear Out)—he lived a quiet, industrious life, happy with his church, his parochial work, his wife and two children and, not least among his joys, the rectory garden. Yet, for all his contentment with things as they were, he had one ardent desire: that the family connection with the church, broken for two hundred years, should, now it had been resumed, continue from generation to generation.

This aspiration showed promise of fulfilment when Harold, his elder child, took Holy Orders, for Andrew Micheldever held the patronage of the church and would therefore have the right to select his successor. But Harold was seemingly of more adventurous spirit than his father, and took the first opportunity to go into the mission field. Under the Downshire Missions in Asia, he sailed for China a week after his twenty-fourth birthday. That was in 1945.

Fourteen months or so later, when the time for his retirement approached, Andrew Micheldever wrote a long letter to his son, then at the D.M.A. Mission at Haolaofen, in the province of Honan, begging him to come home and assume the rectorate of Yateham. This entreaty was unanswered, the charitable assumption being that, with the conditions prevailing in China at that time, Harold did not receive it. His father followed it with another, more urgent than the first, and to this there eventually came a reply—not from Haolaofen, but from an address in Nanking—which contained nothing more definite than "I'll have to think about it." In any event, it was so long delayed that, by the time it arrived, the opportunity had gone and a new rector, the Rev. Angus Donaldson, had taken Mr. Micheldever's place at St. Anselm's, Yateham.

The father bore this bitter reverse bravely, salving his wounded feelings by frequent mention of "my missionary son in China."

The Rev. Angus Donaldson had a wife and four children, which left the Micheldevers no alternative but to surrender the comfortable rectory, which stood nearby the church—an upstart neighbour of no greater antiquity than the reign of the second George. Perhaps the wisest course—in fact, as things turned out, there was no doubt about it—would have been to move right away from the district, but Andrew Micheldever had his roots in Yateham and was reluctant to begin again elsewhere. Mrs. Micheldever kept her own feelings to herself, yet it might well have been with secret vexation that she received the news that Medlar Cottage, in the High Street, had fallen vacant through the death of the elder Miss Sumner and the removal of her surviving sister to a home for aged gentlewomen.

Medlar Cottage, of rather greater size than its name implied, was two-storeyed and with a thatched roof. The back garden was extensive enough to satisfy Mr. Micheldever's love of horticulture and neglected enough to provide vigorous employment for several pairs of hands, while the front garden was no more than a small square of lawn, with a low, hedge-crowned wall of Downshire flint, a little white gate giving immediate access to the High Street without the intervention of a pavement. In the middle of the front lawn was the medlar tree from which the cottage got its name.

A tenancy was arranged and the Micheldevers took occupation. Mr. Micheldever settled down to augment his modest pension by writing theological books and articles for the religious press, his daughter also contributing to the maintenance of the household by acting in a secretarial capacity at the Lulverton War Memorial Hospital, a sixpenny bus ride from Yateham village.

Angus Donaldson, B.A., B.D., a tall craggy Scotsman, was of the fire-and-brimstone school, and took all his texts from the Old Testament—a favourite of his was "My father hath chastised you with whips, but I will chastise you with scorpions"—which was not much to the liking of his predecessor, who, a milder man, saw fit to remonstrate. Mr. Donaldson, however, was not to be deterred, and that he had his supporters in the parish— those who, however much they might condemn corporal punishment, seemed nevertheless strongly in favour of chastisement by scorpions—was evidenced by the fact that during the darkness of one winter's night some unknown person crept with a piece of chalk up to the gate of Mr. Micheldever's new home and turned "Medlar" into "Meddler."

Mr. Micheldever erased this mischievous amendment with his own hand, and it was noted that thenceforward he attended divine service not at the parish church, but at All Saints, in Lulverton. As his wife and daughter dutifully followed his example, and as the bus fare was sixpence each way twice every Sunday, this added not a little to the financial burdens of the Micheldever *ménage*.

Meanwhile Mr. Donaldson, from the seventeenth-century pulpit of magnificently carved oak, the cresting of the canopy above his head symbolizing Charity and Mercy, preached in a thunderous voice of destruction and the flaming pit to a congregation that, torn between ecstasy and fear, gazed up at him open-mouthed from pews that were old when the body of Sir William Chatthume was borne to Yateham after the disaster at Stow-on-the-Wold in the spring of 1646. Word of this new force in the life of Yateham was slow in getting round, but before two months were out Mr. Donaldson had a full church for every service.

In the winter of 1951 came tragedy. Mr. Donaldson, returning one evening from a visit to a sick parishioner, old Mrs. Barlow, was drowned in Dark Hollow millpond, not very far from Yateham village. Subsequent investigations produced no definite proof as to how this had happened, nor any witness of the occurrence, but the night had been foggy and the ground slippery, which suggested that Mr. Donaldson, while making his way along the footpath skirting the millpond, the direct route from the Barlows' cottage to the rectory, had strayed off the path, missed his footing and pitched over the steep bank into the water below. Though it was on private property, the millpond was used from time to time by the public for the stealthy disposal of unwanted articles, and the medical evidence at the inquest, which dealt inter alia with an abrasion on the dead man's temple, supported the suggestion that drowning had been precipitated by his being knocked unconscious by an ancient ploughshare fished out of the mud by the police. On this evidence, with the added fact that a heel-mark on the edge of the grass bank of the pond had been identified with the pattern on Mr. Donaldson's goloshes, the coroner's jury returned a confident verdict of accidental death, with the recommendation that the millpond be fenced off on the footpath side. This was not done, nor was there locally full agreement with the finding of the coroner's jury.

Until a new rector could be installed, Mr. Micheldever was called in to deputize, and saw in it an opportunity to undo some of the harm—as he understood it—that had been done under Mr. Donaldson's rectorship. His sermons were like the cooing of doves after an earthquake, yet in a few weeks attendances began to decline. Perhaps an explanation of this falling off was to be found in a remark of old Tom Smart as he and Mr. Micheldever worked together one afternoon in the garden of Medlar Cottage.

"Mr. Donaldson," said Tom wistfully, adding a forkload to the bonfire, " 'e were a proper 'ot un."

Although he did not mention it to anyone, not even his wife, it might well have been that Mr. Micheldever thought hopefully again of his son as rector of Yateham. His only open reference—and that a guarded one—was in a letter to Harold, one of the weekly communications penned by either Mr. Micheldever or his wife, a devotion to duty in no way equalled by their son, whose letters home were very infrequent and then no more than a few scribbled lines. Having mentioned the sad and sudden passing of Mr. Donaldson, he went on:

"I am now endeavouring to fill the breach—inadequately, I fear, for the years have taken their toll, but this cannot continue indefinitely. I have been somewhat alarmed by a note from the bishop to the effect that difficulty is being experienced in finding a suitable successor to poor Mr. Donaldson. His unfortunate widow and children are still residing in the rectory, but will have to find other accommodation, of course, when a new man is appointed. You will remember the rectory as a very comfortable home, the more so now that electricity has been laid on and a new hot-water system installed, such an improvement on things as they were during our time there!..."

Ten days after the dispatch of this letter—too soon for a reply to it—an air-mail letter from Harold arrived, but not from China. When he saw that it came from Bangalore,

Mr. Micheldever's first thought was that his son had been transferred from China to the mission field in India, but a quick glance through the hastily written scrawl inside gave him more unwelcome news than that.

"I am sorry to tell you, Dad," wrote Harold, "that I found I hadn't the call. I've always tried not to be a hypocrite, so now I've given up the church and have taken a job with a silk merchant—a Frenchman who's been in business here for years. ..."

This came near to breaking Andrew Micheldever's heart, but Harold's mother was more philosophical and at length persuaded the stricken father that perhaps it was all for the best; that Harold was nearly thirty-one and old enough to know his own mind; and that, after all, India was safer than China nowadays. Notwithstanding this, she had a little weep in private, for she too had fallen into the habit of referring to "our son Harold, who's a missionary in China, you know." An even more practical view was taken by the daughter of the house, Janet, who was Harold's junior by almost two years, and who said on hearing of her brother's apostasy:

"Now he can send us some stockings and things."

But no such feminine necessities were sent from India to Yateham, nor did any other letter follow the first. Instead, late one Saturday evening in the first July of the reign of her Majesty Queen Elizabeth II, there arrived at Medlar Cottage, without a single word of forewarning, Harold Micheldever himself. And he was monstrous drunk.

Chapter Two

BREAKFAST AT MEDLAR COTTAGE

ONE tends to think of a country rector as a man of cheery, rubicund countenance, with an inclination towards an agreeable plumpness, his hair thinning, perhaps, or maybe fled for ever, and his whole being aglow with kindliness. Such was not Andrew Micheldever. He was a spare little man, his clothing having the appearance of being suspended from a wardrobe hanger, his thin neck, with prominent Adam's apple, protruding from his clerical collar with the irresolute, skinny looseness of a tortoise's from its shell. His features were sharp, his nose hooked, his grey hair frizzed; and his light blue eyes surveyed the world through gold-framed bifocals. He was once disrespectfully likened to a moulting goshawk, but as the speaker was young Sir Timothy Chatthume, who, if things had been different, could have claimed kinship with the gentle, gracious lady who was now Mrs. Micheldever, the description was not unbiased.

It could never have been said of Andrew Micheldever:

"The service past, around the pious man,
With steady zeal, each honest rustic ran;
Even children followed with endearing wile
And plucked his gown, to share the good man's smile."

Apart from the fact that the honest rustics of Yateham

avoided such antics, he himself would have been embarrassed by these attentions. Yet he had been popular enough in the parish during his years as rector—an esteem enhanced by the deep affection in which his wife was held for miles around, and, too, by his own wily skilfulness in lawn tennis, badminton and bridge. This popularity would doubtless have continued after his retirement had he not—or so it was affirmed—interfered in church matters no longer within his province. While rector, he had shown a "steady zeal." "The service past," a number of the parishioners lamented that this zeal had not abated—or, rather, that it had not been diverted into some channel less bothersome for Mr. Donaldson. Some even murmured over their teacups or tankards, when news came of that gentleman's death by drowning, "He was driven to it," but this was mere malice. Pin-pricks do not impel to suicide men of his sturdy rampageousness.

Breakfast on the Sunday morning following the return of the prodigal son was an uncomfortable meal for three of those at the table in a front room—attractive, chintz-curtained and, that morning, sun-blessed—of Medlar Cottage. Janet, the fourth, was not similarly distressed, for she had been in bed and asleep at the time of her brother's home-coming. Dark, vivacious, brown-eyed and still on the marriageable side of thirty, she chatted gaily, while Harold tried with no success to do the same, but they could not loosen the tight lines of their father's face, banish the bright spots of colour on his sharp cheek-bones, or alleviate the pensive sadness of their mother. That Harold had returned in such a disgraceful condition had been bad enough, but Mrs. Smart, old Tom's wife, who came each day to help with the housework, had brought tidings before breakfast that destroyed any hope Mr. and

Mrs. Micheldever might have had that they alone knew of Harold's transgression.

Mrs. Smart had had it from Mrs. Battle, helpmate of the landlord of the Seven Stars, Yateham's only inn, that at nearly half past eleven on the previous evening, Harold Micheldever, carrying a fibre suit-case, had rudely aroused the Battle household by beating with his fist upon the door of the saloon bar and demanding entrance in a loud and very alcoholic voice. Mr. Battle, said Mrs. Smart, had endured this assault for some minutes, in the hope that the late and unwelcome visitor would give up and go on his way, but this Harold had not done. Mr. Battle had then got out of bed and gone to the window. On recognizing the man below as the son of Mr. Micheldever, he had feared that something more serious than after-hours refreshment was involved and, putting on his dressing-gown, had gone downstairs.

The door was scarcely unlatched before Harold had pushed his way into the bar, calling in no moderate tone for a large Scotch. The firmness of Mr. Battle's refusal had been tempered with a friendly politeness—though he had promised himself a few sharp words when Harold would be sober enough to take them in—but Harold was not to be turned from his purpose, and Mr. Battle, sweet reasonableness having failed, was preparing to resist an onslaught on his liquor stocks, when P.C. Bristo, roused by the hubbub, had come across from his cottage opposite with his blue tunic pulled on over his pyjamas.

The united efforts, both vocal and physical, of Mr. Battle and the village policeman had got Harold out into the street again. A solemn threat that if he gave any more trouble he would be up before the Lulverton magistrates on Monday morning had had a quietening effect on him, and he had submitted to being escorted by Bristo, who had carried the suit-case, to the gate of Medlar Cottage, this not without difficulty and some divergence. Here, having in mind his unconventional attire, Bristo had left Harold to make his erratic way up the front path, had watched him being taken in by his horrified father, and had then gone back—though this did not emerge during Mrs. Smart's breathless recital to Mrs. Micheldever—for a night-cap with Mr. Battle in the Seven Stars.

Mr. Micheldever was the first to finish his breakfast. With a word of apology, he rose from the table, saying he was going upstairs to his study to put the finishing touches to his notes for the morning sermon. In that, before his son's arrival, he had chosen as his text Proverbs, xx. i—"Wine is a mocker, strong drink is raging: and whosoever is deceived thereby is not wise"—this meant the selection of another text and the preparation of a completely new address.

"Perhaps," he added before he left the room, "you'll follow me up in a few minutes, Harold?"

His son, the victim of the malady known as alcoholic remorse, agreed without much eagerness.

As soon as the door had closed behind Mr. Micheldever, Janet, in defiance of his frequently expressed disapproval, lighted a cigarette before she asked:

"When are you going back?"

Harold's answering laugh was a failure.

"It's always the same! As soon as a fellow comes on furlough, everyone seems to want to get rid of him again."

Mrs. Micheldever tried to explain.

"It's only that we want to know, dear, how long we're going to have you all to ourselves."

She had once been dark and beautiful, this wife of Andrew Micheldever, and she would have been Lady

Chatthume if John, the tenth baronet and direct descendant of that Sir William who had died in the Civil War, had not lost his life in another and greater conflict, the first battle of the Marne. They had become engaged in August 1914 and when, a little over a month later, he had fallen in the attack on Coulommiers, Mary Boyd's life had also ended, though her body had continued to go through the actions of physical existence. After the war, without quite knowing why, she had married Andrew Micheldever and had been a true and dutiful wife to him ever since, the years transmuted her dark hair into a lustrous silver grey, and if her complexion and lips were over-pale, it was because her husband was much against cosmetics—a dislike that did not deter their daughter from their judicious and artistic use. The Chatthume title had passed to John's younger brother, on whose death his son Timothy became the twelfth baronet. Greatly attached to Mrs. Micheldever, it was the custom of this gay and likeable young man to call her "Aunt Mary," but only when they were alone together and there was no one else to hear. She loved him for it.

Mrs. Micheldever now went on:

"How much leave have they given you?"

"As a matter of fact, I'm not—well, I'm not actually on leave."

They both looked at him inquiringly. He lighted a cigarette very slowly before he spoke again.

"I'm not going back to India."

"Harold!" cried his delighted mother. "I'm so glad!" Janet asked with a sister's forthrightness: "Did the Frenchman give you the push?"

"What, old Courvaisier? Oh, I left him some time ago."

"You're dodging the question," said Janet.

"Janet, don't be rude," reproved her mother. "I'm sure

Harold had a very good reason for leaving."

If he had, Harold seemed not disposed to reveal it at this juncture. He said instead:

"I drifted around for a bit, but soon got fed up with it, so here I am—turned up again like the bad penny."

"Have you any plans, dear?"

"Give me time, Mother! I've only just got here. I'll look round and find a job."

"How are you going to live in the meantime?" demanded Janet. "I hope you brought some money back with you, because we haven't any—not to spare."

Harold gave a short laugh and jumped to his feet.

"I think I'll be safer with Dad," he said, and strolled out of the room, a lanky young man, his black hair worn too long, his good looks impaired by over-full lips and a weak chin.

Janet said after he had left them:

"I shouldn't be a bit surprised to hear that he got into trouble in India. He's so undependable."

They began to clear away the breakfast things.

"Janet, dear, you're too outspoken sometimes. You might easily have offended him by suggesting he'd been dismissed."

"I'll bet he was and, couldn't find another job, or he wouldn't have come back. I know Harold, Mummy. What he's going to do now is live on us—or on Daddy. I'll make sure he doesn't live on me."

"We'll have to help him until he can get a position somewhere. What about the hospital?"

"Please, not the hospital. I don't want him there."

"Then Boyson's. I wonder, if I spoke to Mr. Boyson"

"Mummy, don't start arranging things! Let Harold do it for himself. All we've got to do is keep on prodding him.

Otherwise he'll just be a what Dick—what one of the surgeons at the hospital calls reptilia sofa, a lounge lizard."

Mrs. Micheldever looked unhappy, then changed the subject.

"Are you going to be in for tea, dear?"

"What's the food position like?"

"There's a fruit cake, and some strawberries out of the garden. Harold's always been fond—"

"I'm not bothering about Harold. I just wanted to be sure it won't be Starvegate Hall."

There was a slight smile on Mrs. Micheldever's face as she asked:

"Another of your Dr. Dick's expressions?"

"No, but I want to ask him to tea."

"Is this something new, dear?"

"Something? He's more than just that. He's—he's ..."

"Yes, dear? He's what?"

"You'll see. May I ask him?"

"Why, of course. Do you know his other name—or is it too soon for that?"

"Naughty. The nicest mothers don't mock their offspring. His name's Farringdon and he's assistant house-surgeon. I hope you'll like him. I know you will, because it's important."

"You haven't mentioned him before."

"No, I suppose I haven't."

"Have you known him long?"

"Not really. About a fortnight. He's new."

"So I thought."

"I mean, new at the hospital."

Janet went to the door with a trayful of crockery.

"What happened to the last one?" her mother said after her.

26

The girl paused at the door.

"By the way you say it, anyone would think I poisoned him. If you mean Jack Phillips, he was a major blunder. I found out something too awful about him."

"But he seemed such a—"

"He keeps his money in a purse—and that's unbearable in a man."

She was raising her knee to support the tray while she opened the door, when her mother said:

"Don't go, dear. I want to talk to you."

Janet brought back the tray and laid it on the breakfast table with a sigh.

"Oh, heavens. I wilt when you use that tone. Another lecture?"

"Janet, dear, you're twenty-nine."

"Only just."

"That doesn't matter. You'll soon be thirty—and if you don't hurry up, you'll ..."

"Be an old maid all my life."

"You've had so many men friends, and they come so quickly one after the other that it takes my breath away. You know they're always welcome here, but you simply can't go on like this—that is, if you want to get married. And some of them were very nice young men. Lewis Potts—"

"Yes, good at tennis, but I had to decide against him when he proposed."

"You didn't tell me he got as far as that."

"Didn't I? Well, he did—and quite prettily, too. But I had to tell him there was only one thing against it—that I couldn't bear the thought of answering to Mrs. Potts."

"You might have been more tactful, dear. The Pottses are a very old Downshire family."

"There! Pottses—in the plural. It shrieks of the nursery. No, Mummy, it would be too much."

"Then there was Frank Barrett and Trevor—"

"Have pity! Spare me the list, *please*! You make me feel like Jezebel, wife of Ahab, that poor Mr. Donaldson used to get so cross about."

Mrs. Micheldever went to the window and looked out over the lawn in thoughtful silence before she said, without turning back:

"Dear, you know about my first engagement ... It would please me more than anything else in this world if..."

Her voice faded off. From the table Janet said:

"I know what you mean, but it's no good. I simply couldn't live up to being Lady anything. Besides, he's not interested."

"Are you sure?"

"Well, *I'm* not, then."

She came up behind her mother and put her arm round her, her manner much less abrupt as she said:

"Mummy, dearest, you know I'd never hurt you if I could help it. . . . I'm trying hard to find the right one."

Mrs. Micheldever turned, smiled a little, then kissed her on the cheek.

"Don't leave it too long," she said.

Meanwhile, upstairs in his study, Andrew Micheldever was talking earnestly to his son, his only grounds for satisfaction being that his notes on Proverbs, xx. i were not to be entirely wasted.

Chapter Three

THE MAN WHO OWNED A VILLAGE

AS, a few paces behind their parents and under a blazing sun, they walked back home from church after the morning service, Harold murmured to his sister:

"Can you lend me a pound? All my ready cash is in rupee notes."

"How much is a rupee worth?"

"Say one and six."

"So if you give me—let's see . . . Thirteen plus six and six ... If you give me thirteen rupees, I'll give you a pound. I'll let you off the odd sixpence."

"That's fine."

Janet stopped, opened her handbag and extracted a pound note. Harold held out his hand.

"Thirteen rupees, please," said Janet.

"I haven't them on me."

She replaced the note, clipped the handbag shut and started walking again, saying:

"When we get home, then."

"That's the trouble, Jan. They're all in my trunk, which is still on the railway. In a couple of days I'll be—"

"Harold, I admire cleverness—even at lying—and you're not clever. People don't keep money in trunks, where they can't get at it. Why don't you say will I give you a pound?"

"Well, will you?"

"No."

"Thanks very much."

They walked in silence for a while. Then Janet said:

"I'll give you ten shillings—like an idiot."

Half a pound is better than no cash, so Harold instantly accepted. As soon as they reached Medlar Cottage, he changed out of his dark clothes into a suit of khaki drill, brought from India, and slipped out of the house with the murmured excuse that he was going to buy some cigarettes.

"Lunch is at quarter past one," Janet called after him.

Mr. William Battle, licensee of the Seven Stars, was by nature a genial, kindly man, yet something very like a scowl disfigured his big, ruddy face when Harold Micheldever came into the low-raftered saloon bar. Whether he would have refused to serve him, or said the few words he had promised himself, was not to emerge, for Harold had not taken more than two or three paces towards the counter before a voice hailed him:

"Well, if it isn't the old evangelist himself!"

Harold turned and saw a tall, lean-featured, fair-haired young man, clad in the flawless elegance of white shorts and a tennis shirt, who was standing with a breath-taking blonde, her summer frock of such sweet simplicity that it must have cost someone a lot of money. This was Miss Sabina Danbury, star of musical comedy and with the finest legs in the business, who was doing a season at the Empire Theatre in the nearby seaside resort, Southmouth-by-the-Sea. Her companion was Sir Timothy Chatthume.

"Why, hullo, Tim!" said Harold and walked across to them.

Sir Timothy introduced him to Miss Danbury, then asked:

"What's your poison?"

Harold glanced at their glasses, saw that they contained pink gin, and answered:

"A pint of bitter, please—in a tankard."

"Another, Bi?"

"Yes, please," came the prompt answer from the victim of this ungraceful contraction, and she added more crimson smears to the brim of her glass.

As Sir Timothy went up to the counter, she said to Harold:

"I adore gin and angostura. I hope they have it in heaven."

"'Fraid my taste is rather low. It's grand, though, to get back to English beer after years out of the country."

"Oh," said Sabina brightly, putting two and two together, "have you been abroad?"

"Yes—India."

"I'd love to go to India and see the Taj Mahal by moonlight. They say it's one of the best places to stay at in Bombay—right overlooking the sea."

He was wondering whether it was worth while enlightening her, when she prattled on:

"Ensa want me to go to Singapore to give shows to our boys out there. I don't know what to say."

At the counter, customers with a prior claim were having to wait while Mr. Battle attended to the requirements of Sir Timothy, for this young man owned not only Chatthume Place and many acres of farmland, but also most of Yateham village, including the ground on which stood the Seven Stars.

With the two gin glasses in one hand and the tankard of beer in the other, Sir Timothy came back to Harold and

Sabina, who said as she took her glass from him:

"Tim, darling, Ensa want me to go to Singapore. Shall I?"

"I'd stop here if I were you. We all say England's the foulest country in the world—until we're out of it."

"Would you mind if I went?"

"I should be heart-broken."

"Would you come with me?"

Somewhat embarrassed by the drift—or, rather, purposeful direction—of the conversation, Harold drank some beer.

"No can do," replied Sir Timothy. "The idea seems to have got round that I'm a social butterfly instead of the hard-working farmer I really am. Well, Badger, how's tricks?"

This to Harold, who had earned that nickname in his schooldays, not because he was akin to the weasel family—though there were those who would have supported this interpretation—but because his second name was Bagehot.

"Not too rosy."

"Still converting the heathen Chinee?"

Sabina interjected: "He said India. Do they have Chinese in India? I thought they were all punkah-wallahs or something."

"I thought you were in China," Sir Timothy said to Harold.

"I was—for some time. Then I went to India. Now I'm back in the U.K. for good." He grimaced. "If you can call it that."

He sipped his beer again, mindful that he must not finish it too quickly. If he took it slowly—whatever effort the restraint cost him—Tim and the girl might go before it became necessary for him to buy a round. With pink gins involved, Janet's ten shillings would not go far.

"Won't they find a church for you somewhere?" asked Sir Timothy.

Harold looked at him and shook his head slightly. The hint was taken, and the conversation deftly turned to other things.

In the kitchen of Medlar Cottage, Janet was shelling the peas while her mother chopped the mint.

"Harold's a long time," said Mrs. Micheldever.

"Probably gone for a walk."

"I hope he doesn't..."

"Hope he doesn't what?"

"Oh, nothing, dear—only it pains your father so."

"That's not sense. I suppose you mean that Harold may be knocking them back in the Seven Stars."

"Dear, some of the phrases you use—"

"You're afraid he'll get drunk, then—as he did last night. Is that what you mean?"

"But I didn't think you knew. Has somebody—"

Mummy, my poor pet! The church was so buzzing with it this morning that it nearly drowned Daddy's sermon. But I shouldn't worry. If you like I'll slip along to the Seven Stars a little later on, and bring him back."

"Don't let your father know."

Janet transferred the peas from the colander to a saucepan.

"I think you worry too much about the feelings of my respected pater. If he couldn't find something to disapprove of, he'd think the day wasted. He's not a bad old stick in many ways—"

"Janet!"

"Well, he has got some good points, you must admit."

Mary Micheldever looked at her daughter, then her lips

twitched as she scraped the chopped mint off the board into the sink-basket instead of the silver sauceboat.

In the Seven Stars, lovely Sabina was saying:

"I'm going to be late for lunch at Southmouth."

Sir Timothy finished his drink.

"I'll run you back. Go out and hop into the car. I shan't keep you a tick."

When, with a half-questioning glance at both the men, Sabina had left them, Sir Timothy said in a low tone to Harold:

"Let's have it. What's the trouble?"

"I'm up against it, old boy. India didn't want me. I worked my passage home."

"Are you still a parson?"

"No."

"You or they?"

"A bit of each. I wasn't cut out for it."

"Want a job?"

"Anything to keep alive."

"Come along and see me first thing tomorrow."

"Right."

Sir Timothy was about to follow Sabina, when Harold said:

"Under the Old Pals' Act, can you—"

He did not have to go any further. Sir Timothy slipped his hand into a pocket of his snowy shorts and pulled out a couple of pound notes, which he passed over to Harold.

"On account," he said and strolled out, a slim, athletic figure, more like a tennis international than the most prosperous and progressive farmer in Downshire.

Almost before the engine of the long-snouted two-seater had burst into deafening life, Harold was at the counter, asking for a double Scotch, and talking to Mr.

Battle as if he had not seen him for years. Mr. Battle had been prepared for an apology, even for a renewal of the dispute—was, in fact, word-perfect in a short speech to meet either event; and this ingenuous approach took him completely by surprise—so much so that all he could say was:

"Things are much about the same, Mr. Micheldever, thanks for asking."

Yet the explanation was simple enough. Harold was subject to a not uncommon complaint. It may have another name in high medical circles, but "alcoholic amnesia" is a sufficient description; and if the unpleasant incident of the previous evening would remain fresh in Mr. Battle's mind for some time to come, Harold retained of it no recollection whatever. In the light of what was to follow, it is a point worth bearing in mind.

With a pint of bitter and a sizeable chaser busy within him, Harold was in no mood to heed the scriptural injunction: "and whosoever is deceived thereby is not wise." Notwithstanding this, he had enough common sense to know that the Seven Stars was too close for comfort to Medlar Cottage and that Nemesis, in the person of the Rev. Andrew Micheldever, might come upon him at any moment. Accordingly, with a friendly word of farewell to the still stupefied Mr. Battle, he left the Seven Stars and went across to the bus-stop, so that by the time Janet arrived to collect him and take him home, he was on his way to Monk Jewel, the next village, where, at the White Lion, he dallied happily until closing time at two o'clock, and then committed the crowning indiscretion of going home.

Fortunately for him, by that time his father had gone out on some parochial mission, having previously unburdened himself of some testy remarks about Harold's failure to return at the proper time for meals. As she helped her mother to get their protesting relative up to the bedroom hurriedly prepared for him the night before, Janet said:

"What beats me is how he got like this on ten bob."

But the answer came to her later on and, when her mother was in the garden picking strawberries, she slipped upstairs, ran through the snoring Harold's pockets and relieved him of four half-crowns.

At half past four, Richard Farringdon, M.R.C.S., L.R.C.P., arrived for tea, and met with Mrs. Micheldever's immediate approval. His voice was of the kind that reassured the most nervous of patients, even those with nothing wrong with them, who are often more anxious than any. Dressed in a sports coat, grey flannel trousers and suede shoes with buckles instead of laces, he was tall, broad-shouldered and dark-haired, with good looks that fell short enough of classical perfection to make him as acceptable to men as to women. The epithet is to be deplored, but among the girl probationers at Lulverton War Memorial Hospital, he was described as a smasher.

Under a tree in the back garden, tea had been laid on a table. "No balancing on knees," Janet had said firmly. The wasps were already busy carrying out daylight reconnaissance, but, as Janet had said when Mrs. Micheldever had suggested having tea indoors on that account:

"We'll suffer from them wherever we have it, unless we close all the windows and suffocate."

Janet was in all things a realist.

Mr. Micheldever joined them for tea.

"Where is Harold?" he asked as he let himself carefully down in a canvas-seated chair.

"Upstairs resting, dear," replied his wife serenely. "He went for a long walk after church and couldn't get back in time for lunch." She lifted the teapot and added with a light laugh: "You know what Harold is for punctuality."

Janet said, extending two plates towards Dr. Dick:

"Harold's my brother, just back from abroad. Bread and butter or a home-made scone?"

"Yours?" he smiled, taking a scone.

"No—Mother's. I'm a rotten cook."

"You're not, dear," protested Mrs. Micheldever. "Don't you believe her, Dr. Farringdon."

"Why," asked Mr. Micheldever with more than a trace of asperity in his voice, "is Harold not down to tea?"

"I told you, dear. He's upstairs resting. We mustn't forget he's only just finished a long sea voyage."

Had they not had a visitor, Mr. Micheldever would doubtless have pursued the matter. As it was, he contented himself with a grunt and, reaching forward, had a brisk engagement with three or four wasps for the possession of the jam.

They had come to the strawberry stage before Harold emerged from the house and slouched across the grass towards them, his hands in his pockets. He was without a jacket, and his khaki-drill trousers and open-necked shirt looked as if he had slept in them—as indeed he had. The sight of Dick Farringdon, whom he had not expected, took him by surprise. When Janet, not without some diffidence, had introduced him to the visitor, he took his seat at the table, saying:

"Hullo, Dad. Sorry I wasn't on parade for lunch. I thought Janet said it was at quarter past two."

This was not entirely in accord with the excuse put forward by his mother, but Mr. Micheldever's only comment was:

"I trust you will soon accustom yourself to our way of life, different though it may be from that prevailing in India."

"India?" said Dick, looking interested. "Where were you?"

"Bangalore, down in the south—where all the white sahibs go when they retire. A sort of Bournemouth."

"There long?"

Harold took the cup of tea passed to him by Mrs. Micheldever.

"Quite some time," he replied.

This not very informative answer was followed, after a slight but noticeable pause, by a remark from Janet.

"He was with a firm of silk merchants—and the horror didn't send us home a thing."

"It wasn't easy, Jan. Export duty, permits, and so on."

"Hooey," said Janet.

"Have you been abroad, doctor?" inquired Mrs. Micheldever.

"During the war and just after it. I was a surgeon-lieutenant until the Sea Lords gave me a reasonably honourable discharge."

"Did you visit China?"

This question was from Janet, and only she would have put it. China had been little talked about in Medlar Cottage for some time past. It may have been that Dick sensed a tenseness in the other three, for he looked quickly at each in turn before he answered:

"Yes, I was there for several months. When I was due to come out of the Navy, there was nothing much to bring me back home, so I got my release at Hong Kong and toured round China. Then the Reds began to look like winning, so I came away." He turned to Harold. "Not so comfortable as Bangalore."

Janet said with a sweet smile: "Oh, Harold knows that. He's been to China, haven't you, Harold?"

Mr. Micheldever frowned at her. Mrs. Micheldever said: "Janet, dear, we want some more hot water for the pot." The girl rose from her chair.

"Tell him about it, Harold," she said and, taking the jug from her mother, went off towards the house.

But Dick Farringdon's attention was not on anything Harold might have to say. His glance had followed Janet, whose gosamery frock—one that her father would have roundly condemned had he ever noticed it—did not obscure the fact that this delightful, spirited little person had nothing to concede to the gorgeous Sabina Danbury. There drifted into the young doctor's mind Ben Jonson's line: "O so white! O so soft! O so sweet she is!" No, not white; the summer sun had seen to that.

That very observant lady, Mrs. Micheldever, smiled gently as Dick, remembering that his attention should be elsewhere, turned back to Harold, but that young gentleman's only comment on his experiences in China was:

"I'd rather not talk about it. It's like a bad dream."

As Janet came back with the hot water, unconsciously demonstrating that she was as attractive a picture from the front as from the rear, Mr. Micheldever said:

"Which church do you attend, Dr. Farringdon?"

"C. of E., sir."

Mr. Micheldever's brows creased slightly; the abbreviation pained him.

"I meant which church in Lulverton."

"Well, I've not quite made up my mind. You see, I've

only been in the district a couple of weeks."

"We have a charming church here at Yateham, dating back to before the Norman Conquest. Why not join us at evensong?"

Dick looked at Janet.

"Yes, do come!" she said. "Daddy's taking the service."

"My husband has retired," explained Mrs. Micheldever, "but is having to deputise until a new rector is appointed."

"Can't they find you a successor, sir?" smiled Dick.

"It's not quite that," answered Mr. Micheldever. "I have already been succeeded—by a certain Mr. Donaldson, who lost his life in—ah—very tragic circumstances."

"He was drowned in a millpond," added Janet.

"A shocking accident," said her father. "Entirely misadventure. He lost his footing one foggy night and fell into the water. I—and others too—have urged upon the local authorities the need for a fence to prevent further—ah—mishaps, but nothing has yet been done. The footpath is not a public right of way, though it is used to no small extent by local people. The owner of the land is not disposed to accept responsibility for fencing off the pond. He is Sir Timothy Chatthume. You will have heard of him, no doubt?"

Mrs. Micheldever spoke in defence of her honorary nephew.

"I'm sure Timothy has excellent reasons for refusing."

"I trust, my dear," said her husband thinly, "that they will bear examination when the next tragedy occurs."

Janet threw in: "After all, it's private property. People use the footpath at their own risk. He could have it barb-wired off—and that wouldn't please anybody much."

Harold broke a long silence.

"Did I tell you I've a date with him tomorrow?"

"No, dear," said his mother, looking interested.

"I met him this morning in the—I met him down the road, and he suggested I should pop along and have a chat with him."

No one, not even Janet, appeared ready to put a direct question. Harold's rather thick upper lip curled slightly.

"Nobody going to ask? Then I needn't tell you."

He drained his cup and got up.

"If you'll excuse me, I must go and make myself a bit more presentable."

A wasp buzzed round his head. He fought it off with waving arms.

"Get away, you brute!"

Mrs. Micheldever said: "Don't anger it, dear."

"Shall we see you at the service, Harold?" inquired Mr. Micheldever.

"But it nearly stung me. It's safer indoors."

He was about to seek that sanctuary, when his father said:

"I spoke to you, Harold."

"Sorry, Dad. What was it?"

"Are we to have you with us at evensong?"

"If you don't terribly mind, no. I—er—I've some writing to do."

"Very well," said Mr. Micheldever frostily, and Harold, with a nod to Dick Farringdon, left them and went into the house.

Chapter Four

DARK HOLLOW

THE slight breeze sounded like Nature's sigh of relief that the sun's cruel glare was dimmed and that the unbearable blue of the sky had faded into the softer hues of a July night.

Standing in the front porch of Medlar Cottage, Dick was taking his leave.

"You should just catch the bus," said Janet, who was in the open doorway.

"Where's the stop? I'm a child with buses."

"You men! Quite helpless. I'd better show you."

She called back to her mother, then closed the door and led the way down the garden path, saying:

"It stops opposite the Seven Stars, then comes this way."

From his superior height, he looked over the hedge and down along the High Street.

"And it is, too," he said.

"Oh, dear. It's early."

She pulled open the gate, stepped out into the road and waved; but, this not being an authorized stopping-place, the bus -a single-decker—went straight past, the driver looking down from his high seat with the distant expression of Lazarus in the bosom of Abraham, as bus-drivers do when the regulations are to their advantage.

"Bother," said Janet.

"When's the next?"

"That was the last."

"Then I must walk."

"I'll come a little way with you if you like."

"Will you? That's great."

They strolled along together side by side. Soon they left the village behind and, some two hundred yards beyond the last cottages, came to a bridge where a stream ran under the road. Northward, visible over the low parapet to their left, lay rough, uncultivated, marshy land through which the stream threaded its course among reeds and willows, but to their right a high and ancient wall of dark red bricks cut off the view, so that the slow-moving water gave the impression, as it flowed under the bridge, that it was passing into an underground conduit.

"What's the stream called?" asked Dick.

"Snare Brook—usually just the Snare. It comes out on the other side of that wall and wanders off towards the sea. It's a tributary of the Itchen or Hamble or something— one of those rivers that run into Southampton Water."

Thirty yards farther along, they drew level with a break in the wall—the entrance to a well-kept drive that led to a white mansion, of noble proportions and simplicity, set back among the trees. As they passed the pillar-flanked gates, Dick softly chanted a stanza from the song by Mr. Noel Coward:

> "'The stately homes of England,
>   How beautiful they stand,
>   To show the upper classes
>   Have still the upper hand...'"

"That's Chatthume Place," Janet told him, "where Sir Timothy Chatthume lives."

"Marvellous how these old die-hards hang on to their feudal castles."

"He's not old—he's quite young, only about thirty. He hasn't been a baronet long."

They strolled on past the gates.

Janet added: "Lady Chatthume's a dear."

"Lucky fellow. Some men aren't so fortunate with their wives."

"No, it's his mother. Timothy's a bachelor—and very eligible."

"So I should imagine."

"We've known him since we were children. Mother— my mother—was once engaged to his uncle, but he was killed in the First World War."

"And now, I suppose, this Sir Timothy chap is living on the inheritance."

"Dick, that's unkind and not true."

"Sorry."

The road, fairly level thus far, now led them uphill.

"The Chatthumes," said Janet, "used to be the richest family for miles around, but they've not had much these last fifty years. Timothy, I know, is well off, but he's made it all himself—out of scientific farming and breeding race-horses and polo ponies. He works frightfully hard. Up at six every morning."

"Is he the fellow Mrs. Micheldever stood up for about the fencing of the millpond?"

"Yes."

He laughed shortly.

"I'm on dangerous ground. 'Fraid I'm a little prejudiced

against idle lordlings.'"

"Which he's anything but."

"I can see that now. And another thing I can see is that he has more than one staunch champion in the Micheldever family."

"Dick, you sound quite cross."

This time his laugh had lost its edge, though his tone was still aggrieved as he demanded:

"Wouldn't you be if you were in my position, with an affluent, eligible young baronet lurking in the offing?"

Over the brow of the hill loomed the headlights of an approaching car.

Janet said: "I don't see what you mean."

"Don't you? Are you sure?"

Any reply was prevented by the dazzling glare of the headlights. As they moved over to the left-hand side of the road, the lights were dimmed, but the car, instead of passing them, slowed down and stopped level with them—a long, low sports model.

"Hullo, there!" said its only occupant, a bare-headed young man in a dinner-jacket.

"Why, hullo!" replied Janet and walked across to him, followed by Dick.

"Had to stop, you know," said the motorist. "Couldn't just shoot past."

Janet introduced him to her companion.

"This is Dr. Farringdon from the hospital. Dick, Sir Timothy Chatthume."

The two young men exchanged greetings and shook hands.

"Excuse the recumbent posture," said Timothy. "The Bug's an anti-social barrow."

"A car," smiled Dick, "in which two's company and three's an impossibility."

"Not quite. She's taken three in her time—and an Alsatian! Remember, Janet?"

She was saved from replying, for he turned his head towards Dick.

"A doctor, eh? You know, I'd much rather have your I handle than mine. You've worked for yours."

"And *you* work, too," said Janet stoutly. "I was just telling him about the farm and the training stables, and you getting up at six every morning."

"Quarter past, dear. Not too much flattery."

Dick said to him with a slightly puzzled frown:

"Haven't I seen you somewhere before?"

"Not that I remember."

"Perhaps it was abroad," suggested Janet. "You were in China, weren't you, Tim?"

He looked at her sharply.

"What makes you think that?"

"But you were, weren't you?"

"No, not China. While the war was on, I toured the hot spots with the Hill Billies—"

"That's the Royal Downshires," Janet explained to Dick. "He was a major."

"War substantive lieutenant," was Timothy's modest amendment. "We went practically everywhere else, but not China. Burma, mostly."

"I must have thought Burma was in China," Janet laughed, then bent forward to murmur in his ear.

"Have I?" he said. "Oh, Lord."

Janet turned to Dick.

"We'd better be going or you'll be terribly late home."

They said goodnight to Timothy and went on their way, leaving him fumbling for his handkerchief.

As they went on up the hill, Janet said:

"Did you like him?"

Dick parried with another question:

"Why did he jump like that when you suggested he'd been to China?"

"The sudden question must have taken him by surprise."

They walked a few paces in silence.

"Dick," said Janet at length.

"Yes?"

"You mustn't get any foolish ideas about—well, about Tim and me."

"Can I help it?"

"You mustn't—really. Do you know what I whispered to him just now? I told him he had some lipstick on the side of his mouth. So you see?"

Dick was silent. A few yards short of the top of the hill, Janet pointed down a narrow lane to the left, on the corner of which was an A.A. telephone-box.

"That leads to the millpond we were talking about," she explained, for want of anything better to say.

"Shall we have a look at it?"

"Come on, then."

They turned into the lane—a shadowy tunnel formed by trees interlocking their branches overhead. As they went down the flinty slope, she gave a little shuddering sound.

"Frightened?" he asked.

"Terrified."

She slipped her arm into his, adding:

"No wonder country people still believe in goblins.

47

This is called Dark Hollow."

Beyond the foot of the hill, the big trees grew fewer, but to each side of them the undergrowth and shrubs grew thick and high with a lushness that spoke of marshy ground. Old man's beard—the wild clematis——climbed and twisted everywhere.

In a little while, they came suddenly upon a cottage, which stood on their right and was set so far forward that it was but a single step from the public thoroughfare into the front parlour. The ground floor was in darkness, but the dim, flickering light of a candle showed between the curtains of the upstairs room.

Instinctively, as if they were intruding on the privacy of others, they stepped more lightly as they went by the cottage, and it was not until they had passed it that Janet said in almost a whisper:

"That's where the Barlows live. She's a dear old soul."

"I don't envy them. This valley smells like Slimy Creek at low tide."

"That's from the millpond.... It was Mrs. Barlow that Mr. Donaldson came to visit the night he was drowned. She has chronic arthritis and can't leave her bed. They say she never will."

Dick grunted sympathetically. Janet went on:

"The pond's just a little farther along."

They came to a humpbacked bridge, but instead of crossing it, Janet drew him to the left, with the warning:

"Mind, it's a bit steep."

Between the end of the bridge and the bushes bordering that part of the lane there was a gap through which she led him. They stepped down a grass bank, worn bare by many feet over the course of years, on to a footpath that led along the edge of the brook. This soon widened out into the millpond, which, covered with blanket-weed—except for a central channel kept fairly free by the main flow of the water—looked pleasanter then than in daytime. But the night could not hide its other ugliness: the stench of it.

The water was about two feet below the level of the path, and here and there, close to the bank, were clumps of flag and reed-mace, which is so often wrongly called bulrush. On the far side were willows and thickets of alders.

"This is the part Daddy thinks should be fenced," Janet said as they skirted the pond.

"Certainly perilous on a black and dirty night. What's that infernal row?"

"Why, the water-wheel, of course."

"Sounds more like a bulldozer with asthma."

"It's very old. It never stops and it's been doing it for years—ever since I can remember. No wonder it's crotchety and clanky. You'd be."

The mingled sounds of machinery and rushing water increased as they drew near to the end of the pond, where they left the path and passed on to a narrow footbridge. Here they paused side by side, their hands on the wooden rail, and looked back, across the pond. Just below the planks on which they stood, the water passed between the rusty iron bars of the trash-rack and flowed into the gut, the concrete gully leading to the wheel. In the bedroom of the Barlows' cottage, the only habitation in that dank little valley, the candle still burned. To the right rose the trees that, even in daytime, shut off all view of the road on which they had met Timothy Chatthume. In the clear sky, the stars seemed not as pin-holes in a dark parchment, but as tiny floating spheres of silver.

Dick said: "So this is where poor old what's his name was drowned."

"Mr. Donaldson, yes. He must have come from the cottage the same way as we've just come, except that he didn't get as far. Just about there"—she pointed to a section of the bank on their right—"the police found the mark of one of his goloshes, and they decided that he thought he'd got to this bridge before he actually had."

"But why did he choose this route?"

"It's a short cut back to the rectory."

"And he fell in the pond, just like that. Seems curious."

"Don't forget it was foggy. You get all sorts of funny delusions in a fog. Dark Hollow's famous for its fogs in the winter-time and autumn. But don't let's talk any more about Mr. Donaldson." She looked around and gave a happy sigh. "What a marvellous night it is!"

In his deep, attractive voice he quoted:

"" As when, upon a tranced summer night,
   Those green-rob'd senators of mighty woods,
   Tall oaks, branch-charmed by the earnest stars,
   Dream, and so dream all night without a stir.'"

"Darling, that was lovely! Who wrote it?"

"Say that again."

"I asked who wrote it."

"A youngster called John Keats. What did you say before that?"

"I said it was lovely."

"Evasive child."

He edged nearer to her, taking his hand off the rail,

but—as if by chance—she escaped his encircling arm by turning suddenly and moving across to the other rail.

"Isn't it quaint?" she said.

Not at all interested now in their surroundings, Dick stepped to her side.

"Janet—" he began.

"Do look at it. It's the only one for miles."

With an impatient ejaculation he complied.

Dark Hollow mill was an ancient building of Downshire stone, which, nearly white when quarried, weathers to a smoky grey. The roof had once been entirely covered by red tiles, but was now by no means waterproof. From the lower left-hand wall—though Janet and Dick could not see it from where they stood—projected the shaft for the water-wheel, which was directly ahead of them, but on a lower level.

He felt in his pocket for cigarettes.

"Smoke?" he asked, proffering the packet.

"You've only two left."

"Just the right number."

"No, not your last."

"They're not. I've a hidden reserve."

When they had lighted up, he tossed the empty packet into the gut and they watched its sedate progress towards the wheel.

The water was only a foot or two deep; freed of weed and rubbish by the trash-rack, it flowed smoothly along the gut until, at the far end, it reached the gate, which could be raised or lowered according to the flow, but had the appearance of not having been adjusted for years. At the gate, the water lost its serenity again and leapt excitedly over on to the vanes of the wheel, which, of the type known as overshot, was turned by the weight of the water rather than by its velocity.

The cigarette-packet reached the gate and was flung over it.

"Can't see much of the wheel," said Dick.

"Follow Auntie."

She led him along the bridge, back the way they had come. The gut was not the water's only means of egress from the pond. Close to the bank was a spill-way, where it poured over an adjustable sluice-gate and cascaded down a steep little rocky channel, to rejoin Snare Brook on the lower level beyond the mill. Between this miniature Niagara and the lichened brickwork supporting the gut was a flight of uneven stone steps.

"Be careful," she warned before they descended. "They're steep and may be slippery."

"Just a minute, then."

He pulled out a pencil torch and directed a slim beam of light down the steps.

"It's probably alive with frogs," said Janet as she started down.

They reached the foot. On their left, alders and lank weeds were held back from further encroachment by the spill-stream. Before them was a narrow strip of grass, marshy from the spray thrown off by the wheel on their right.

"What an ugly monster!" said Dick, playing the light on it.

The great wheel, its supported axle not far above the level of the ground, was rusty and blotched with green, particularly round its circumference, which had the same slimy appearance as the surface of the millpond; the chlorophyceae are not an attractive genus. From the ends of the vanes trailed weeds that had slipped through the trash-rack, and the wheel was revolving at a much higher speed than might have been imagined from the stagnancy of the pool that fed it.

"Funny," said Janet, "but it's not so noisy down here. Not exactly quieter, but it's all water noise."

"The machinery part will be inside the building. See where the shaft goes through the wall. What's the mill used for, do you know?"

Janet shook her head.

"No, I don't. I suppose they ground corn with it once upon a time, but they don't now. I'm sure of that."

"Then why keep it running? "

"I've no idea. Timothy Chatthume could tell us. It's his."

Despite the warmth of the night, she shivered and looked around them with an apprehension unusual in so matter-of-fact a young woman.

"I don't like it here," she confessed. "So clammy it gives me the horrors. I keep on thinking of snakes and big lizards."

He laughed reassuringly.

"Not in Downshire. I'm glad almost, though. You're so—so ruthlessly efficient that it's nice to discover some feminine weaknesses."

"Do I seem like that?" she asked, genuinely surprised.

"Just a little, but not nearly enough to make you a Medusa. Can we go this way?"

"No, it's all bog this side of the brook."

He shone the torch again for her to precede him up the steps. Back on the footbridge, Janet gave a sigh of relief.

"That's better. Look, the moon's coming up."

53

The moment seemed suitable, but he had no chance to take immediate advantage of it, for she went swiftly on:

"The Snare bends to the left a little farther down, then goes under the bridge—you know, the one we crossed over—and runs right through the grounds of Chatthume Place. When we were kids—and our parents weren't watching—we used to sneak the skiff from the boathouse, and come all the way up as far as here. Sometimes we fished, but we didn't often catch anything."

"Who's we?"

"Harold and I—and Tim, of course. It was his father's skiff, so we had to invite Tim."

Her little laugh found no echo.

"Janet, dear," he said gravely, "would you mind very much if I kissed you?"

"No, I think I should like it."

Three or four minutes later, she gently disengaged herself.

"Now we must go."

"Just another moment or two. Look, I'm far too incoherent a wooer to put it into words, but you know how I feel about you, don't you?"

"Yes."

"Is that all you can say?"

"I'm incoherent, too."

"Do you . . .? Do you . . .? Dammit, you know what I mean. Help me out."

"We've only known each other a fortnight."

"Five minutes was long enough for me. I want you to be my wife. Will you, Janet?"

"I don't know . . . I'm not sure. . . . Dick, you said I'm ruthlessly efficient. I'm not really—not ruthless, but I can't bear people who won't face facts."

"But I—"

"No, not you. But marriage is serious—and permanent, if you don't want one of those beastly divorces. Daddy would be terribly shocked if he heard me say it, but I believe there's a lot to be said for trial marriages."

He laughed half-humorously.

"I'm shocked, too. Do you really mean it?"

"Yes, up to a point. Marriage isn't just having babies and—getting ready to have them. It's living together. We might get dreadfully on each other's nerves after a month or two—and then what?"

"I'm sure we shouldn't."

"That's what all men say."

"And how do you know?"

"Well, that's what all the ones who've proposed to me have said."

"So I'm not the first?"

"Of course you're not."

"Oh, Lord. I'd hoped I was."

"You're the seventh—no, eighth. I'd forgotten Trevor Kennard. He's so easy to forget. That's why I didn't marry him."

Dick chuckled.

"What an amazing child you are! But seriously, dear, think about it. I won't stampede you."

Tactfully he changed the subject by turning towards the mill.

"This old thing intrigues me, rumbling and grunting away all by itself, like a lonely hippo in a swamp. I wonder what's inside. Shall we peep?"

"It's getting awfully late."

Disregarding this reminder, he walked along the bridge. The footpath did not turn immediately, but skirted the eastern mid northern sides of a stone-flagged yard, now overgrown with weeds from long disuse as such, which was below the level of the footpath and protected by a brick wall. Having turned the comer of the wall, the footpath sloped fairly steeply and I rejoined the brook a short distance below the mill. Though normal users of the footpath kept to it on leaving the bridge, a flight of stone steps, similar to that on the southern side, gave direct access to the yard for those whose objective was the millhouse.

"Another suicide pact," said Dick as they went down them.

In the yard, away from the water, the sounds of machinery were much more pronounced. The millhouse's heavy wooden door was firmly secured by a massive and businesslike padlock, out of keeping, in its modernity, with its surroundings. To one side of the door was a small window. The panes were covered with cobwebs inside, but, with the help of the torch, they could see part of the building's interior. Immediately in front of them was a wooden staircase leading up to a hole in the upper floor. To the left of the staircase, where the main shaft came in through the southern wall, were the gears and wheels for transmitting the power from the water-wheel. A pulley carried an endless belt, which ran under the staircase to a piece of machinery, causing a plunger to move backwards and forwards. This was working smoothly enough, but the pulley geared to the water-wheel shuddered at every third or fourth revolution, as if the shaft was loose in its bearings.

"Looks like a reciprocating pump," said Dick as they peered through the grimy panes. "Why the devil anyone should—"

A man's voice spoke.

"What be ee doin' daoon there?"

Janet jumped and gave a startled cry. Coming down the steps was an elderly man dressed in the square-crowned hat and black suit appropriate to a rural Sabbath. His wrinkled old face was clean shaven, but tufts of grey beard grew down each cheek. He carried a stout stick and was followed by an Airedale terrier.

"Good evening," Dick smiled politely, as the old man hobbled along the yard towards them.

With nose down, the dog went excitedly in search of rats or other prey among the weed-cloaked rubble, millstones and such discarded debris as rusty farming implements that littered the yard.

"What be ee doin' 'ere?" his owner demanded of Dick.

"Oh, just having a look round."

"This be proivate praarperty. Ee'd do best to keep ayoot."

"May I ask what business it is of—"

Janet's hand on his arm restrained him.

"Dick, this is Mr. Barlow."

The old man bent forward and peered into her face.

"Aw, it be ee, Miss Micheldever."

He raised the knob of his stick to his hat.

"We were just walking past," she explained, "when we—when we thought we heard something funny going on inside, so we came down."

"That be on'y the wheel, miss. 'Er do maake queer noises in 'er sleep, loike. 'Er'll boide till mamin', when mebbe Oi'll give 'er a drarp o' oil."

"Do you look after it, then, Mr. Barlow?"

"Oi do thaat, miss. Sir Timothy, 'e put me in chaarge

of 'er."

Dick said rather impatiently: "But what's the purpose of it? What does it do?"

His tone seemed to offend Mr. Barlow, who looked at him with disfavour as he replied:

"Oi told ee Sir Timothy put me in chaarge of 'er. But 'e didn't tell me to answer naw questions. That be Sir Timothy's concam, nart youm or moine."

"Dick," said Janet, fearing a scene, "we must go. Good night, Mr. Barlow."

"G'noight, miss. Taak care 'ow ee go."

Janet took Dick's arm and drew him away. As they walked across the bridge, Dick muttered:

"What was he warning you against—the perilous steps or me?"

"We mustn't vex him, Dick," she murmured back. "He's very old."

"But we weren't doing any harm."

"He's responsible for it to Timothy. You know how jealous of things old people get. He probably lives for the mill."

They reached the footpath on the other side of the pond. Dick was not entirely mollified.

"What's that pump bringing up?" he demanded.

"Water, I suppose."

"Coals to Newcastle."

They came back into the lane and passed through the tunnel into the road.

"This is where we say good night," said Janet.

"Oh, no, it isn't. I'm not letting you go off alone at this time of night."

When they reached the front gate of Medlar Cottage, a

light still shone from one of the upper windows.

"The parents are waiting up for you," said Dick. "What an inconsiderate ruffian I am."

"That's Harold's room," explained Janet. "He said he was going to do some writing, but it can't have taken all this time."

"Writing a book about China, perhaps."

"The very last thing he'd do. I must go in."

"Just a final one?"

"No, not here."

"Right. But don't forget what I asked you, will you?"

"Yes, I'll think about it. Don't be too . . ."

"Too what?"

"Pessimistic."

As she turned and ran up the garden path, the light in Harold's bedroom was switched off.

殺

I cannot keep Yi Cheng out of my mind. That inquiring expression on his flat face, changing to horror as I raised the rifle to my shoulder. ... He was a faithful servant and I shot him down in cold blood. Why? So that I might escape from China and the terrors of Communism. Now I am back in peaceful England. Have I found contentment of mind? Freedom from the aching suspense of every waking minute at Haolaofen—the sickening fear of what the next minute might bring. Freedom from that, yes; but now I am prey to doubts and uncertainties no less oppressive, but of a different kind, for then I had the moral support of my two companions. Whatever we suffered, we would suffer together and in the conviction of righteousness. Now there is a great barrier between us. No, not a barrier, but an abyss.

Hamlet says: "Thus conscience does make cowards of us all." It does more—and worse: it forces us into a life of deception that grows increasingly difficult to maintain. All my actions, all my words are lies. Every day is an eternity, and without drugs or drink I cannot sleep at night. A knock on the door of our hovel at Haolaofen might have been a summons to go out and dig our own graves and then be buried in them alive. Would it have been more horrifying to open the door then than to open it tonight and discover on the threshold one or both of those comrades I so shamefully deserted?

I am acting a part—and acting it badly. Some day someone will suspect the truth. And then . . .? Can I be hanged for the murder of Yi Cheng? Is there proof? Dead men tell no tales, but. . . Let me consider it dispassionately.

While Yi Cheng was fetching the water, I killed the Pa Lu soldier with the butt of his own rifle, then shot Yi Cheng with the same weapon. Those are the facts. How can they be twisted to my advantage?

Yi Cheng could have killed the soldier. Seizing an opportunity, he clubbed him to death before I could prevent him. Our only course then was to escape. We took the rifle with us, Yi Cheng carrying it. After some distance, he tripped and the rifle, which the careless soldier had left cocked, went off and the bullet went through Yi Cheng's head. "What did you do then?" they are bound, to ask. Made my escape across the Shanho by bribing a boatman. "And the rifle?" Tell them the truth: I threw it in the river. No, unconvincing rubbish, especially Yi Cheng's accident.

Another version. The three of us were on our way back from Tsinhotun. Yi Cheng suddenly tried to escape and the soldier shot him. In a fit of unreasoning rage at the loss of my devoted and beloved servant, I snatched the rifle from the soldier and clubbed him to death. Then, knowing what I should suffer at the hands of the Communists if they were to capture me, I fled to Nationalist-controlled territory. There is a discrepancy: I left the bodies nearly half a mile apart. Put it this way. The soldier was so frightened by my anger at this brutal murder that he fled, dropping the rifle in his haste. I snatched it up, ran after him, caught up with him at length and dispatched him.

There is still a serious weakness. If the soldier shot Yi Cheng as he tried to escape, the bullet would have entered through the back of his head. Well, then, Yi Cheng flung himself suddenly at the soldier, who shot him in self-defence. Will those who knew gentle Yi Cheng believe that? "For ways that are dark and for tricks that are vain . . ." But Yi Cheng was a devout Christian, and physical violence was abhorrent to him . . . Hsi-lo? Yes, in her defence, or in the defence of her honour, Yi Cheng might have struck, but this was not such an emergency.

One ray of hope. Undoubtedly the Communists would have discovered the bodies and placed the blame on me, but those of my own race, those who could now condemn and punish me, perhaps they did not see Yi Cheng or which way the bullet had passed through his head. It might well be that they do not know how he died—or even that he is dead. They would not believe anything the Communists told them about me.

Then what is the strength of the case against me? There were no witnesses. It is my word against the word of two Chinese who will never speak again. Yet, proof or no proof, there may be those who are convinced of my guilt. Could I face them, those two missionaries whom I left to their fate at Haolaofen? With the best story ever concocted, with the strongest alibi ever forged, could I stand up to them as a man of honour, conducting myself in such a way that they think me innocent? I doubt it—I gravely doubt it. Their condemnation might not be spoken, yet I should see it in their eyes—as they would see guilt in mine. A greater punishment than the gallows.

But do my fears carry me too far? Five years have passed. Even if they too escaped, perhaps I shall never see them again. I have not dared to make inquiries about them. If they did escape, but were killed by the Communists, I should have nothing to fear. . . . 'Greater love hath no man than this' . . God, what a contemptible cur I am.

Chapter Five

DEAD MAN'S SHOES

ANDREW MICHELDEVER'S lean features denoted conflicting emotions as he read through the only letter that came to Medlar Cottage on the Monday morning. When he had thoroughly absorbed its contents, he looked across the breakfast table through his gold-framed spectacles, first at Harold and then at his wife. Harold's attention was on his plate, but Mrs. Micheldever said with a smile:

"Andrew, dear, you look glad and sorry at the same time." Janet said: "Then I can guess what it is."

Mr. Micheldever, though he had not yet put it into words, was not pleased with his daughter. Dr. Farringdon seemed a nice, gentlemanly young fellow, but that was no reason why Janet should be out so disgracefully late with him. He now glanced at her, his pale blue eyes half hidden by the lids, then slipped the letter back in its envelope without a word. Janet grimaced.

"Aren't you going to tell us, Daddy?"

"It is a business communication," he replied and put it away in the pocket of his grey alpaca jacket.

Harold was moodily working his way through his bacon and egg. His mother said to him:

"What time are you seeing Timothy, Harold?"

He looked up from his plate.

"He said first thing, whatever that means."

"Then," said Janet, helping herself to toast, "you're two hours late. Tim's first thing is six ack-emma."

Harold's heavy mouth fell open.

"Good Lord! It isn't, is it?"

"Six-fifteen, to be exact. That's when he gets up, anyway."

"Janet's joking, dear," said Mrs. Micheldever. "I'm sure he didn't expect to see you then. I should go as soon as you've finished breakfast."

"I'll go when I'm ready," was the sour reply.

"Harold," said Mr. Micheldever, scarlet patches on his high cheek-bones, "I prefer you not to address your mother in such a tone."

Harold threw down his knife and fork on his plate, rose to his feet, glared at his father, then slouched, silent and resentful, out of the room. They heard him go upstairs and slam his bedroom door.

"Oh, dear," said Mrs. Micheldever, glancing at the plate, "he's left most of it, and food's so hard to get. Andrew, dear, I think you're just a little—"

"You know my views. That should suffice. Janet, I wish to see you in my study before you leave for the hospital."

"If it's about last night, Daddy, you can say it now. No— I'll say it. Dr. Farringdon and I went for a little walk to Dark Hollow mill. Why? Because he wanted to see it and I wanted to go with him. He brought me all the way back to the front gate, sound in wind and limb."

"I am averse to such behaviour. It is one thing for you to invite Dr. Farringdon here—your mother and I are always pleased to welcome your friends—but it is quite another thing for you to be—ah—dallying with him in Dark Hollow well into the night."

"Daddy," replied Janet with sweet firmness, "I'm going

to be perfectly frank with you. I'm twenty-nine, not seventeen, and I'm going to live my life as I want to live it. If you disapprove so strongly, I'll move to the L.W.M.H. hostel."

It was Mrs. Micheldever who protested: "Janet, don't be silly. This is your home until some nice husband takes you away from it. Daddy gets so worried—and so do I, darling—when you're out late and we don't know where you are or when to expect you. In the newspapers every day—"

There was no anger in Janet's voice when she said:

"That's not what Daddy's getting at. His real grouse is that I don't ask his permission before I do anything. If he was a bishop, people'd say I was tied to his apron strings. I'm sorry I was late last night; I'm sorry if I made you anxious: but I'm not a child and I don't intend to be treated like one. Now I must go."

She left her seat and went across the room, pausing at the door to add before she left them:

"You funny old darlings, but I love you both for it."

Alone with her husband, Mrs. Micheldever said with a faint smile:

"Our consolation, dearest, is that this has been going on ever since Adam and Eve—except they had no daughter."

An apparently casual remark, yet made with feminine guile. Her husband leant back in his chair, bringing his splayed fingers together across his narrow chest.

"There is variance of opinion on that point. Certainly in the fourth chapter of Genesis we read that Eve bore two sons, with no mention of daughters. It is, however, a tradition among the Mahometans—and a tradition of no little antiquity—that both Cain and Abel had twin sisters—Aclima, the twin of Cain, and Jumella, the twin of Abel. Cain wanted Aclima for his wife, but it was their father's desire that each son should marry the other's twin."

"Even that wasn't very respectable."

Mr. Micheldever gave a dry chuckle.

"If we are all descended from Adam and Eve, there must have been mothers for their grandchildren. The Mahometan story is that this so angered Cain that he slew Abel to prevent him from marrying Aclima."

"Which means we're descended from Cain—a murderer."

"So we must suppose if we attach any credence to this story."

The door opened, but neither noticed.

"It's dreadful to think," said Mrs. Micheldever, "that we've a murderer in the family."

A sharp ejaculation made them turn towards the doorway, in which stood Harold. Mr. Micheldever gave him no more than a casual glance, for he was now well in the saddle of his hobby-horse.

"Modern theological thought—"   "

"Just a minute, dear. I think Harold . . ."

"I—er—yes, Mother. I came back to apologize for my infernal rudeness just now. Dad, I'm sorry."

His ill-temper quite dissipated by this interesting discussion, Mr. Micheldever came near to beaming.

"Thank you, Harold. Let us consider the incident closed."

"Jolly decent of you. I'm just off to Chatthume Place."

His mother asked: "Will you be home to lunch, dear?"

"It all depends. May I leave it open?"

"Yes, of course, dear. It will be here if you want it."

Mr. Micheldever wagged a jocular finger at him.

"And remember, my boy—one o'clock."

Harold grinned sheepishly and left them. Mr. Micheldever took up his theme once more, his wife, with her mind on other things—Harold, chiefly—following the disquisition with every appearance of attention. At length Mr. Micheldever said:

"And now, my dear, I must tell you the news. I hesitated to mention it too precipitantly in the presence of the children."

He drew the envelope from his pocket.

"This is from the bishop. He tells me that a successor to Mr. Donaldson has been found at last."

"Dearest, how splendid!"

"Earlier you read my feelings aright, Mary. I am both glad and sorry. Glad because I am a tired man and getting old; sorry that, after my short—ah—Indian summer, if I may so describe it, I can no longer serve the parish."

"Who is the new rector?"

His brows creased.

"That is another cause for regret. You will share my feelings when I tell you that he was formerly a missionary in China. The bishop informs me that he was taken prisoner by the Communists and treated with the greatest brutality until, by some fortunate chance, he managed to make his escape."

She asked with some hesitation: "Which Society?"

"The Downshire Missions in Asia."

She drew a sharp breath. He went on:

"Yes, as was Harold. I pray that it is not so, but it may well be that he was acquainted with Harold and aware of his—ah—calamitous dereliction"

"Dearest, you mustn't take that so much to heart. I think Harold acted very honourably by resigning as he did. He needn't feel ashamed—and nor should you." She controlled a sigh and added inconsequentially: "And China's a vast country."

"All we dare hope is that Harold will not further disgrace us. If the new rector were to come upon him in the condition in which he returned here on Saturday night, I should never hold up my head again."

"You haven't told me who he is, dear."

He referred to the letter.

"The Reverend Bruce Gault, Master of Arts and Bachelor of Divinity."

"Bruce Gault. What a hard, uncompromising name!"

"Yes, indeed. I trust we shall not find him so dogmatic and overbearing as—ah—certain others we have encountered. He will be inducted at the beginning of August and will take occupation of the rectory as soon as Mrs. Donaldson can be—ah—prevailed upon to relinquish it."

Harold, meanwhile, was on the way to keep his appointment. It was quicker to walk than to wait for the bus, so he set off along the road and reached the entrance gates of Chatthume Place just as Timothy was coming down the drive in the car he called the Bug. The fearsome monster was brought to a stop and Timothy shouted over the engine, which ticked over like a quick-firing anti-aircraft gun:

"Hop in. I'm going to Lulverton."

Harold obeyed.

"So you want a job?" said Timothy as they moved forward.

He swung the wheel and they turned to the right into

the road.

"Very much so. I've come back from India without a bean and can't live on the parents."

"Are you fussy about what you do?"

"I'm desperate enough to try anything."

"Fancy yourself as a rent collector?"

He changed gear and they roared up the hill.

"Yes, I should think so."

"Then you're the man for me. Sipworth and Parrack have been our agents for years, but they got so slack that I took the business away from them. You've turned up at just the right moment."

Ahead of them, out of the tunnel of trees that led down to Dark Hollow, hobbled a bent figure. He waved his stick at the approaching car, which Timothy brought to a stop.

"Good morning, Barlow."

"Marnin', Sir Timothy," said the old man, touching the soiled and ancient Panama hat that was the week-day substitute for the Sunday boxer.

"Lovely day again."

"Oi were on me waay raoond to see ee."

"What's the trouble?"

The glance from Barlow's watery eyes transferred itself to Harold, then went back to Timothy.

"It do be confidential loike, sir."

"Out with it. I'm in a hurry."

"It be abaoot the mill, sir."

He jerked his head backwards, then turned and went a few yards down the lane. Timothy gave an impatient ejaculation and got out of the car, a manoeuvre similar to alighting from a hammock. He walked round the car and joined Barlow, who held him in earnest conversation for some minutes. Then Harold, who had missed the rest, heard Timothy say:

"Right. I'll see what can be done."

He returned to the car.

"I heard a story once," he said to Harold as he slid back into his seat and they started off once more. "You know these old cannons you see standing in parks and places? Well, there was one in a town where an old war veteran lived—nearly as old as the cannon. Somebody took pity on him and gave him a quid or so a week to look after the Crimean fieldpiece—an unnecessary job, if ever there was one. After a while, the old chap fell sick, and when visitors came to see him in hospital, the first anxious question he always asked was: 'Is all well at the gun? ' Barlow's the same with that confounded mill."

"Lives for it, eh?"

"He'd live *in* it if I gave him half a chance. Now, about this rent collecting. Being a bloated aristocrat, I own most of the cottages round here. I make about tenpence a year on each, but that's beside the point. Your job will be to go round every Monday to collect the rents—or try to. I can fix you up with a bicycle."

"That sounds fine. I prefer an open-air life."

"There's more in it, mind, than shovelling up the specie. There's a ten-minute chat at every cottage door. If the roof's not letting in water, there's a funny smell coming up through the parlour floor. Or you may have to listen to a full acccount of Mrs. Jones's internal disorders, and exactly how, when and why she was took bad."

"I'll put up with that," laughed Harold.

"Repairs will be your pigeon, too. If you think anything needs doing, you'll fix it up with the builders or get the plumber to call round. In other words, as we used to put it in the Army, you'll be i.c. Cottages. By the way, Badger, I hope you've got over the old failing?"

"Meaning?" Harold asked sharply.

"The one you had at school—putting the pound after the figures instead of before them."

Harold looked relieved.

"Not entirely. I've tried to break myself of it."

"Bad thing when you're trying to keep books. Is it a deal?"

"You bet. I can't say how grateful I am."

They discussed the question of salary. Harold was glad that he was not called upon to name a figure, for the one suggested by his new employer was much in excess of what he would have dared to ask—was, in fact, twice as much as the job was worth. Trying not to show too much eagerness he accepted.

"Good," said Timothy. "Today's Monday, so you start this afternoon."

They rounded a bend before he asked casually:

"Who's this doctor chap Jan's got hold of?"

"Just that. He's a doctor chap and she's got hold of him. Richard Farringdon."

"Will anything come of it?"

"Not if I know Jan. With men, she's like a woman at a bargain sale, picking up this and that, testing for quality then chucking them back on the pile till she finds the right colour and not too shop-soiled. If Jan spends much longer picking and choosing, she'll have to take what's left—or nothing at all."

Sir Timothy Chatthume's only response was a grunt.

At this same time Mr Micheldever was called upon

at Medlar Cottage by Mrs. Donaldson. Though her late husband had been a Scot of Scots—withal a priest of the church of England—she was a London woman, hers a complete contrast to his masterful personality. Slight of build, with greying Whispy hair, she was usually vague and irresolute in her department and was that morning tearful also.

The trouble was, of course, the rectory. She too had received a letter from the Bishop of Whitchester.

"Where am I and the children to go?" she almost wailed, her gestures and whole bearing remindful of a butterfly balked by a window-pane.

"Have you not made inquiries elsewhere, Mrs. Donaldson? I should have imagined that, knowing your tenure might be brought to an end at—well, one might say—at any moment—you would have—'"

"But I have! I've tried everywhere. Ian and Margaret are at boarding-school, but the two younger ones ... What am I going to do? Where are we to go?"

"As a temporary expedient, perhaps some relative—"

"No, never that! Don't ask me to explain." Her tone changed slightly. "Do you think Mr. Gault will really want the rectory?"

"I fear he is entitled to it. It is a part of the living. If he is a married man with a family of his own—"

"He's not. He's a bachelor. I've made inquiries. Surely he won't need that great house?"

"We cannot tell at this juncture, Mrs. Donaldson. If I may be permitted to advise you, I urge the continuance of your attempts to find another house, either here or in some other locality."

This counsel did little to alleviate the poor lady's

distress, and she went away uncomforted. Mr. Micheldever, however, had not been disposed to reassure her—and for a simple and quite human reason: with the news that Mr. Gault was unmarried, the thought had come to him that, on some not far distant day, the Micheldever family might move back into the home that he still considered to be rightfully theirs.

An hour later, a small saloon car of the vintage of 1935 was brought to a stop outside Medlar Cottage, and a tall, bearded man alighted. As he opened the front gate and came up the path with long, purposeful strides, Mrs. Micheldever had time to notice through the curtains that his grey suit was well cut, that he was bare-headed, and that he wore a clerical collar.

"Good morning," he greeted her unsmilingly when she answered his ring. "Is Mr. Micheldever at home? My name is Gault."

"Why, yes. I'm Mrs. Micheldever. I'm sure my husband will be pleased to see you. Won't you come in?"

There was no need to inform Mr. Micheldever, for he came down the stairs just then, welcomed this new visitor in the hall, and took him up to his study.

"I am delighted you have called, Mr. Gault," he said as they sat down. "I received a note from the bishop this morning to the effect that you had accepted the benefice of St. Anselm's. I wish you every success."

"Thank you."

The words were polite, but they were delivered so abruptly that Mr. Micheldever felt repulsed. If first impressions were my thing to go by, he did not think he was going to like the Rev. Bruce Gault, whose appearance was as grim as his manner—forbidding, almost. The black pointed beard—a rarity among Anglican clergy—was trimmed in the court style of Queen Elizabeth I, though covering more of the cheeks, and made him look older than his thirty-six years. Gaunt and hollow-eyed, as if from privation or suffering or chronic insomnia, he had a chilling effect on Mr. Micheldever—as, indeed, he had had on the lady of the house when she had answered the door to him. His right eye had a curious droop in it.

"Now," said Mr. Micheldever in as friendly a tone as he could manage, "is there anything I can do for you? I am, of course, entirely at your service."

With a few terse questions, Gault sought information about the church and the parish. One of these concerned the rectory.

"Is it vacant yet?"

"Dear me, no. Mrs. Donaldson, widow of your predecessor, is still in residence with her children. Housing difficulties are acute and this unfortunate lady—"

"She must find somewhere else."

"That is what I told her, if not"—Mr. Micheldever allowed himself the dig—"in quite such forthright terms. She came to me in great distress earlier this morning and I had no alternative but to advise her to increase her efforts to secure other accommodation. ''

"And the sooner the better."

"It is scarcely within my province, Mr. Gault. . ."

"Very likely not, but go on."

"I am given to understand that you are unmarried."

"Yes. Why?"

"The rectory is far from small. A fine Georgian house, to be sure, of most handsome appearance and with a magnificent outlook, but the rooms are too large and numerous for a single man to live there in comfort. A solution might be—"

"I shall decide that for myself."

Mr. Micheldever bit his lip at this rebuff, but persevered: "Another problem is staff. A large house like— "

"I have my own Chinese servants."

"Chinese? God bless my soul!"

The visitor rose to go.

"Can I offer you some refreshment?"

"Thank you, no."

"Would it be as well for me to have your present address?"

"Seaview Hotel, Southmouth."

"A little vacation before taking up your duties?"

"I would not call it that."

He was escorted down to the front door. In the porch he asked curtly:

"Are you related to Harold Micheldever?"

Mr. Micheldever contrived to answer in a steady voice: "He is my son."

"I imagined so," said Bruce Gault, and stalked off down the garden path.

Chapter Six

BAILIFF AT PLAY

THAT afternoon, Sir Timothy took Harold around the village and its neighbourhood, going from cottage to shop and from shop to poultry-farm or the workshop of some rural craftsman, at each of which he introduced him to the tenants, so that all could confidently hand over future dues to "the new bailiff," as Sir Timothy was pleased to dub him.

It being Monday, they took the opportunity to collect such sums as were forthcoming, sympathetically or gravely considering the explanations concerning those that were not. Harold was shown how to make the entries in the rent-books and had his first exercise in listening to complaints, which covered such varied matters as cesspits, the strawberry crop, chimney-stacks, Jim's Edie, wallpaper, and the Ministry of Agriculture; to drink tea from six different cups; and to inspect, admire and make cooing noises at two new-comers to the parish, both of whom expressed their resentment by screaming violently, which, their proud parents explained, was a sign of good health.

"Phew!" said Timothy as they walked to the car after making their final call. "I'm glad that's over. Worse today, probably, because I was with you. They took the opportunity to trot out all their grievances."

"And got what they wanted."

"Prince Mug—that's me. Sob on my shoulder and half my kingdom is yours, less income-tax."

They got into the car and turned towards Chatthume Place. "Free this evening, Badger?" Timothy asked.

"Free as air. Something you want done?"

"No, we down tools at six. 'Now comes the turn of Taste and the Fine Arts,' as the old opium-eater himself put it. Tonight I'm going to see the show at the Southmouth Empire. Like to come with me?"

"Very much so. Who's in it?"

"Bi Danbury. I've been twelve times."

"The thirteenth may be unlucky."

"I'll chance it. The comedian is Beverley Bott."

"Don't know him. I've got terribly out of touch."

"He's quite good and can be funny without a script, which is more than most of them can. Overdoes it a bit, really. Bi says he's difficult to play opposite because you never know what he's going to do or say next."

At that particular moment, Beverley Bott was saying quite a lot, all unscripted and unrehearsed, in the dingy greenroom of the Empire Theatre. The great, flabby, moonlike face, which could reduce audiences to a condition of hysterics by its comical contortions, showed genuine anger now; and though, ready for the first house, he wore mountaineering kit of extravagant cut and pattern for the Swiss Alps scene in Act I, nobody even so much as smiled at him as he ranted and gestured before them, his enormous head out of all proportion to his thin body and short, skinny legs.

"This show's the biggest flop it's ever been my bad luck to play in. And why? We've got the book, we've got the music, we've got the costumes, we've got the scenery, we've got the cast. The season started well. Now look at it. Take one good look at it."

As the season was not there for their inspection, the others present at this informal conference did no more than avoid each other's eyes—all save Leonard, the stage-manager, who was sitting at the piano and, as proof of his fixed conviction that he was a great composer in the making, was picking out an air with one finger.

"How's that?" he said to Maisie, the little soubrette, who was standing by. "Touch of freshness. Might go big."

"That?" scoffed Maisie. "Why, it's 'Roses of Picardy'."

"Is it? Thought I'd got something."

He poised his right forefinger over the keys, decided to start on a black note this time, and tried again.

"And what's the trouble?" Beverley Bott demanded of the others. "I'll tell you what the trouble is. I'll tell you who it is. It's about time someone said what I'm going to say and even though I'm not the one who should say it, I'm going to say it because it needs saying if we're not going to finish up the season in the red."

"Then for heaven's sake, say it, Bev," said the languid voice of Sabina Danbury, who sat smoking a cigarette, one shapely leg over the other. "We can't *wait* to know who it is."

"Then I'll tell you. It's you."

She gave a trilling laugh.

"Me? Poor little me? Bev, darling, don't be ridiculous!"

"You go through the show like Lady Macbeth at a whist drive. You're dead. Where's the life? Where's the sparkle? They're not paying good money to see you with night starvation, with no more interest in what you're doing on the stage than a flea-bitten performing bear in a two-anna, small-time circus in the Corn Belt."

"Jake!" cried Sabina to the producer. "Don't let him talk to me like that."

Jake held his peace. As Bott had rightly observed, someone had to tell her, and he was relieved it was not he.

Beverley Bott surged on in full spate:

"It's about time you got it into your head, Bi Danbury, that you're not Lady Chatthume yet."

"Oooo, you beast!"

"That's what's wrong with you. You're in a pipe-dream, living up to the title before you've got it. Keep that la-di-da, high-tone stuff till you open the new wing of the orthopaedic hospital or receive the French ambassador, but get this into your head right now: the women come to hear you sing songs about desert-island lovers, the men to look at your legs. They're away from the washtub and the office desk. They want glamour, glitter—"

"He's right, you know, Bi," said Jake, greatly daring, then resumed nibbling a finger-nail.

"Bubbling over with romance," declaimed Bott. "That's what you ought to be, Bi Danbury. But you—you're as bubbling over with romance these days as a glass of fruitsalts that someone's forgotten to take. You've turned so aristocratic in three weeks that now you dance like a thoroughbred mare in foal and your— "

He did not get any further, for Sabina rose from her chair like Tisiphone the Avenger, took one swift stride and smacked his face with such vigour that a crimson patch spread over the dead whiteness of his fleshy cheek. Then, with a whirl of nylons, she was gone.

"Now you've done it, Bev," said Jake placidly, transferring his attention to another finger.

Bott was rubbing his cheek. He said with a wry grin:

"She's got a swipe like a humane-killer."

Maisie giggled.

"She won't go on tonight."

"I'll lay you ten pounds to a penny she does. When Bi's on form and got her heart in it, she could make a Trappist sit up in his seat and think he was a bit hasty about those vows, but when she's not trying, she's a dead loss. She'll try all right this evening, just to show I'm wrong. Now look, Jake, the fault's not all Bi's. You don't give her all the chances you might."

"Starting on me now?"

"Bi's wishing-well scena—it's all right for children's matinées, but why not cut it out—just tonight, as an experiment?"

"And put in what?"

"Let Bi do her Salome number."

"Oh, no. Not me, Bev. Never again. No more up-and-downers with Watch Committees for me."

"People are more broad-minded down here in the south. Besides, it's art, isn't it?"

"You tell me. Any event, she wouldn't do it—not now."

"You ask her. Got the costume, I suppose?"

Maisie giggled again: "She keeps it in a matchbox."

"You ask her, Jake. Say the Maharajah of Gongapore's going to be in front tonight and is particularly partial to that sort of thing. Rub in the art. She'll bite, I'll bet you. Then see how the house fills up tomorrow, when it's got round."

Jake chewed at a nail for some time.

"Certainly wants something like that," he conceded.

On the piano, Leonard had just evolved another tune.

"How's that, Maisie?"

She, now convinced of his talent, cried:

"Len, darling, it's beautiful!"

"Simple, homely—that's what gets 'em. Listen while I run through it again."

With the light of inspired creation in his eyes and a little smile of triumph on his lips, he tapped out the first eight notes of Schumann's "Traumerei."

"Len, you *are* clever!"

"Should fetch 'em," said he modestly.

Sir Timothy had reserved a box for the second house, and a few minutes before the curtain went up, he and Harold took their seats. The auditorium was far from full.

Though described as a musical comedy, *The Folly of Polly* was not much more than a series of turns strung loosely together, and the "book" of which Beverley Bott had spoken favourably was discarded, as occasion demanded, to make way for a juggler or an exhibition of ice-skating, continuity being maintained by the chorus, who stood round in graceful attitudes while these acts were in progress, pretending that they themselves were the audience. Even Beverley Bott's performing bear would not have seemed—indeed, might not have felt—out of place. The only cue needed would have been for one of the chorus to scamper into the Palm Beach Lido or the foyer of the Hotel Stupendous, crying:

"Here comes Lord Fanhaven—and he's brought his performing bear!"

Consequently it was not thought at all incongruous that in Act II, when the party had come back from Switzerland and were now grouse-shooting in Scotland, the irresponsible Polly saw fit to desert her friends and go through the graceful motions of the Dance of the Seven Veils in the seclusion of the library of Fitzmanock Castle.

In his poem, "The Light of Asia," Sir Edwin Arnold wrote:

> "Shall any gazer see with mortal eyes,
>   Or any searcher know by mortal mind?
> Veil after veil will lift—but there must be
>   Veil upon veil behind."

There was a similar piquant element in this performance by Sabina Danbury, which proceeded to the increasingly enthusiastic accompaniment of shrill whistles from the cheaper seats, and the mounting annoyance of Sir Timothy Chatthume.. In the wings, the producer was nervously biting his nails, wondering whether he had done the right thing in talking his leading lady into this change of programme for that evening's second house. Her fierce "I'll show 'em—and that misshapen clot" had not brought him much comfort, and now he was beginning to fear that, art or no art, if anyone's head was going to be demanded in a charger after this exhibition, it would be Jake Harris's.

However, the hearty applause that came from all parts of the house when the dance reached its *ultima Thule* reassured him somewhat, as did the cries of "'Core!" that continued until Beverley Bott came out in front of the drop to show what could be done by a clever comic with no more properties than a couple of false moustaches and a piece of black felt that, in his hands, was miraculously transformed into hats for a variety of characters, from Sairey Gamp to the Duke of Wellington.

And so the show proceeded to its illogical conclusion.

When the artistes had taken their calls and the curtain had gone down for the last time, Sir Timothy said to Harold with an unnaturally grim expression on his handsome young face:

"Let's go behind."

They found Sabina and Maisie in the dressing-room they shared. Sabina, who was at her mirror removing grease-paint, said over her shoulder:

"Shan't be a tick, darling. There's gin and glasses on the window-ledge."

Maisie did not wait for a formal introduction, but immediately engaged Harold in a lively conversation, while she made her few remaining preparations for departure. Timothy poured out the gin.

"Well," said Sabina, turning away from the mirror, "what did you think of it?"

He held out a glass without answering.

"Did you like it? Salome, I mean."

"No."

The glance from her lovely eyes was reproachful.

"Darling!"

"I thought it was cheap."

"But they all loved it."

"I didn't. Making a spectacle of yourself."

Maisie said to Harold: "I simply dote on the seaside: bathing and donkeys and the pier and getting sunburnt, don't you? Last summer we played Manchester and Sheffield and it was frightful."

Sabina said: "Tim, you've wounded me dreadfully."

"What about my feelings? You had me sweating blood, with all those slobbering oafs cat-calling like a lot of—"

"Stop it!"

Maisie said to Harold: "I adore going out after the show and absolutely gulping down ozone, and there's always something going on even when it's ever so late. The coloured lights on the esplanade, and the fun-fair, the moonlight trips in the speedboats—oh, and everything!"

Timothy said very seriously: "Bi, my mother. Do you want her to like you?"

"Of course I do. Don't be silly."

"Do you want her to like you enough to have you as a daughter-in-law?"

"I'm sure I've never done anything"

"Oh, yes, you have—tonight. Do you know this? Mother, told me this morning that she wants to come and see you act? I promised to bring her on Thursday. If she hadn't had a bridge-party, it would have been tonight."

Sabina drew a sharp breath and chewed her lip.

"Jake Harris made me do it."

"That's not the point. You're not doing it again."

"But Jake—""

"Damn Jake! Look, Bi. How would you feel now if Mother had been there tonight? And how would she be feeling?"

Sabina did not reply.

Just then there was a cursory knock on the door and Jake entered without waiting for an invitation.

"It's done the trick, Bi! Dozens of them went straight out to the box-office and booked again! We're on a winner now!"

It was Maisie who cried: "Goody!"

Belatedly realizing the presence of the two visitors, Jake mumbled an apology, adding lamely:

"Thought you'd like to know."

Timothy set down his glass on the window-sill, then stepped across to Jake.

"That Salome dance must come out," he said crisply.

Jake was immediately on his guard; this might be worse than the Watch Committee. He forced a friendly smile.

"You can't mean that, Sir Chatthume. Why, it's charming!"

"I didn't find it so."

"Artistic presentation—"

"Drip! Get this clear, Harris: it's not going to happen again."

Jake waved a placating hand with chubby fingers spread.

"Easy, now—easy. We're all entitled to our opinions, Sir Chatthume, and I'm not stopping you from having yours, but I'm running this company and it's up to me to make the decisions. Let me think it over. Maybe I'll come round to your point of view; maybe I won't. Fair enough?"

Timothy looked from Jake to Sabina, who turned her blonde head away. He walked to the door, where he said:

"I'll be at the first house tomorrow—and the second. Good night."

The door closed behind him. Harold murmured his excuses to Maisie and hastened after him, but the Bug roared out of the car park before he could reach there, and bore his angry employer off towards Chatthume Place. Harold, thus forgotten and abandoned, was wondering how he was going to get home, when a little voice said at his elbow:

"The wretch! Fancy ditching you like that!"

It was Maisie. He did some quick thinking.

"I'm not a bit sorry. It gives me the excuse I was looking for. How about a moonlight trip in the speedboat?"

"I'd adore it!"

"Come on, then."

But others had the same idea, and there was such a queue waiting to buy tickets at the pay-box at the head of the beach that Harold and Maisie went instead to the fun-fair farther along the front, where they paid good money for the opportunity to be thoroughly uncomfortable in or on a variety of contrivances calculated to turn the stomach and bring the heart into the mouth.

"I was absolutely terrified," Maisie said as they came away from the Great Dipper. "Wasn't it lovely? What shall we go on next?"

Harold was not feeling too good.

"I suggest a quiet sit down to give our insides a chance to—"

"Look! Swing-boats!"

She caught hold of his arm and drew him with some difficulty across to them. Soon they were facing each other in one of the boats. Harold would have preferred a rhythm as gentle as the old rocking-chair, but Maisie, by the way she tugged on her rope, seemed set on swinging higher and higher until, presumably, they fell out and rounded off the evening by breaking their necks. But some time before this climax was reached, Harold's expression, which up to then had denoted only a mild uneasiness, suddenly became really frightened and he lost his grip on the rope.

"Windy!" jeered Maisie.

It was not, however, the motion of the swing-boat that had caused him such swift alarm; it was the sight of a man who stood watching them. Maisie could not see him, for he was behind her, but he came into Harold's view on every backward and upward swing. He was a tall, spare man, bearded and bare-headed. Though he wore the collar and tie of a layman and when they had last met had been clean shaven, Harold recognized him in one swift glance of dismay as the Reverend Bruce Gault.

Maisie soon tired of the swing-boat and suggested they tried something else. Harold, having no wish to meet the man who stood so motionless below, continued to pull on his rope with a methodical persistence that at first puzzled the protesting, Maisie, then angered her, and finally scared her. Even when the attendant called up that they had now had their money's worth, Harold still kept on. Maisie, now convinced she was, trapped with a maniac, threatened to jump out if he did not stop "acting so silly" and doubtless would have done so had not Bruce Gault suddenly turned and walked away. Only then did Harold consent to alight.

It took him some time to placate Maisie, yet he managed it at length and left her at her hotel after extracting the promise that she would meet him after the show on the following Saturday evening.

As he was making for the railway station, and estimating whether he had enough money to hire a car if the last train for Lulverton had left, he was brought up short by a voice saying behind him:

"Micheldever, I want a word with you."

Harold turned and assumed a perplexed expression:

"We must have met before, but—"

"You know who I am."

Harold came closer.

"Bruce Gault! The beard had me guessing. Well, you're the last man I expected to see."

"That doesn't surprise me."

"Look, I'm dashing off to catch a train. Perhaps we can'

have a chat when we've more time."

"A minute now will be enough. Where are you living?"

"With my people at Yateham."

"Just as I feared. This morning I called on your father,"

"You didn't . . .?"

"No, I didn't. I've been appointed rector of St. Anselm's. which means we'll be living in the same village." He gave a harsh ejaculation. "The irony of it."

"What are you going to do about—you know what I mean."

"Have you told your parents the truth?"

"No; it would hurt them too much."

"Then understand this: if they ever hear, it won't be from me. For their sake, not yours. That's all."

Without a word or nod of farewell, he turned and stalked into the summer night.

Chapter Seven

SALOME DANCES

"LOOK, Sir Chatthume," said Jake Harris with a wave of his cigar.

"And you look, too. I'll answer to Chatthume, but not the other barbarism."

"Say 'Sir Timothy,' Jake," prompted Sabina. "It sounds nicer."

This conversation was taking place, at midday on the Tuesday, in the Wine Lodge, which was at the more exclusive end of Southmouth front. Timothy had been invited on the telephone by Sabina to meet her there for a sherry, and had been disappointed but not surprised to find Jake Harris in attendance. They had found a free table in the fairly crowded, red-carpeted lounge.

"Darling," Sabina went on, turning to Timothy, "Jake thought we'd better have a little talk with you."

"What about?" he asked, knowing full well.

Jake said: "It's the Salome number. We're in a spot."

"Getting complaints?"

"Only from you. We know how you feel, but let's face it. Business is business."

"The position is, Tim, dear," said Sabina in the saccharine tone of one soothing a fractious infant, "that we're sort of committed—or Jake is. We just can't take out the Salome dance now."

Jake said: "I wasn't taking no—I wasn't taking any chances. First thing this morning I was along at the Town Hall, seeing the chairman of the Watch Committee. We laid on a special showing in the theatre and they gave it the O.K.—said it was very nice, and with class."

"I don't give a tosser," said Timothy, "whether it's been passed by the Lords and Commons. I'm not having Bi undressing herself on the stage."

"But I don't, darling—not quite."

"If she doesn't go on with it," threw in Jake, "we'll be in trouble—big trouble. Taking money under false pretences, that's what. She's billed to—"

"Jake," said Sabina hastily, before he went too far, "why don't you leave Tim and me to talk this over quietly together?"

She jerked her head slightly. The situation had possibilities that had not previously occurred to her.

"Right," said Jake, "I'll be getting back to the theatre." He drained his glass and rose to his feet. "So long, Sir Chatthume."

As soon as he had left them, Sabina drew her chair closer.

"I love you more than ever for the way you feel about this, darling," she murmured. "You don't want to share me. But Jake's right. He's got to live—we've all got to live, to give people what they'll pay to see."

"Which makes it more blasted sordid than ever."

"I think you're being a tiny little bit unreasonable—and selfish. What's going to happen to me if the show comes off? It will, you know, if we can't play to something like capacity. Have you thought what would happen to me then?"

"You'd get something else, with your looks and talent."

Sabina thought it was time now to show her dainty claws.

"Is that quite nice of you, Tim? I'm sure it's not the real you. I simply won't believe that if—and only to please you—I refused to dance Salome again and the show went phut or Jake fired me, which he'd have every right to do—I just can't think that you'd leave me to go round from agents' office to agents' office, and all because of you."

His head bowed, he revolved the stem of his glass between his thumb and forefinger. Her tone was a little sharper as she went on:

"It's time we faced the facts, my sweet. Look at me, Tim, and answer this question: do you want me or not?"

Slowly he raised his head.

"More than anything else I can think of."

"Then you must do something about it, mustn't you?"

He laughed shortly.

"Quite frankly, I'm in a cleft stick. It would have been much easier if you hadn't—"

He broke off, for there had come an interruption. They heard a man saying in a loud voice:

"Read your Bibles daily. Hell is eternal."

He was a thin, sharp-featured little clergyman, his black suit shabby and baggy at knees and elbows, his shoes cracked and down at the heels. From beneath the broad brim of his shovelhat, which was green-tinted by age, sprouted untidy tufts of grey-white hair. He walked with the aid of a stick held close to his left leg and fitted with a large rubber ferrule, and in his right hand he carried a Bible, its leather cover worn and tattered. For such a small man, his voice was surprisingly deep and resonant;

his accent Welsh.

Repeating the same words—and no more than those—he went from group to group at the counters and tables. Some thanked him, some laughed at him, some ignored him, some turned their backs on him, but he made the complete circuit, then passed out again into the sunshine, his stick taking the weight off his left leg.

Timothy and Sabina resumed their discussion.

"You said you were in a cleft stick."

"Mother's the trouble. She can't stop me marrying, but I want her to like my wife. It's damned awkward when a mother-in-law disapproves of her daughter-in-law. She told me after I'd introduced you to her that she thought you were very beautiful, intelligent and dignified—yes, dignified, which she meant as a compliment. Don't be offended when I tell you that I had to break it to her very tactfully that you're on the stage. It shook her badly at first, but she's got used to the idea now. What she'd say if she knew about the Dance of the Seven Veils, I'll leave you to guess!"

"Tim, I don't want to hurt you, but I've got to go through with it unless ..."

"Yes . . .?"

"You know."

"Unless you find escape in marrying me. Is that it?"

"There you go again, stupid! I shouldn't be escaping from anything. Anyone'd think the Salome dance was worse than death. Tim, precious, let me go on with it. It's not just me. There's Jake and Bev and Maisie and the others. They'll all be in trouble if the show flops. I can't let them down. Let me do it for the rest of this week—"

"Mother's coming on Thursday."

"You'll have to persuade her not to. Say I'm ill or something and won't be appearing. ... If the box-office takings aren't much up on last week, Jake can't possibly mind me going back to the wishing-well scene."

He was silent for a long time.

"Say you don't mind, Tim."

"All right—till Saturday."

"Tim, you're an angel! Later on, if we can manage it, I'll dance it just for you alone and—"

She bent forward and whispered in his ear.

"Would you like that?" she said aloud, drawing back.

"Do I have to tell you?"

They laughed together, happy once more.

At the first house that evening, there was an incident proving the prudence of Jake Harris in having sought the approval of the Watch Committee. To soft music from the orchestra, Sabina was going through the Salome dance, and the library of Fitzmanock Castle was becoming strewn with diaphanous gauze, when from the auditorium came a strong, resonant voice:

"The reading is from the second chapter of the First Epistle of Paul to Timothy, beginning at the eighth verse. 'I will, therefore, that men pray everywhere, lifting up holy hands, without wrath and doubting. In like manner also, that women adorn themselves in modest apparel, with shamefacedness and sobriety ...'"

There was murmuring all over the house, all craning their necks to see who spoke. On the stage Sabina was going on with her dance and the orchestra still played.

" '. . not with broidered hair, or gold or pearls, or costly array; but (which becometh women professing godliness) with good works. Let the woman learn in silence with all subjection.' That is the end of the reading. You, shameless woman, abide by the Scriptures. 'For if the woman be not covered, let her also be shorn.' Go and cover yourself. Go I command you!"

Poor Sabina could not keep it up. She stopped dancing gave a few helpless gestures, then, with a little cry, ran off into the wings. The curtain was lowered and the house lights went on. Two uniformed men appeared, but before they could reach the little clergyman standing in the gangway with the open Bible, he closed the book and said, his voice and manner compelling attention and bringing the attendants to an embarrassed stop:

"Let us pray."

Having led the whole respectful audience in prayer, he cried out:

"Read your Bibles daily. Hell is eternal."

Then, his stick held close to his left leg he quietly made his departure, and all those around him rose to their feet as he passed. Three minutes later, our nation being what it is, they were laughing heartily at the antics of Beverly Bott.

The Dance of the Seven Veils was not repeated at Southmouth Empire. Though protected by the formal sanction of the Watch Committee, Jake Harris had had enough.

Chapter Eight

STORM-CLOUDS

I

DURING the afternoon of the first Saturday in August, in the presence of a large congregation, the Reverend Bruce Gault, M.A., B.D., was inducted and instituted by the Bishop of Whitchester into the spiritualities and temporalities of the parish of St. Anselm's. On the following morning he conducted his first service, which was, of necessity, not so well-attended, for then the worshippers were all local folk.

It was the general hope that, after the troubled period through which it had passed, the parish would soon settle down under its new rector. This hope, however, was not to be immediately fulfilled, for a number of things contributed to the creation of a condition of unrest. Most important of these factors was, perhaps, the personality of Mr. Gault, which inspired fear rather than respect, doubt rather than confidence, suspicion rather than trust. The late Angus Donaldson had been a terror in the pulpit, but human and friendly enough out of it; Bruce Gault was unsmiling, stern and unapproachable. There seemed a gulf between him and the rest of mankind. Old Tom Smart's verdict on Mr. Donaldson has been recorded. Of Mr. Gault he said:

"Wi' that there beard and them dayvilish oyes, it be fer arl the warld loike Ole Nick 'isself waar praychin'."

Nor were the Chinese retainers well received in the village. Nothing could have been more innocuous or respectable than Yi Liu-ying in his quiet Western clothes, and no young woman more charming in appearance than his wife, in her white silk blouse and black skirt; but Yateham residents, to whom even a visitor from ten miles away was suspect, looked askance at them and found excuse to cross the road when Mrs. Yi came their way, or leave the village grocer's when Yi Liu-ying called in for supplies.

Then there was the treatment of Mrs. Donaldson, who was so offended by Mr. Gault's uncompromising manner when he called to see her that she removed from the rectory within three days, stored her furniture and, at the generous invitation of Sir Timothy and his mother, found sanctuary for herself and children in Chatthume Place. It might have been that the aggrieved lady magnified the offence of her husband's successor, but the incident, and Mrs. Donaldson's ceaseless references to the cruel treatment she had received at his hands, served only to increase his unpopularity.

He was, too, at loggerheads with Andrew Micheldever right from the start. Mr. Micheldever dutifully attended the induction ceremony and the services on the day following, but during the ensuing week his doubtless well-intentioned attempts to assist and advise Mr. Gault were received more and more coldly until the crisis was reached on the Friday, when Mr. Micheldever offered some guidance on the rights of such pewholders as arrived at the church after the entry of the choir, and Mr. Gault told him, in the presence of the verger and three churchwardens, to mind his own business. Mr. Micheldever's instant resolve was to resort to his former and expensive practice of going to All Saints, Lulverton. Similar tactics in his treatment of the late Mr. Donaldson had made him disliked in more than a few quarters, but now he appeared to have the majority on his side.

If no more, Mr. Gault had two champions in Yateham. One was the anonymous sender of a postcard, which read:

> "Mr. Andrew Micheldever,
> Are you, sir, retiring never?
> Must you interfere for ever,
> Mr. Andrew Micheldever?"

The other was Janet.

"I don't think it's fair on the man," she said at tea in the garden of Medlar Cottage. "Everybody's against him and it makes my blood boil. Why can't we give him a chance? Daddy, you're behaving like a sulky schoolboy."

Mr. Micheldever did not like this at all, but he had no opportunity to emit more than an angry exclamation, for Janet swept on:

"You can do what you like about attending All Saints—and Mummy'll have to do the same, I suppose—but I'm going to go on going to St. Anselm's, even if there's a congregation of one and I'm it."

When his duties permitted, Harold was much at Southmouth, his friendship with Maisie having developed satisfactorily in every way except financially. As he had admitted to himself since, he had acted foolishly in the early days of their acquaintance by posing as a well-to-do friend of Sir Timothy Chatthume. He had not actually said that he was a rich young man-about-town, but had tried to give that impression and had been so successful that now he was faced by the serious problem of acquiring enough ready money to keep up the deception. Timothy, whose courting took him in the same direction, could not help noticing this, and it was beginning to cause him some concern, not as a friend, but as Harold's employer.

Some of these fears he confided to Sabina while, early on the Thursday morning in the last week of August, they were sitting in the train at Southmouth terminus, waiting to leave on a shopping expedition to London.

"You might give Maisie Brown the quiet tip," he said without troubling to lower his voice, for they were alone in a first-class compartment, "that Harold Micheldever's not a millionaire. No fellow likes to show up badly to his girl friend, and poor old Harold's having as much as he can do to cope with Maisie's enormous appetite for expensive amusements. He has a decent income, but—"

They heard, coming from farther down the platform, a voice that was now only too familiar to them.

"Read your Bibles daily. Hell is eternal."

Sabina gave a sobbing cry of distress.

"It's him again."

Timothy rose to his feet and stepped across to the window. Compartment after compartment, the little Welsh clergyman, looking seedier and hungrier than ever, was working his way with Bible and stick along the train. Timothy closed the window and went back to his seat.

"Turn the other way," he told Sabina.

When the evangelist reached their compartment, he took hold of the handle and opened the door.

"Read your Bibles daily. Hell is eternal."

Gazing through the opposite window, they waited for

him to go on his way, but Sabina was of such striking appearance that she was not easily forgotten, and now she was recognized, I even though her face was partly hidden.

"So it is you, is it, young woman?" The singsong voice! had become more conversational, but there was no approval in it. "Have you repented your sin?"

Timothy jumped up and went to the open door.

"I respect your cloth, sir," he said politely, "but we'd rather not hear any more. You've caused enough trouble already."

"The woman had to be shown the error of her ways."

"After your last effort, she nearly had a nervous breakdown."

"That was the voice of the Lord speaking within her."

"Whatever it was, we don't want any more of it. Good day, sir."

He caught hold of the door and pulled it to with a slam. Further embarrassment was prevented by the starting of the train. As Timothy came back to his seat, Sabina said in a voice that shook:

"He terrifies me."

"More than somewhat potty, I'd say."

"Do you think he's a real clergyman?"

"If he is, he can't give much time to his flock." He laughed lightly. "Let's forget him and talk about that hat you're going to buy."

"I just can't forget him, Tim. I even have bad dreams, about him at night. They're all mixed up with the Salome dance—oh, and horrible things."

He moved across to sit beside her and slipped his arm around her.

II

Yateham rectory was pure Georgian: of creeper-clad red brick, with a hooded doorway in the centre of its plain facade, tall, small-paned windows and, in the front slope of the roof, three dormers.

Some hours after Sabina and Timothy had departed for London, Mrs. Yi knocked on the door of Bruce Gault's sparsely furnished study, which overlooked the lovely garden at the rear, and was told to enter. Both she and her husband spoke excellent English, having been for a number of years at the D.M.A. mission at Haolaofen.

Mr. Gault, who had been writing at a plain wooden table, laid down his pen and turned to her with a smile that would have astonished his parishioners.

"A caller, Faith?" he asked in a kindly tone, using the English equivalent of her name. "I heard the bell."

"It is Mr. Price."

He stiffened.

"The Reverend Dafydd Price?"

"Yes."

He stroked his beard for a moment or two.

"Show him in, please," he said, rising to his feet.

He was standing in front of the empty fireplace when Mrs. Yi returned with the visitor, and stepped forward with outstretched hand as the little Welsh clergyman limped in.

"Dafydd!" he welcomed him warmly. "What a nice surprise! Why, my dear fellow, you don't look too good."

He pulled up a chair for Mr. Price and remained standing himself.

"That old leg of yours giving trouble?"

"No more than usual. I had no breakfast and am weak."

"Then we can soon put that right. Faith, some sandwiches, please, and some—coffee, Dafydd?"

Mr. Price addressed his reply to the young woman.

"Yes, if you will be so kind."

While they waited for the refreshment, he continued to his host:

"I was surprised by your beard, but it did not deceive me. Why have you grown a beard, man?"

Mr. Gault's steel-blue eyes narrowed under his heavy brows.

"For much the same reason as you carry a stick, but I prefer not to discuss it."

Mrs. Yi soon came in with the tray, then left them alone together. Mr. Price attacked the sandwiches as if he had fasted for twenty-four hours—as, in fact, he had.

"Now tell me everything, Dafydd," urged his host in a friendlier tone when the last mouthful had been consumed and the coffee drunk. "It's years since we met. I heard you managed to slip out of China and I tried to get in touch with you, but even the D.M.A. couldn't—"

"We will not trouble ourselves with that," said Mr. Price, his words and manner strangely out of keeping with a reunion of old friends. "Having read in the newspaper of your recent induction, I have walked this morning from Southmouth—"

"Walked? But my poor old—"

"Not all the way. A kindly motorist offered me a lift for some distance. Now you must listen to me, Gault."

"It used to be Bruce."

"Bruce or Gault, it is to you I am talking. After you went from Haolaofen so suddenly—"

"Yes, what actually happened was that—"

101

"After you went so suddenly, a Christian Chinese from Taochiaching, at great risk to himself, came to Haolaofen and, by bribing the sentries, was able to talk to me. The news that he brought from Taochiaching was sad and shameful to hear. I will tell you what he said."

As the singsong voice continued with the terrible indictment, Bruce Gault went over to the window and gazed out into the sunlit garden, his mind far away in Communist China. When Mr. Price finished speaking, he asked harshly:

"Do you believe him? His word is no better than—"

"He is a Christian and he swore to me on this same Bible which I now carry that what he told me was true. With his own eyes, he saw the clubbing of the soldier and the brutal shooting of Yi Cheng—poor Yi Cheng, who had in him nothing but loving-kindness, shot down in cold blood and left to—"

"Please don't go on."

Gault turned back into the room and went over to stand in front of Mr. Price.

"What action do you propose to take?"

"It must be left to you, Bruce. I am weak with suffering for the Communists were not gentle after you left. Since I came back to this country, my life has not been easy. I wonder, perhaps ..."

"Yes, go on."

"I am wondering whether you have knowledge of anyone who would give me some small employment. Scripture teaching at a school—a temporary post of that kind. Having you own parish here, you will know of something, perhaps?"

"Not off-hand."

Gault took a turn up and down the room.

"Look, Dafydd, I know what an independent, fiery little Celt you are, and you'll probably resent the suggestion, but I'm going to make it. I'm far from being a second Croesus, but if can help you to get on your feet again . . ."

He paused inquiringly.

"That is most kind and I gladly accept," said Mr. Price then added with an impish smile: "It is gratifying to know that we understand each other."

Chapter Nine

THE PILLARS OF HERCULES

I

WHERE shall we go?" asked Dr. Dick Farringdon.

"Let's walk to the mill, shall we?" Janet suggested.

"As good as anywhere, I suppose. On a glorious day like this, everything might not be quite so clammy as last time we went."

He had lunched with the family at Medlar Cottage, and now The whole Sunday afternoon was before them. They set off in the same direction as on that night in July, but had not gone many yards before Janet said:

"We go left."

Here a secondary road. Church Lane, formed a fork with the High Street. This took them, after fifty yards or so, past the church, which was on their left, and, a little farther along, on the other side of the road, the rectory.

They soon left behind the two or three straggling cottages beyond the rectory, and made their way along the winding, hedge-bordered road until they came to a stile on the right.

"This is where we take to the bush," said Janet.

"And don't forget ladies allow their escorts to be first across."

"Then I'm not a lady," she said, swinging her leg over the bar.

The footpath along which he then followed her soon began to lead them downward, and the gorse bushes on either side were succeeded by marshier growths. Before many minutes, they reached the point where the Snare Brook turned southward, and were just about to proceed along the northern bank, which would lead them upstream to the mill, when a voice called:

"Hullo, there, you landlubbers!"

In mid-stream, on the lower stretch below the bend, was a skiff. In the stern, with her back to them, was Sabina Danbury, in a new frock, while at the oars was Sir Timothy, who had hailed them. As Sabina turned her head, Janet waved and called a greeting. Then, as they were about to continue their walk, Timothy shouted:

"Wait a tick! We've some news for you."

He got the boat turned round and brought it alongside where they stood.

"Show 'em it, Bi," he said. "They can be the first to congratulate me."

"Timothy, you're engaged!" cried the delighted Janet.

"I'm so glad. I do hope you're both very happy."

Dick added his good wishes to hers.

"We've just rowed up to the mill," Timothy told them "and there I popped the pertinent query."

Janet said: "That's where we are going."

"Verb, sap.," laughed Timothy, taking up the oars again! "And," he called out after them, "if it comes on to rain, don't try to get in. It's dangerous."

"We'll keep out," Dick assured him, and he and Janet went on their way.

They reached the mill and went round on to the footbridge, where they paused by tacit consent.

"Do you remember that night?" she asked, her elbows on the rail.

"I'll never forget it. Janet, I asked you a question then. We've been out a lot together since, but I haven't worried you for an answer. I wanted you to be the first to mention it again. But," he smiled, "Chatthume's success gives me' courage. Have you an answer for me?"

"Dick, I think you're a dear—quite the nicest man I've ever met—but ..."

"I suppose that means no."

"It doesn't, nor does it mean yes—not yet. I know I'm being silly and unreasonable, but give me a little more time, dear. It's such a very serious decision, isn't it?"

"Why, of course."

"Then let's go on just as we've been these last weeks. What do they call it—the period between just being friends and being engaged?"

"Walking out?"

"That sounds very old-fashioned. I heard a girl on a bus say, 'He's my regular.' Would you mind very much being my regular for just a little while longer?"

"Will you be my regular as well?"

"Naturally. One can't be a regular if the other isn't."

Dick laughed ruefully.

"Then I'll have to be content with that. But you're an exasperating little devil. Here am I, offering you—"

"Dick, dear, it's settled. We're regulars and you mustn't say any more about marriage for at least . . ."

"How long? Don't make it too interminable."

"A week. I'll tell you definitely yes or no next Sunday."

"What time?"

"How very precise. Do you keep an appointment-book?"

"Call it an engagement-book."

"Well, half past nine's always been a favourite of mine."

"Where?"

"Here, on this very spot."

They resumed their walk, going onward in the direction of the Barlows' cottage. Janet said as they strolled along:

"Have you heard we've a new rector?"

"Vaguely. 'Fraid I'm not very much up in church matters."

"Yes, he came some weeks ago and there's trouble already. Mrs. Donaldson was living in the rectory and there was unpleasantness before she'd move out. People are saying the rector's a hard man, but it was really her fault, because she must have realized that sooner or later she'd have to go. Anyway, it was a bad start. Then Mr. Gault   "

"Gault? . . . Who's he?"

"Why, the new rector—the Reverend Bruce Gault. They're frightfully cagey and reactionary round here, and they all took exception to his Chinese servants."

"Good God!"

He paused to light a cigarette before he went on:

"Chinese servants! That must have shaken the residents rigid."

"It did. Nobody's quite sure, because they haven't liked to ask Mr. Gault, but we think they must be husband and wife. His name's Yi something or other, and when we talk about her at home we always say Mrs. Yi, though she may not be."

For a while they walked on in silence. Then Janet said:

"I can't bear anything unfair or not sporting. They're not treating Mr. Gault justly. Do you know he's practically been sent to Coventry?"

"Has he?"

"They're all going to other churches or not at all, and St. Anselm's is almost empty—just the old country people who've been there all their lives and will go on till they die. Even Daddy's started going again to All Saints and poor old Mummy's had to do the same. . . . Dick, I'm very, very sorry for Mr. Gault. It brings a lump into my throat. I feel I want to help him all I can. I'm going to the service this evening. . . . Would you like to come with me?"

The answer was so abrupt that it startled her.

"No, I wouldn't."

"Dick, that wasn't nice."

"Well, I couldn't help it. I don't want to be unpleasant about it, Janet, but I'm jealous enough to wish you'd spare a bit more of your sympathy for me and not waste it on this parson fellow. Last time we came here, all you'd talk about was Chatthume; now it's the parson's turn. I was going to suggest we went to Southmouth this evening to meet an old shipmate of mine, and all you can do is go to church."

"I asked you to come with me. Will you?"

"No, thank you."

The rest of that lovely afternoon was darkened for both of them.

Evensong at St. Anselm's on that day—the twelfth Sunday after Trinity—was poorly attended. As Janet had remarked to Dick Farringdon, some of the elderly villagers were there—old Tom Smart and his wife, Miss Frost, who had kept the sweetshop for forty years, Mr. and Mrs. Ovenden from Patchworth Farm, Mrs. Wilkins from the post office, Mr. Allen from the curio and art shop, and a handful of others; but those of higher degree were absent. Even Lady Chatthume, a staunch church-goer, was absent—maybe prevailed upon by the injured Mrs Donaldson. In a rear pew, half hidden from the pulpit by the ancient font, were Yi Liu-ying and his wife, and a few rows forward, on the other side of the aisle, sat Janet Micheldever. Mr. Mullett, the village schoolmaster, was at the organ, but on that Sunday the choir stalls were empty.

Under these dispiriting conditions, Bruce Gault went through the service with the inhuman efficiency of a machine. His sermon was on the text: "For now we see through a glass, darkly; but then face to face: now I know in part; but then shall I know even as also I am known." His treatment was out of keeping with the hopeful theme, his voice hard and austere; gone the friendly note that had warmed it when Dafydd Price had called at the rectory.

Mrs.Yi leaned sideways towards her husband to murmur in Chinese:

"What ails him? His harshness breaks my heart. In Haolaofen, before the Pa Lu came, he was gay, inspiring, and the sunshine of the soul went with him always."

"Our poor master," Yi Liu-ying muttered back, "he's under a great heaviness of the spirit. He grieves."

She was going to speak again, but he warned her to be silent.

On the other side of the aisle, Janet's handkerchief, crushed into a tight ball, was pressed to her mouth.

In All Saints, Lulverton, the Reverend Andrew Micheldever was sitting beside his wife, listening with close attention to a sermon on the text, "but the greatest of these is charity," nodding his head with approval from time to time.

At Southmouth, Maisie Brown was saying to Harold:

"I'm getting ever so tired of gentility. Shall we go slumming?"

Harold, holding a mental review of his financial resources, expressed entire agreement and suggested Old Town, by which name the original seaport of Southmouth was now known, as distinct from Southmouth-by-the-Sea, the prosperous seaside resort that had grafted itself on to its ancient and disreputable parent, and extended away from it for some distance along the coast.

Here, in Old Town, was dockland, where Harold now escorted Maisie. They had a look at the shipping in the port, then went in search of a drink. They did not have to go far, for right down on the waterfront, at the end of a narrow street, was the Pillars of Hercules, a drab little tavern that did nothing to live up to its splendid name, with a fried-fish shop on the opposite corner, from which emanated the fragrance of hot, stale nut-oil.

Wishing to be thoroughly democratic, they went into the public bar, where Harold called for gin.

"No spirit, sir," said the landlord. "Only a beer licence."

This pleased Harold immensely. He looked inquiringly at Maisie, who, having expressed the wish to go slumming, had no alternative but to put a brave face on it and—remembering the favourite drink of Leonard, the stage-manager—said she would adore a brown ale.

She was sipping this with a not very convincing show of enjoying it, and Harold was busy with a pint of bitter in a glass as thick as a jam-jar, when Dr. Richard Farringdon came in with an officer of the Royal Navy.

II

As if shamefaced at their fewness, the congregation drifted out of St. Anselm's at the end of the service. Some went off home immediately, while others paused to gossip in the gathering dusk. In the little gabled porch, Janet murmured to old Tom:

"Where was the choir, Mr. Smart?"

He pushed back his hat to scratch his head.

"Reckon they be on stroike, Miss Janet. Woan't come no more, nary a one of 'em."

"Why on earth not?"

"There be no tellin', Miss Janet," Tom answered evasively, and went on after his wife.

Janet lingered in the porch until Bruce Gault emerged.

"Good evening, rector," she smiled.

Her sweet voice and the delightful picture she made should have brought an answering smile, but he retorted through tight lips:

"Have you come to mock me?"

"Why, of course not. I wanted to thank you for the inspiring sermon."

"Inspiring?" he almost barked at her.

"'... but then shall I know even as also I am known'"

It was gently and sincerely said.

"Tell your father that," he snapped and strode off between the encroaching gravestones, shouldering roughly past Miss Frost, who was standing in talk with Mrs. Wilkins.

As he turned towards the rectory without a backward glance, Yi Liu-ying and his wife came out through the church door. Janet, with tears in her eyes, turned towards them, but the words she would have said were frozen on her lips by the deep hatred in the large black eyes of Mrs. Yi.

III

After a chat and a drink or two with Harold and Maisie, Dick and his friend went on their way, in search of something more comfortable than the hard wooden forms provided in the public bar of the Pillars of Hercules.

"I couldn't tell you in front of them," Harold said when the door had swung shut, "but Farringdon—the civvy one—has been running after my sister Janet."

"Ever so handsome in a mannish way," replied Maisie, "but he's not very sociable, is he? Sitting there not saying hardly a word."

"From which," said Harold grimly, "I can only draw certain conclusions."

"What do you think's happened?"

"No, not now. I've other things on my mind." He took a long swig at his beer, not the first long swig that evening. "Maisie, I've got something to tell you. I don't think you'll like it."

"Oh, is it something horrid? I was so happy."

"Then I'll keep quiet."

And he decided that he would. That was the trouble with drink: it made a fellow open his mouth too wide.

Maisie moved along the form and nestled against his side.

"Tell me, sweety."

"No, I've thought better of—"

A loud voice declaimed in the private bar:

"Read your Bibles daily. Hell is eternal."

Harold smothered an ejaculation, rose to his feet and stepped across to peer cautiously round the partition that divided the two bars. He came back to Maisie.

"Come on, quick!" he whispered urgently. "He'll be in

112

here next!"

Maisie could not see the force of this, but allowed herself to be hustled out of the Pillars of Hercules. Perhaps the next place they went to would have gin.

I feel the net drawing in around me, ever closer and closer. Dafydd has appeared suddenly in Southmouth. He will never forgive. I remember his last words to me at Haolaofen—remember them as if they were cut into my brain with a cruel knife. "Remember to come back, man, for if you do not, vengeance will follow." What did he mean by that? Whose vengeance? The Communists'? Or had he guessed what I was going to do? "Vengeance will follow"—and it has. Old sins have long shadows. Shall I ever escape from him? ... Dafydd .. . Dafydd ... He will be everywhere around me—in loneliness, in crowds, night or day, in the sea or in the air. Everywhere Dafydd ... I think I am going mad . . . How can I tell her? How would she take it? Would she stick to me or run from me? . . . No, it was a temptation, but I did right not to tell her. . . . What will tomorrow bring, and Tuesday, Wednesday, Thursday . . . Days, days, days, waiting for the blow to fall. . . . Dafydd . . . Dafydd . . . AND THE OTHER ONE?

Chapter Ten

CRISIS

A DISCIPLE of Lancelot Brown, the landscape gardener who earned himself the nickname "Capability" and flourished in the eighteenth century, Sir Francis Chatthume, forebear of Timothy, had been a hater of the formal garden. He had remodelled the extensive grounds of Chatthume Place and, after a lifetime of loving attention, had passed them on to his descendants, who had maintained the naturalistic traditions Walking through, the visitor might well imagine that this was not a private estate contained within high brick walls, but a stretch of undulating and varied countryside, with clumps of trees in which brown squirrels sported, here and there little clearings of velvet-smooth grass, beds of flowers so cleverly placed and arranged that they seemed accidental, and the Snare Brook trespassing across the property on its leisured way to Southampton Water. Even the pool, where there were swans and herons and ever-greedy ducks, though carefully looked after, had the appearance of natural scenery.

"Where?"

Sabina Danbury tried to keep a conspiratorial note out of her voice as she and Timothy came out of the big white house, she in a summer frock, he in his white shorts and tennis shirt.

"This way."

Carrying a small leather case, he led her round the houses across the kitchen garden and under the trees beyond, their leaves showing the first hint of autumn.

It was the first Sunday in September, which had begun with rain, but had grown into a glorious day. Now the night was as glorious; warm, scented and, for lovers, with magic in it. The moon was up.

They walked on until they came to a circular clearing.

"I mowed it myself yesterday," said Timothy.

"Specially?"

"Specially."

Alone in the centre of the clearing stood a great plane tree, and around the circumference were other trees and laurels—an unbroken ring except where Snare Brook skirted it.

Timothy handed Sabina the case.

"Off you go."

"Suppose somebody comes?"

"They won't. I'll give you thirty seconds."

As she went among the trees, he strolled across to the plane and squatted down at the foot of it.

Not in thirty seconds but very soon, Salome appeared and came on dancing feet into the natural amphitheatre. There was no music from an orchestra now; instead the ceaseless chirrups of the crickets and the lonely hooting of an owl.

One by one the veils were discarded until the seventh floated to the ground. Timothy drew a long, deep breath, for he saw that Sabina had kept the whispered promise she had made.

For a full minute she danced—not Salome now, but Eve. Then, with a final pirouette, it was over.

115

Timothy jumped up, but as he ran towards her, she turned and darted away with a laugh into the shadows under the encircling trees.

He found her and carried her out into the moonlight again.

"Where are you taking me?" she whispered.

"For a row."

"What, like this?"

"I'm mad tonight, darling. Let's both be mad."

He placed her in the skiff, then rowed up-stream until she saw ahead of them the dark semicircle at the foot of the boundary wall, where Snare Brook ran under the public thoroughfare.

"This is as far as we go," she said.

He laughed softly.

"Mind your head."

He took the boat under the low bridge.

"Don't go any farther, Tim."

"We'll pop our noses out, just for fun. Listen first, though."

All was silent above, no sound of approaching footsteps or motor-cars. He propelled the boat gently onward, and they came out into the open on the other side.

Then the beam from a flashlamp shot suddenly down.

"You naked harpy without shame!" thundered the voice of Dafydd Price.

Sabina gave a scream of terror and crouched down.

"I have again caught you at it!"

"Oh, Lord," said Timothy, working the boat back towards the bridge.

"And you, man! Do not think I do not recognize you, Sir Timothy Chatthume! What did we say in Haolaofen?

Tsui t'ien hsin k'u—The words are sweet, but the heart is bitter."

By now they were under the bridge. They heard him shout: "I shall make a report to the police!"

They floated into the safer waters within the grounds.

"That's done it," Timothy muttered, pulling hard on the oars.

"I begged you not to," sobbed Sabina. "There'll be a dreadful scandal. What are we going to do?"

"Think quickly," he said, "then act."

In the small private bar of the White Lion in the village of Monk Jewel, which lay between Yateham and the town of Lulverton, and where he had come to avoid meeting any of his acquaintances, Harold Micheldever was resentfully drinking himself into a stupor.

That afternoon, Maisie had thrown him over, and for no more apparent reason than that he had persisted in his refusal to let her into the unpleasant secret that he had almost disclosed a week ago in the Pillars of Hercules at Southmouth. Which was hard on him, he felt, for if he had told her while she was in that mood, she would have thrown him over just the same.

But Maisie was not the only problem on his mind. There was another and greater one: Money. He was in a mess. Tomorrow, Timothy Chatthume had told him, they would run through the figures after Harold had completed his Monday round of the tenants, to ensure that Harold was conducting the rent-account in the right way. He was not; that was the trouble. What was Timothy going to say about the fifteen pounds, the last few shillings of which were now finding their way over the counter of the White Lion? Where could he get fifteen pounds in a hurry? His father? Very unlikely and too big a risk, for other issues were involved. His mother? She would not have so much in the house; the domestic budget never did more than just balance. Janet? Definitely not; she was hard as nails, that sister. Then who? . . . Dr. Farringdon? Probably ribby himself; sawbones were seldom rolling in it. Anyway, Farringdon had fallen out with Janet and had not been near Yateham for a week. To hell with the fellow. . . . Then who? . . . Then who? . . . Was there some other way? He could confess to Timothy. No, Timothy would never trust him again; he would sack him.

So ran his thoughts, round and round, backwards and forwards. He felt he was getting fuddled. Fresh air would clear his head, he decided, though experience should have told him that fresh air very often has the opposite effect. With some difficulty, he got to his feet and lurched across to the bar with his tankard.

Mr. Taske, the landlord, looked at him dubiously, wondering whether to serve him with more. Harold, however, did not require the tankard refilled. He asked instead for a bottle of light ale to take home with him. This seemed to Mr. Taske a request with which he could safely comply, so he said:

"Quart, sir?"

Harold had not enough money left for that.

"No, a pint, please."

Mr. Taske turned and reached down for a bottle from one of the lower shelves. This he stamped with the amount of the deposit, but as the first impression made was not very clear, he inked the stamp again and pressed it elsewhere on the label. Harold paid over the required sum, which left him with insufficient for the bus-fare to

Yateham, then wished those present a decidedly slurred "Good evening" and left the White Lion.

With the bottle weighing down the right-hand pocket of his jacket, he swayed off in the direction of Yateham, his problem still unsolved.

Oddly enough, Mr. Dafydd Price took no steps to report the scene he had just witnessed, but proceeded direct to Yateham rectory. He was taken by Mrs. Yi into the study, where books stood piled on the floor for want of a case or shelves.

It had been a bad day for Mr. Gault. Some time during the previous night, some person had daubed in enormous letters, high up on one face of the square tower of St. Anselm's:

> "HOP IT GORLT
> US DONT
> WANT YOU"

He and the verger, who had come to him early with this disquieting news, had managed to scrub enough of the lettering away to make it illegible, yet it must have been seen by many local people, and a small crowd collected to watch rector and verger taking it in turns at the top of the ladder. The morning service had been very poorly attended, as had evensong. And Janet Micheldever had not been there.

Perhaps as a result of these things, his manner towards Mr. Price was frigid.

"What brings you here again, Price?"

The little Welshman looked pained.

"Who is it now who is using surnames?"

"I'm worried and dead tired. What do you want—more money?"

"Bruce, man, is that proper treatment of an old friend? "

"You came to me last Thursday week and I gave you five pounds. On the following Tuesday, you came again and had another five pounds from me. Now—"

"When you and I were in Haolaofen, we did not speak to each other like this."

"I can't afford to keep on paying out money. Ten pounds in just over a week—and now you ask for more."

"I have not. It was you who raised the matter."

"Then that disposes of it." His manner warmed a trifle. "Have you found a post yet?"

"Not yet, I am sorry to say. I have replied to advertisements, both by post and personal application. That is the stumbling-block, man—personal application." He looked down at himself as he sat in his chair, and grimaced. "When they see me, these employers are not impressed by my appearance. I have been thinking that if I could contrive to purchase some new clothes—in particular, a suit; this one is threadbare and a disgrace to our calling—I might meet with greater success in my search for profitable occupation."

He noticed that Mr. Gault's face had hardened again and swiftly changed the subject.

"I have been thinking about that terrible tragedy at Tao-chiaching. The murder of poor Yi Cheng must not be allowed to go unpunished. There are two of us who can bear witness that the third of us left Haolaofen with Yi Cheng, in order to visit an old man who lay gravely ill at Tsinhotun. And there are two of us who can bear witness that the third of us did not return to Haolaofen. The Chinese Christian from Taochiaching will be able to give direct evidence concerning the murder of Yi Cheng by the third of us, which he saw with his own eyes. The name of this man is Feng Lin-tso."

"He could never be produced as a witness."

"Why not, man? I have the address where he is now living. It is at Jesselton in North Borneo. He was fortunate enough to escape from China."

He leant forward in his chair.

"There is another tragic thing that I have not yet told you. Yi Cheng had a daughter. No doubt you will remember her?"

"Hsi-lo."

"Yes, little Hsi-lo—our English Joy, and what a joy the sweet child was to all of us at Haolaofen, until calamity struck her down."

"That must have been after I left."

"Several months after. I can scarcely contain my feelings when I tell you that little Hsi-lo came to me and told me something that she had kept from everyone else, including the members of her family. I could not but do my best to comfort her and she went away. . . . That afternoon she flung herself and her unborn child into the well."

Mr. Gault chewed his lip.

"Did she tell you who it was?"

"It was the man who had murdered her father, though she was unaware of that. She told me that if I ever met him again, I was to say that she still loved him very dearly."

The rector of Yateham sat in thoughtful silence for a long time, while Mr. Price waited patiently, his fingers gently tapping on the flat crown of his shovel-hat, which he nursed in his lap.

"I think the first step," Mr. Gault said finally, "is to get your own affairs into satisfactory order. You're quite right,

I'm afraid, when you say your appearance is against you, so I will give you ten pounds for you to—"

"Ten pounds? Will that be sufficient? Clothes are expensive, you know, man."

"Then I'll make it fifteen. And that must be all, Dafydd. I simply cannot afford any more. I drew some cash yesterday for house furnishings from my small account at the bank, but they'll have to wait. You shall have fifteen pounds—on the understanding that you don't come back for any more. Is that agreed?"

"Indeed it is."

Mr. Gault withdrew his wallet from his pocket and extracted some new five-pound notes. He unfolded them, then stepped across to Mr. Price and dealt three of them on to the outstretched palm.

"Thank you, Bruce."

Mr. Price removed the top note, folded it and slipped it into his breast pocket. Then, taking his hat from his lap, he rose to his feet and stowed the other two away in his hip pocket, saying as he did so:

"It is an old saying that one should not keep all one's eggs in a single basket. Now I must go back to Lulverton, where I am lodging with a widow whose late husband should consider himself fortunate."

He looked round for his stick, and Mr. Gault handed it to him.

"Bruce, man, I am truly grateful to you. If our positions were reversed, you know that I would do the same for you."

Mr. Gault kept his thoughts to himself.

"Let me show you out," he said, moving towards the door.

By the time he reached it, Yi Liu-ying, who had had his

ear against the panel, was back in the kitchen. He waited until his employer had returned to the study after seeing his guest off the premises, then slipped out of the side door of the rectory and followed Mr. Price, allowing the limping yet spry little figure in the wide-brimmed hat to keep some distance ahead of him.

Chapter Eleven

MIST IN THE VALLEY

I

DURING that last week, there had been a constraint between Janet and Dick Farringdon, but on the Saturday morning she had found opportunity in the Lulverton War Memorial Hospital to murmur to him:

"I shall be there at half past nine tomorrow."

Now it was nearly that time and, hastening past the rectory, she knew that she was going to be late in keeping their appointment. When she reached the stile, a young man was endeavouring to climb over it from the other side.

"Harold, you beast!" she said with subdued anger. "You're drunk again."

"Def'ly not, Jan. Argument wi' shtile, thass all."

With difficulty, and with no help at all from him, she managed to pull him over it.

"Where have you been?" she demanded.

"Talking to a frien'," he answered with a beery chuckle. "Very goo' frien', too—charm' fellow."

"You ought to be thoroughly ashamed of yourself."

"Always am, Jan—nex' morn', b'not now."

He thrust his hands in his jacket pockets and stood swaying.

"'D anyone shay I'd been on the jag?"

"Don't you dare go home in that condition."

"Home, ol' dear? Not while Shem Shtars shtill open."

He looked at her, trying to get her into focus. With one eye closed, he said:

"Providenshl, Jan. Thass what it was—provi—what I said." With a wave of his arm, he swung away from her and staggered off along the road. Poor Janet did not know quite what to do. After a moment or two of hesitation and a glance at her wrist-watch, she made up her mind and, with a last glance at her brother's retreating form, she climbed the stile.

Though the night was clear on higher ground, an early autumn mist lurked in the damp little valley known as Dark Hollow. This did not hinder her progress, but it was twenty minutes to ten before she reached the footbridge. Dick Farringdon was not there. Her first thought was that he had deliberately failed to keep the appointment, for his answer to her assurance on the previous day had been a grunt that might have meant anything. But so many things can delay a medical man that she decided against this possibility and, after waiting a few minutes at the bridge, walked on. Before she had gone very far, his tall, broad-shouldered figure took shape in the mist ahead as he hurried towards the mill.

"I'm terribly sorry, dear," he said. "I got held up."

"I thought it must be that."

"You bet it was. And while I'm grovelling I want to throw in a bit about my unforgivable behaviour this last week."

"Me too. Shall we forget it? Even regulars have rows sometimes."

She slipped her arm into his and they walked back to the bridge.

"Darned thoughtless, some people," he said.

For a moment she wondered what he meant, then he bent down and—cautiously, for it was jagged—picked up from the boarded floor the lower portion of a pint-size beer-bottle. This he threw out into the pond, then shone his pencil torch, but there was no sign of the neck or other dangerous fragments.

"That's cleared the decks," he smiled.

"For action?"

"Why not?"

Appropriate measures were taken.

"Now we're regulars again," Janet said.

"Not for too long, I hope. What about the next step?"

"Yes, the next step. I've thought a lot about love—real love, I mean. I've always imagined it was a sort of thing that suddenly overwhelmed you—that when it came, there couldn't be any possible doubt about it. Have you ever read a book by Gene Stratton-Porter called *The Harvester?*"

"Years ago, yes."

"So did I—and I've just read it again. David Langston tells old Granny Moreland that he doesn't think the Girl—with a capital 'G'—understands what he means by love, and Granny says, 'Aw, bosh!' I can't remember the exact words, but she tells him that a woman can't be a wife till she knows what love means, it would stop nine-tenths of the weddings in the world. He took Granny's advice and . .

"And. . .?"

"I'm going to do the same."

"Which means that your answer is—"

"Thank you very much for your kind invitation to be your wife. Having no other engagements, I am very pleased to accept."

II

With the graceful carriage and sense of direction of the bull calling in at the china shop, Harold Micheldever entered the saloon bar of the Seven Stars and went up to the counter. Mrs. Battle viewed him with disapprobation as, with difficulty, he brought out a five-pound note, which he slapped on the counter and demanded a pint of mild and bitter. Mrs. Battle did not hasten to comply. Like a bank cashier retiring for a word with the manager before cashing a doubtful cheque, she withdrew into the back parlour, while the other customers in the bar—all save young Tony Morris of the Downshire County Herald, who made it his business to observe and record—pretended to be interested in everything but Harold. He, half sprawled across the counter, fumbled in his jacket pocket for his last cigarette. He tossed the empty packet on the floor, and was trying to light the cigarette with a second match when Mr. Battle emerged.

One glance was enough.

"I'm sorry, Mr. Micheldever, but we can't serve you."

"Why not? Money's on the counter."

Mr. Battle picked up the note, unfolded it, folded it again and held it out to Harold, who refused to accept it.

"Wass matter with it?" Harold demanded, bending over the counter with an aggressive expression on his face.

"Nothing, sir. If you want it changed, I'll change it, but I'm not serving you with any drink. If you'll take my advice, Mr. Micheldever, you'll go home and get to bed."

"Bloody imper'nence! Gimme a pint o' mile and bidder or I'll—"

"We don't want that sort of language in here, sir, and I

must ask you to leave."

"An' I'm not going till I've had a pint o' mile and bidder." Mr. Battle turned his head to murmur to his wife, who went and fetched P.C. Bristo from his game of darts in the public bar.

III

Janet said to Dick: "I told the parents that I would bring you home. If I know Daddy, he's got a little future-father-in-lawly speech ready for you."

"I can take it."

"But it's getting rather late now. The last bus—"

"The walk won't kill me. I've done it before, remember."

As they went along the footbridge, Janet said:

"We can cut off a corner by going through the yard."

Dick shone the torch and followed her down the stone steps, saying as he did so:

"Nothing's settled yet, so don't breathe a word to a soul, but I'm well in the running for a post at Exeter—much better paid than" He broke off and said in a very different tone:

"That's curious."

They had come down the steps and were about to pass the millhouse door. From beneath it projected a segment of the curled brim of a black hat.

The padlock was hanging by its open shackle from the staple bolted to the door-post. The door, which opened inwards, was shut, the hasp on it unattached to the staple. No sound of machinery came from within.

"Funny," said Janet. "It looks too big for an ordinary bowler—more like a clergyman's hat."

"But how did it get in that position?"

"Dropped there—or perhaps it was thrown across the floor and slid under the door."

"Which means there's someone in there. Opening the door would have shifted the hat. And there's no clatter now. Wonder what's going on."

He tapped with his knuckles on the door. There was no reply. He took out his pencil torch and they peered through the window, just as they had done on the previous occasion. Things inside, however, were different now. The shaft of the water-wheel still revolved, but to no purpose. The pulley and gears had been dismantled, and the pump, which had been to the right of the staircase, now stood on wooden blocks some feet away from its original seating. From one corner of the long rectangular sump on which it had formerly rested rose a pipe to which a hand-pump had been temporarily connected. Engineers' tools and gear lay about.

"Repairs," said Janet.

"And high time, too, from the row it was kicking up last time. But it doesn't explain the Father Brown hat."

He cautiously pushed on the door, looked round the edge of it, then stepped inside.

"Anyone here?" he called, then suddenly strode to the wooden staircase and went up, the thin beam from the torch lighting the way.

Trying to persuade herself that all was well, Janet stood in the doorway until he began to come down again.

"No one up there?" she asked.

"No. I thought I heard someone moving about. The window overlooking the wheel is unfastened, but—"

He stopped speaking and paused on the third stair from the foot, where he played the torch-beam into the sump.

"Good God!"

Instinctively Janet moved forward to see the cause of this shocked exclamation. Dick waved her back.

"It isn't pleasant."

He was coming down the remaining stairs, when a voice said behind Janet:

"What the devil's going on here?"

Janet gave a cry and turned to see Sir Timothy Chatthume, now in grey flannels and a sports coat.

"Tim! You made me jump."

"What's happening, Jan?"

Now on one knee by the sump, Dick said over his shoulder:

"Come over here, please, Sir Timothy. Janet, you stop where you are."

Timothy walked across to the sump. Face upward in the foot of water it contained lay the body of the Reverend Dafydd Price.

"A clergyman," murmured Dick. "Do you know him?"

"Very much so, but not his name. Shall we get him out?"

"We can't do anything for him. He's dead. Better leave him and call the police."

"Right. I'll get to the nearest phone. You wait here."

IV

Mr. and Mrs. Micheldever heard the front-door bell ring.

"There they are," she said, rising to her feet. "I'll let them in. Janet must have forgotten her key. Try not to be too long-winded with him, dear."

"I am never long-winded," retorted her husband, who

130

had prepared for the occasion some notes on the rights and responsibilities of matrimony.

It was not Janet and Dick in the porch when Mrs. Micheldever opened the door. It was P.C. Bristo, in civilian clothes.

"Evenin', m'm," he said, raising his cap.

The welcoming smile vanished from her face.

"Good evening, Mr. Bristo."

"Is the rector in?"

Mr. Micheldever was no longer the rector, but was still so called by many in the parish.

"I hope nothing ..."

"Not serious, m'm. Just a bit awkward, like."

Mrs. Micheldever invited him into the hall, then went back to her husband, closing the door behind her.

"It's Bristo," she said with a worried frown. "He wants to speak to you."

Mr. Micheldever went out to Bristo, who was fiddling with his cap and looking at a picture on the wall without taking it in.

"What is the trouble, Bristo?"

"I thought I'd best come and tell you meself, sir."

"Yes, yes," said Mr. Micheldever impatiently. "What has happened?"

"It's Mr. 'Arold, sir. 'E's caused a bit of a to-do along at the Stars. Very much under the influence, I'm sorry to say, sir. I left a couple o' chaps looking after 'im in a back room, so's not to 'ave too much of a scene."

Mr. Micheldever's thin features had hardened still further.

"Is he liable to arrest?"

"Only if 'e's too drunk to look after 'imself."

"Is he in that condition?"

"Well, 'e's pretty far gorn, rector."

"Then I urge you to arrest him."

He stepped forward and opened the front door.

"If," he continued, "there is a question of bail, I am not prepared to stand."

Bristo looked worried.

"You're quite sure about this, sir?"

"Completely so. Goodnight."

Chapter Twelve

INSPECTOR BRADFIELD TAKES OVER

THE telephone call from Sir Timothy Chatthume to the divisional headquarters at Lulverton of the County Constabulary had rapid results. Detective-Inspector Bradfield and Dr. Lorimer, the divisional surgeon, were immediately summoned from their homes. Bradfield, in his turn, called out one of his assistants, Detective-Constable Emerson, and, after collecting photographic equipment, they were driven by a police driver to Dark Hollow, arriving a couple of minutes before Dr. Lorimer. By this time, Sir Timothy was back at the mill.

Leaving the cars near Barlow's cottage, where lights glowed behind the curtains, both upstairs and down, the surgeon and the two detectives walked to the millhouse. When Dr. Lorimer had satisfied himself that Dafydd Price was dead, and his confrère had confirmed that life had been extinct when he had made his tragic discovery, the body was photographed and then removed so that the doctors could carry out a closer examination.

Accompanied by Emerson, Bradfield went out to talk with Janet and Timothy in the mill yard. Emerson was a young giant—a hard worker, but without his superior's education, intelligence or sense of humour. "Damned dumb, damned dim, damned dogged," as someone had once described him. Detective-Inspector Peter Bradfield was tall and in the early thirties, broad-shouldered, but not so burly as Emerson. Any pretensions to good looks were somewhat spoiled by a nose that was wide and rather flat. For all that, he was a great favourite with the other sex, and Janet found him quite the nicest policeman she had ever met—at first.

Her answers to his questions can be condensed into a paragraph.

"My fiancé—Dr. Farringdon—and I were walking past here when we noticed part of the brim of a hat sticking out from underneath that door. We thought it was very peculiar, so we looked through that window, but couldn't see anybody inside. We thought there must be somebody because of the hat. The door wasn't locked, so Dr. Farringdon pushed it open and went in. He thought he heard somebody moving about upstairs and went up, but there wasn't anybody there. He found one of the windows open. As he was coming down again, he happened to glance into the hole and told me not to come near. Then Sir Timothy arrived and he and Dr. Farringdon decided the poor man was dead. Sir Timothy went off to telephone you, and we stayed here. While we were waiting, Dr. Farringdon picked up the clergyman's hat and found from the name inside that he was the Reverend Dafydd Price, which sounds Welsh. I don't recognize the name. I might know him if I saw him, but Dr. Farringdon hasn't let me."

During the course of this, at an upward jerk of the head by Bradfield, Emerson had left them and gone into the millhouse to inspect the upper floor.

"There's a private telephone system," said Timothy when his turn came, "linking up various points on the estate. One line runs to Barlow's cottage, which is over there. Barlow is an old pensioner of ours. He's worked for my family all his life. When he got too old for hard manual labour, I found a quiet job for him, which was looking after this mill—not very vital, but it pleases the old fellow to have something to do. He rang me this evening at Chatthume Place and asked me to come here at once, because a curious thing had happened, so I got out the skiff and rowed up, which is the quickest way. When I reached here, I found Miss Micheldever and Dr. Farringdon, who had just discovered the body."

Bradfield asked: "What was the trouble here, sir? Did Barlow say?"

"Yes, he did. You can see for yourself that some repair work's going on in there. The machinery's got old and wonky and I'm having it overhauled, with new bearings and so forth. Under the mill there's a spring, and the mill-wheel supplies the power to pump the water up—fresh, clean water fit for drinking, which is more than the Snare is. It's carried from here by pipes, one to Chatthume Place, one to our dairy farm, one to the stables, and the fourth to Barlow's cottage. My father had this done before we had mains supply to the house. The cottage isn't on the mains, so Barlow has to depend on water from the spring. Now the pump's out of action, there's no water going through to the cottage, so Barlow has to come down here with buckets and draw up water with the hand-pump the engineers have lent us."

Bradfield, who had listened very patiently to this, now said: "You were going to tell me, sir, why Barlow phoned you."

"I was working up to that. Barlow came this evening with his bucket and filled it from the hand-pump, but when he went to lock up afterwards he couldn't find the padlock, which he'd left hanging from the fastening—or so he said. I see it's there now."

"What about the key?"

"He didn't mention it. All he told me was that the padlock had disappeared, that he thought someone must have pinched it while he was working the hand-pump with his back to the door, and that if they had pinched it, they must have had a good and probably naughty reason for doing it. So he debated whether to stand guard over the mill all night or send out a call for help, decided on the call for help and hurried to telephone me."

He frowned as if suddenly remembering something.

"He said he was coming straight back here."

"What time did he phone you, sir?"

"Somewhere round half past nine. I didn't really notice."

"Did he say anything about anything else?"

"No, only the padlock. It worried him—and it worried me too when he told me. But the padlock's there now, so either he found it afterwards or the old fellow's going a bit mental. Funny he hasn't come back. I hope he's all right."

"We'll go along to the cottage in a minute or two, sir." Bradfield turned to Janet.

"Was the padlock where it is now when you first got here, Miss Micheldever?"

"Yes."

"No key in it?"

"No."

"Who holds the keys, Sir Timothy?"

"There are two. Barlow has one, which he keeps on a key-chain and guards as if it's for the strongrooms of the Bank of England. The second one's usually kept with the other duplicates in my office, but is now held temporarily by the foreman in charge of the work going on."

"Miss Micheldever's just said that Dr. Farringdon thought he heard somebody upstairs and found a window open. Did you—or you, Miss Micheldever—see anyone near here this evening?

"No," said Timothy promptly.

Janet also replied in the negative, but only after a pause that did not pass unnoticed by the detective. She went on hurriedly, as if to change the course of the conversation:

"It's very peculiar about Mr. Price's hat, isn't it? If he didn't commit suicide by drowning himself in the tank or whatever it is, someone else must have put him in it, and they couldn't have left afterwards through that door because the hat would have been moved by the door being opened. The only other way out's through the unfastened window upstairs. I think we must have surprised somebody, who ran up there and escaped through the window. I don't know whether you've looked at it, inspector, but it's easy to get in and out of, because it's only just above the thing called the gut, which takes the water to the wheel. You can get down on to the ledge of the gut and walk along it to the bridge." She smiled suddenly. "I know because I've done it. Sir Timothy and my brother and I used to play round here when we were children. I don't know why we didn't get killed, the things we did sometimes!"

Bradfield smiled in a way that she liked, then said to Timothy:

"Where did you leave the skiff, sir?"

"Tied up on the other bank. It's easier landing there— not so many reeds. I left it there, came along the other side of the millhouse, up the steps and across the bridge.

Which disposes, I imagine, of any suggestion that someone hopped out through the window. If he had, I'd have seen him."

Janet, with a fear in the back of her mind that she was reluctant to admit even to herself, wanted to foster the idea that the murderer had been in the mill when she and Dick had arrived, and not on his way to the Seven Stars, so she tried to hide her disappointment and said:

"It may have happened just before you got there."

"Possible," conceded Timothy, "but not at all likely. If I hadn't seen him, I should have heard him. I was a minute or two mooring the skiff close by."

The next inquiry of the detective, while relieving Janet, put Timothy on the alert again.

"Did you know Mr. Price, sir? I'm assuming, for the moment, that that was his name."

"I'll have to assume it, too. No, I didn't actually know him, but I've seen him before. The first time was in the Wine Lodge at Southmouth. He came in while I was having a quick one and went round urging everybody to read their Bibles every day. The next time I saw him was one evening a short while back at the Southmouth Empire. He leapt to his feet half-way through the show and kicked up a devil of a fuss about a perfectly respectable bit of dancing by my fiancée, Miss Sabina Danbury. We weren't engaged then, but we are now. Though I ought not to say it, my own opinion is that he was nuts—chronic religious mania."

"Have you seen him since, Sir Timothy?"

It was a formal question, prompted apparently by nothing more than the need to collect as much information as possible.

Timothy hesitated—and again the pause was not lost on Bradfield—then decided that half the truth was better than a downright lie.

"Yes, earlier this evening. Miss Danbury and I were in the skiff, just above the bridge where the Snare runs under the road, when he came hopping along like a sparrow with a crutch—"

"Hopping?"

"He was lame, you know—walked with a stick up against his leg. I'd better be absolutely accurate. We didn't see him arrive at the bridge—or hear him. I said he came hopping along because that's the way he went about it when I saw him previously. Anyway, he was there on the bridge when we rowed out from under it, coming in this direction. He recognized us and ..."

"Yes, sir . . .?"

"Well, he was damned rude, to put it bluntly. Still on the old theme, he called Miss Danbury a woman without shame. I didn't want an altercation with the old—gentleman, so discreetly withdrew under the bridge and left him to go on his way."

"Which way was that?"

"I couldn't tell you. We didn't see him either come or go. When I saw him next, it was in the sump. It's no business of mine to put forward theories, inspector, but I'd say he drowned himself while—how do they put it?—while the balance of his mind was disturbed. Came past here, saw old Barlow busy at the pump, took the padlock off so that Barlow couldn't lock up again, then, when Barlow went to phone me, popped inside and—"

An expressive gesture served instead of the unsaid words.

"Yes!" said Janet eagerly. "That sounds possible, doesn't

it, inspector?"

Bradfield did not reply.

"Excuse me," he said and turned towards the millhouse door.

"Just a moment," said Timothy. "I'm getting concerned about Barlow. Shall I slip along to the cottage?"

"Yes, do, sir," Bradfield agreed, then went inside.

Dr. Stuart Lorimer—slim, dark, keen-witted, forty-two, and a close personal friend of Bradfield's—stood upright and turned as he entered. Bradfield raised his eyebrows inquiringly.

"Drowned," said Lorimer.

"In there?" Bradfield asked, jerking his head towards the sump.

"That's more your section, Peter, but I'd say he hadn't been in the pond, eh, Farringdon?"

"Not from the condition of his clothes. There's no trace of blanket-weed or anything like that."

Lorimer added to this: "A man couldn't fall or be pushed into that noisome mixture without showing signs of it afterwards. Certainly there were traces of water on the floor before we lifted him out. They might have dripped off him as he was carried in."

"There's another possible explanation for those," Bradfield said. "I gather that earlier this evening a bucket was filled from the pump. That would explain the odd splash here and there. It's a pretty safe assumption that if he was drowned anywhere it was in here."

"We can't do much under these conditions," said Lorimer, "and with a flashlamp, but Dr. Farringdon and I have examined him as best we can. A thing that will interest you is that, from the state of his skull, he's had a very severe blow on the head, and fragments of brown glass in his hair strongly suggest that he was stunned with a bottle before he was drowned."

"May I say a word, inspector?" asked Dick.

"Please do, doctor."

"When Miss Micheldever and I were coming across the footbridge, we came upon a broken beer-bottle, which was lying on the floor-boards. I threw it in the pond."

"How was it broken?"

"All we found was the lower part of it, smashed off about half-way up—perhaps more in places, because it wasn't a clean break, but—well, jagged."

"Was there a label?"

"I think so, but I wouldn't like to swear to it."

"There's your weapon, Peter," said Lorimer. "Used with such force that it snapped off at the neck."

"If I'd known that," said Dick, "I wouldn't have chucked it in the pond. I got rid of it p.d.q. because it was dangerous."

"We'll try to recover it," Bradfield told him, then went on to ask for his account of the evening's events.

Dick's story tallied with Janet's, the only supplementary question being:

"Can you describe the noise you heard upstairs, doctor?"

"It sounded like somebody moving cautiously about—floorboards creaking; but I'm beginning to think I was mistaken. That water-wheel going round must cause a lot of vibration. I don't think you'd better quote me on that, inspector. At all events, that's why I went up. There was no one there. The casement-stay of one of the windows was adrift. You know the type: four or five holes in it. If there'd been a breeze, the window would have been flapping in it. I left it as it was."

"You looked out, I suppose?"

"Oh, yes, but I didn't see anyone. I couldn't see anything much, really, because of the mist."

"Did you hear anything?"

"Only the swish of the water-wheel."

"Just about that time, Sir Timothy was mooring his skiff a few yards down-stream."

"Then it was out of my sight and hearing."

"Thank you, doctor."

Lorimer was looking speculatively at the sump.

"I'm no engineer," he remarked at this juncture, "but why is there any water in that thing? Presumably it acts as a sort of drip-tray for the pump, to prevent flooding. Won't it have a hole in the bottom to drain away surplus water?"

They examined it for an outlet pipe, but the base of the concrete trough was below the level of the floor, only about eight inches of the sides showing above it, with projecting bolts to hold the reciprocating pump in position. The water was not clear enough to see to the bottom, so Bradfield took a crowbar left by the engineers and poked around with it until he encountered something soft in one corner of the sump. This he could not dislodge with the crowbar. He took off his jacket rolled up his shirt-sleeves and, with a grunt of distaste, plunged his hand into the water, not quite happy about what it would encounter. After a moment or two of groping, he drew it out again, and, as he did so, there was a gurgle as the water began to run away. He examined the makeshift plug and found it to be piece of greasy cotton waste as used by engineers. By the time he had refastened his shirt-cuffs and put on his jacket, the water had all flowed out of the sump. With the help of a torch, he peered into it, examining the bottom and sides.

"Clues by the thousand," he said over his shoulder.

"What sort? "asked Lorimer.

"Tea leaves."

He had just risen to his feet when Sir Timothy came suddenly in, out of breath, and with a troubled expression.

"What's the matter, sir?"

"It's Barlow. I'm afraid the poor old chap's in a bad way—dead, for all I know."

Chapter Thirteen

THE CLUE OF THE LABEL

SIR TIMOTHY and Dr. Lorimer hurried off together. Leaving Bradfield and Emerson in the millhouse, Dick went out to speak to Janet, who was looking anxious. He endeavoured to reassure her.

"It's very tragic, darling, but you must try not to let it upset you."

Her voice trembled as she answered:

"Dick, I'm frightened."

"Don't be. I'm here to look after you."

"It's not for myself."

She took his arm and drew him away from the open doorway. Out of the detectives' hearing she murmured:

"It's Harold. I'm terrified that he did it."

"Harold? What on earth makes you think that?"

"I told that inspector a lie. I said I hadn't seen anyone near here this evening, but I did—Harold. He was trying to get over the stile and was dreadfully drunk. Suppose he ..."

"Of course he didn't, you dear little silly."

"But he'd just come from here. He must have met him."

"Not necessarily. They might have been both coming in the same direction and not seen each other. Which way did the parson come? We don't know. And another thing we don't know is when the murder was done—if it was murder. Maybe it was much earlier in the evening."

"No, it couldn't have been. Tim told the inspector that Barlow phoned him about half past nine, and all Barlow told him was about the padlock. He'd just come from here and if the body had been here then, surely he would have said so?"

"Padlock? What did he tell him—something new?"

Janet repeated Timothy's report to Bradfield.

"But why take it," asked Dick, "then put it back again? Sounds crazy to me. Whoever did it must have been mad—or drunk."

Immediately he regretted this remark, which increased Janet's fears.

"Harold said he'd had a providential meeting with someone. That means only one thing—that he'd got money from this someone to spend in the Seven Stars. When I met him he was too drunk to know what he was doing. If he hadn't any money in his pocket to buy more drink, and met that poor clergyman and killed him and robbed him . . ."

Dick took her in his arms and did his best to comfort her.

Timothy and Dr. Lorimer were climbing up the bank at the far end of the millpond, when the ambulance pulled up. They showed the men which way to take the stretcher, then went on to Barlow's cottage.

In the millhouse, with Detective-Constable Emerson hovering with the massive immobility of a captive balloon, Bradfield was going through the dead man's pockets and listing the contents. Among the few sodden papers in the breast pocket was a letter addressed to "Rev. D. Price, c/o Mrs. Steadley, 8 Friar Lane, Lulverton, Downshire." From the hip pocket he managed to extract two very limp five-pound notes, the only money, save for a few coppers, on the body.

Next he examined the hat. After glancing at the name inside, he was just about to lay it down, when he sniffed, then brought it to his nose for a closer inhalation. He held it out to Emerson, who drew in deeply before he said:

"Catarrh."

"Helpful fellow. Anything upstairs? "

"Only a dead rat, sarge."

The appellation was allowed to pass unchallenged. Bradfield's promotion had come but a few months before, and it always took a little time for things to sink into Emerson's mind.

"What about the window?"

"Open and unlatched. He could have got out that way easy."

"Did you find anything to suggest he did? Shreds of torn clothing? Mud? We had rain this morning and he might have left footmarks on the sill."

"I didn't get round to a real close look."

"Imbecile," said Bradfield, but as he pronounced it in the French way, his assistant was not at all offended.

As he went up the stairs, Emerson said after him in a tone compounded of satisfaction and hope:

"You won't find nothing, only the dead rat."

Which was true enough. Except for the decomposing rodent, the whole uneven floor was bare. Through the holes in the roof where tiles were missing, the stars could have been seen had it not been for the mist. With the help of his torch, Bradfield satisfied himself that although a reasonably agile person could have left the millhouse through the window, there was no evidence to show that anyone had. Such negative results, however, did not persuade him to dismiss the possibility entirely.

He leant out and shone the beam along the concrete ledge of the gut, which was about on a level with the floor inside, but could detect no footmarks. Just to the right of him the water poured into the trough-like vanes of the water-wheel and bore it round, sounding curiously like the engine of a motor-car.

Without much difficulty he got through the window and walked along the ledge, reaching the bridge just as the ambulance men arrived. Having directed them round, he carried out an examination of the bridge. The first thing he noticed was that the floor-boards had been very recently creosoted; they smelt strongly and were still damp in places. He found one or two small fragments of brown-tinted glass and, held by the pressure of water against and around one of the bars of the trash-rack, the oval, coloured label from a beer-bottle. This he managed to retrieve and, having noted that the principal words it bore were "Trumington's Light Ale," put it carefully away in an envelope, with the glass splinters in another.

He then went down the steps between the spill-way and the gut and made a survey down as far as the point where the Chatthume skiff lay moored against the bank. Then he returned to the yard, where Janet and Dick still waited.

"Do you need us any more, inspector?" Dick asked. "It's getting late."

"I'm so sorry," Bradfield said with an apologetic smile. "I'd forgotten about you. How are you going to get back?"

"I'll take Miss Micheldever home, then pad the hoof to Lulverton."

"If you can wait a minute or two, sir, I'll give you both a lift."

Janet smiled at him, making him feel a knight-errant indeed.

"That'll be lovely," she said. "I've never been in a police car." She turned to Dick. "You can drop me, then go straight on. We'll expect you to dinner tomorrow."

Bradfield went into the building and took Emerson by surprise by appearing from such an unexpected quarter. The ambulance men were covering the body on the stretcher.

"Stop here till you're relieved," Emerson was instructed, "and keep a general eye on things. The engineers will probably turn up in the morning. There's no reason why they shouldn't get on with their work. Explain the position to the man in charge." He nodded towards the sump. "If their slop-basin's anything to go by, you should get a cup of tea."

"O.K."

"And just to keep yourself amused till then, see if you can find a walking-stick lying around anywhere— more than likely with a rubber doings at the end of it. It shouldn't be far away. If you do come across it, remember where it is, because it's quite possible I shall ask you."

Before Emerson could consider the implications of this and make reply, Bradfield had picked up the photographic kit and the package in which he had placed the property removed from the pockets of the victim, and gone out to Janet and Dick. The trio set off for the next objective, Barlow's cottage.

Timothy and the divisional surgeon were waiting for them by the front door. When Bradfield had stowed his burdens in the police car, Lorimer took him on one side.

"He was dead when I got to him. A stroke, probably brought on by hurrying back here—the third he's had. He was a patient of mine and I'll give a certificate."

"Mrs. Barlow . . .? "

"Upstairs in bed. I've broken it to her. I'll get a nurse in tonight. Leave all that side to me."

"I'd better have a quick look round in there."

With a word of apology to Janet and Dick for keeping then, waiting still longer, he went into the cottage. In the kitchen stood a bucket full of water and alongside it a hurricane-lamp; still alight. The door leading into the back garden was open, Barlow had passed away in a chair in the front parlour, on the wall of which was the telephone instrument connected by private line to Chatthume Place. The receiver was on its hook.

The sequence of events seemed clear enough. Barlow had taken the bucket through the back door into the kitchen, where he had set it down before going into the parlour to telephone Sir Timothy. At the end of the conversation, he had replaced the receiver, then, suddenly overtaken by the attack, had collapsed in the nearest chair and died.

Bradfield left the cottage. The uniformed constable at the wheel of the police car had got it turned about and was patiently waiting to depart. Bradfield ushered Janet and Dick into the back, then, after a few final words with Sir Timothy and Dr. Lorimer, took his seat in the front.

They dropped Janet at Medlar Cottage and, after waiting till she was safely indoors, turned back towards Lulverton; As they approached Monk Jewel, with thatched, half-timbered cottages around its little village green, the headlights picked out the post in the forecourt of its only hostelry. Over the white lion rampant regardant painted on the sign were two words that attracted Bradfield's attention: "Trumington's Ales."

"Stop at the pub," he told the driver.

Messrs. Trumington & Co. were Downshire brewers and their tied houses were numerous in the county, but inquiries about the label would have to be started somewhere, so, the lights being still on upstairs, Bradfield decided that it should be the White Lion. He got out of the car saying:

"Shan't be a couple of minutes."

Mr. Taske himself answered the door in his dressing-gown. He recognized Bradfield and, following his usual practice of doing all he could to keep on the right side of the police, invited him in with what was intended to be a bright smile of welcome, which suited neither him nor his dressing-gown. Bradfield produced the envelope and cautiously extracted the label, which he passed over to Mr. Taske with the words:

"Careful with it, please. It's wet. Is that your deposit stamp on it—in two places?"

He was greatly pleased when Mr. Taske nodded his head vigorously and continuously as he replied:

"Yes, that's ours. That's ours all right. Yes, without a shadow of doubt. Yes. Oh, yes, definitely."

Evidently he looked upon Bradfield as a man who would not take "Yes" for an answer.

"Can you tell me who you sold the bottle to—and when? "

"Pint-size light. Hmmm. Now, let me think . . ."

The results of these meditations were not agreeable.

Mr. Taske looked first worried, then disgruntled. He was an insignificant little man with a long moustache, and his tone was more injured than angry as he asked:

"Are you trying to catch me?"

"Certainly not. Why?"

"Seems a funny way of going about it. Yes, a funny way. Why not come straight out with it?"

"I don't follow you."

"If you want to find out whether young Micheldever gave trouble in here tonight, you ought to ask. Yes, you ought to come straight out with it. He was O.K. when he came in here—sober enough to serve. Yes, O.K. he was—quite O.K., yes. How much he had afterwards at the Seven Stars is none of my business. I know Mr. Battle. He wouldn't have called you police in without good cause. I'm not denying that. Don't think I'm trying to deny it. Mr. Battle knows his business, and his business is none of mine. All I'm saying is that there was nothing wrong in me serving young Micheldever. And I don't much care for the way you try to get at it. Labels and the like. Why didn't you come straight out—"

Bradfield had listened to this outburst, during which Mr. Taske had gained increasing confidence in his own rectitude, with something approaching stupefaction, for he had not enjoyed that evening the benefit of the jungle telegraph that operates so swiftly and mysteriously from pub to pub in any district. He tried to avoid showing his ignorance of what had happened in the Seven Stars.

"You're jumping to the wrong conclusions," he said. "I'm not concerned at the moment with whether Micheldever was drunk or not when he left here. I might be later, but I'm not just now. Please answer this straightforward question: Did you sell Micheldever this evening a bottle of beer with this label on it?"

Mr. Taske was off again.

"Yes, quite definitely yes. About nine o'clock, it was. Yes, about nine o'clock. Minute or two either way, perhaps."

Bradfield's tone became more conversational.

"Micheldever has a sister, hasn't he?"

"Yes. Father's the rector of Yateham. Yes, the rector of Yateham. Pretty as a picture."

Bradfield did not question this description of Mr. Micheldever. He said:

"You're sure about the label?"

"I remember it distinctly, yes. There wasn't enough inks on the stamp first go off, so I did it again. Yes, I'd go into the witness-box and swear it on oath."

"Thank you. You may be called upon to do so."

He wished the now very apprehensive landlord of the White Lion good night and went out to the car.

When they reached Lulverton, Dick Farringdon was put down at his request at the gates of the War Memorial Hospital. He said through the window to Bradfield:

"Very many thanks, inspector. You've saved me a long walk."

"Don't mention it, doctor—the least I could do after keeping you kicking your heels so long."

Dick mastered a yawn.

"It's certainly been a tiring day. After a token appearance at the hospital, I'm getting to bed. I hope you'll soon be able to do the same."

"It all depends. Good night, doctor." The smile faded as he turned to the driver. "Friar Lane."

The big black Wolseley moved forward.

Mrs. Steadley was a widow who eked out a living by taking in boarders. Her house was in darkness when they pulled up outside, but Bradfield considered his errand sufficiently urgent to arouse the residents. Persistent ringing of the bell at length brought down Mrs. Steadley, fully dressed. She regarded this late visitor with no favour at all.

"I'm full up," she announced, and was just about to close the door in his face, when he said:

"Are you Mrs. Steadley?"

Something in his tone and bearing made her pause. She pulled the door open a trifle and agreed that she was Mrs. Steadley.

"I'm from the police, madam. Very sorry to bother you so late, but it's a serious matter. Has Mr. Price, a clergyman, been lodging here?"

"Yes, but only a few days. Has anything happened to him?"

"I'm afraid so. He's been found drowned in Dark Hollow."

"Oh, dear," she replied, working out by mental arithmetic how much the tragedy might cost her in pounds, shillings and pence. "I am sorry. How did it—"

"Can you tell me anything about his movements this evening?"

"Yes. I gave him his supper and then he said he was going to Yateham to see his friend, the rector there."

"Mr. Micheldever?"

"No, the new one. I don't just remember his name. Gaunt or something. Anyway, he lives at the rectory, because that was where Mr. Price said he was going. He left here about eight o'clock."

"Was he going to catch a bus, did he say?"

"No. The poor gentleman was lame, but he'd been advised by the doctors to walk as much as possible—without tiring himself, of course. His leg would get worse if he didn't use it regularly. That's what he told me the doctors said. More likely because he was hard up, if you ask me."

"Did he take his walking-stick with him?"

"Why, of course. He couldn't walk without it. Well, I never saw him walk without it, even in the house."

"Can you describe it?"

"It was a good one. Perhaps I oughtn't to say it, but it was better than most of the poor gentleman's belongings. He wasn't at all well off by the look of him, but so long as they pay regularly, I'm the last to—"

"You were telling me about the stick, madam?"

"Oh, yes. It's ebony and the handle's white and"—her forefinger delineated an inverted U—"like that. It looks like ivory, and where it joins the ebony there's a silver band with Chinese writing engraved on it. The other end had quite a big rubber thing on it to stop it from slipping. Mr. Price was very proud of the stick. He told me his parishioners in China gave it to him."

"Thank you. Had he any family, do you know?"

"He wasn't married. I don't know any more than that, He was a missionary and, though he didn't say so, mind, it's likely he got his bad leg while he was in China. He talked about being keen on tennis before he went there. Poor gentleman, I told him to be careful walking in the dark with that leg. Now it's been the death of him."

It was a completely unwarrantable assumption, but Bradfield did not contradict her. He thanked her, apologised once more, and left.

"Is that the lot?" asked the driver as he got in beside him.

Bradfield thought for a moment, glanced at his watch, thought for another moment, then answered:

"Yateham."

Chapter Fourteen

RECTOR'S EVIDENCE

POLICE-CONSTABLE BRISTO was rightly incensed at being got out of bed at that hour of the night, but when he saw that the caller was no less a person than Detective-Inspector Bradfield of the C.I.D., his expression changed entirely.

"You young devil!" he grinned. "Might've guessed it was you. Come in out of the dry."

They were old friends, these two. Bristo was a Cockney and proud of it. What he was doing as a village policeman in the depths of rural Downshire was his secret. As Bradfield was a Londoner too, they had been drawn together when Bradfield, twenty years the other's junior, had come to Lulverton as a detective-constable. In these later days, Bristo was most respectful when formal occasions demanded, but this was not one of those.

In the cottage parlour, he said:

"I'll put the kettle on."

"Fine! I'm about ready for a cupper."

"With a thimbleful o' you know what," added Bristo with a wink, as he went out into the kitchen.

While the kettle was coming to the boil, Bradfield asked:

"What happened in the Seven Stars tonight, Charley?"

"That silly young so-and-so, 'Arold Micheldever, filled 'imself up to the hatches with wallop, then went on the turn. Got proper nasty with ole Battle, 'e did. I was just going to try for eleven, sixteen, double eight, when Mrs. Battle fetches me out of the public bar into the private, where young Micheldever was 'oldin' forth, sayin' if 'e didn't get a pint o' mother-in- law 'e'd wreck the place. Seems from what was said that 'e come in plastered and starts wavin' a fiver about."

Bradfield's interest quickened.

"Does he usually carry money in such large chunks?"

"Not 'im."

"What happened to the note?"

"'E smacked it on the counter. Battle refused to serve 'im and tried to give it 'im back, but Micheldever wouldn't take it. When 'e was whipped orf to the cells at Lulverton, I passed it over and 'e'll get it back tomorrow."

"What's the charge?"

"Drunk and disorderly. I didn't want to do it, 'im bein' local and son of the old rector, but I went along to see 'is dad and 'e said, 'You pinch 'im, Charley, and good luck to yer.'"

"The rector said that?"

"P'raps not in them words, but that's what 'e meant. Prob'ly thought it might bring young 'Arold up with a jerk."

The lid of the kettle began to rattle in the kitchen. Bristo went out to make the tea. When he came back with the tray, Bradfield gave him a brief account of the evening's happenings in Dark Hollow.

"Funny, you know," said Bristo at the end of it. "That's the second padre as 'as bin drowned there, only the other fell and wasn't pushed."

"Who was that?"

"Mr. Donaldson, the rector. Last winter, it was."

Bradfield looked puzzled.

"Let's sort this out, Charley. Yateham seems to run to rectors. This is the third I've heard about within the hour."

"It was like this," said Bristo, and went on to explain.

Then Bradfield asked: "And what of Harold Micheldever, the problem child?"

Bristo pulled his chair a little closer and bent forward.

"There's a bit of a mystery there, Peter. 'E was a padre once, too, and then all of a sudden 'e wasn't. I never 'eard the rights of it, but I've always 'ad the suspicion in the back of me mind as what 'e was unfrocked or whatever it is they do to 'em. Yes, 'e was a missionary in China with the what's its name—the Downshire lot."

"The Downshire Missions in Asia?"

"That's it. Then, by all accounts, 'e left 'em—and China, too. Went to India for some time. Cup more?"

"Yes, please, Charley."

Bristo went on as he poured the tea and added the lacing of Scotch:

"Late one night last June or July, 'e turned up 'ere without a word o' warnin' and as guzzled as a newt. Same sort of trouble I 'ad with 'im as s'evenin'—knockin' up ole Battle and shoutin' the odds for booze. 'E's a proper no-good, young 'Arold. Give 'im a quid and before you can turn round 'e's got 'imself so's he can't see an 'ole in a ladder."

Bristo paused to light his pipe, then said through the haze:

"I don't like the sound of tonight's 'ow-d'yer-do, Peter."

"Wonder where he got that fiver?"

"Number any use to you? I kep' a record of it."

"It might help a lot."

Bristo fetched his note-book while Bradfield consulted his own.

"I'll read it out," said Bristo. "Capital 'B,' then a little 'c' over a little 's,' then one eight four space two seven one nought nought six."

Bradfield compared this with the numbers of the notes he had found in Dafydd Price's hip pocket. These were Bc/s 184 271004 and Bc/s 184 271005.

One last call was essential before Bradfield and his driver went home to bed. They drove along the deserted High Street, forked left and, having passed the church, pulled up at the rectory gates. A few lights were still on, which encouraged Bradfield to walk up the short drive and press the bell-push in its brightly polished brass surround to the right of the handsome front door.

After a short while, the light was switched on in the hall, then the door was opened by Yi Liu-ying in formal black coat and striped trousers. Concealing his surprise at the sight of this young Chinaman in such unexpected surroundings, Bradfield asked with a polite smile if it was convenient for him to have a word with the rector.

"Will you tell me your name, please?"

"Detective-Inspector Bradfield."

There was no change of expression on the flat face of Yi Liu-ying as he said, standing back for the visitor to enter:

"If you will please come in, I will tell Mr. Gault."

Leaving Bradfield in the hall, which had a minimum of furnishing, he went upstairs, and it was some minutes before he returned.

"Mr. Gault is sorry to keep you waiting. He was just getting into bed. He asks me to show you into the study and will come down to you as soon as he is dressed."

In the study, Bradfield was supplied with a wooden chair, offered a cigarette from a box that Yi Liu-ying took from the mantelpiece, then left alone.

Bruce Gault joined him at length—a tall, striking figure, his white hands and clerical collar contrasting sharply with the black of his clothes and beard. Bradfield, having risen from his seat and been told to sit down again, began with apologies for the lateness of his call. Mr. Gault, standing before the fireplace, waved these aside with an impatient hand.

"What brings you here?" he asked curtly, in the same tone and almost in the same words as to his previous visitor that evening.

"A serious matter, sir. A gentleman we believe to be the Reverend Dafydd Price has been found drowned."

"Drowned?"

Mr. Gault seemed more surprised than shocked by this news.

"Yes, sir."

"Where?"

"At the mill in the valley near here called Dark Hollow. I've been to the house in Lulverton where he's been staying, and the proprietress, Mrs. Steadley, told me he left there about eight o'clock with the intention of coming to see you."

"What of it?"

"Did he?"

"He did."

Bradfield waited for amplification of this chilly assent, but none was forthcoming.

"Can you tell me what time he left, sir?"

"About a quarter past nine."

"Did he say where he was going to?"

"Back to his boarding-house."

A little disconcerted by the arctic manner of this austere member of the cloth, Bradfield did his best to enlist his sympathy.

"I'm in some difficulty, sir, and I was hoping you could help me. Mrs. Steadley said Mr. Price proposed to walk here."

"Which he did—or so he told me."

"Did he mention which way he came?"

"He did not. At the end of our conversation, I went with him to the front door, where I suggested he caught a bus back to Lulverton. He told me that he had walked here and was going to walk back. He asked me whether I knew any short cut, and I told him about the footpath through the valley. I strongly advised him not to go that way, but to keep to the road, even though it is a longer way round. From what you have just told me, he couldn't have followed my advice."

"You didn't see which way he went?"

"No. I stood at the front door until he had reached the gate, then closed the door."

"And that was the last you saw of him?"

"That should be obvious to you."

This was heavy going. Bradfield persevered.

"We're very much in the dark, sir, about Mr. Price. Have you any information, please? We'll have to communicate with his relatives."

"I've known Mr. Price for a number of years. We were ' missionaries together in China and—"

"Which Society?"

Mr. Gault gave a testy ejaculation.

"Does that matter? The Downshire Missions in Asia. When the Communists gained control, we came back to this country."

"Together?"

"I fail to see what concern that is of yours, inspector. If you insist on a reply, we came back separately. We were imprisoned by the Chinese Communists, then I was taken to another part of Honan province. I obtained my release, and some months later, Mr. Price was able to do the same. As for his family, he came from Bethesda in North Wales. That's all I can tell you, except that he was unmarried and"—he paused to make a mental calculation—"fifty-three years of age."

"Thank you, sir."

The rector walked across to the table, from which he picked up his pipe and tobacco-pouch.

"I am naturally very shocked," he said as he opened the pouch, "to hear he's lost his life through such a tragic accident."

"There's strong reason to think, sir, that it wasn't."

Mr. Gault stopped what he was doing and turned towards Bradfield.

"Not an accident?" he said slowly.

"Everything points to murder."

"But that's preposterous!"

"I'm afraid it isn't, sir. The medical evidence, which is supported by certain other facts, is that he was stunned with a beer-bottle, then deliberately drowned in a tank inside the millhouse."

Mr. Gault seemed to sag. He felt for the chair and sank down on to it. Bradfield continued:

"That's why I want all the help you can give me."

"Murdered," said Mr. Gault dully, gazing at the floor, his back bent and his forearms on his knees. "I could endure his death by accident without great grief, but murder . . ."

There was silence in the big, bare room for some time. Just as Bradfield could bear it no longer and was casting round in his mind for an expression of sympathy that would not offend this strange man, Mr. Gault rose suddenly to his feet.

"We must discover who did it and see that he hangs for it. Ask whatever questions you like, inspector."

"It was part of my duty to search the body, sir. I found in the hip pocket two five-pound notes."

"Was there one in his breast pocket also?"

"No, sir."

"There should have been. He put it away there this evening, in this room."

Bradfield did not put his question into words; his expression implied it.

"Mr. Price," explained the rector, "was not so fortunate as I. He came to me for financial aid—and got it. This evening I gave him fifteen pounds—three five-pound notes—to buy himself some new clothes and other necessities. Now, you tell me, one of them has gone."

"Did you make a note of the numbers, sir?"

"No. I drew twenty-five pounds from the Southern Counties Bank in Lulverton on Saturday morning, and was going into Southmouth tomorrow to buy some curtains and furniture. Perhaps the bank will have a record."

"These notes were new, sir, and consecutively numbered. If you still have the other two . . .? "

The wallet was produced and the notes extracted and

passed over to Bradfield. Their numbers were Bc/s 184 271007 and Bc/s 184 271008.

"Double 0 seven and double 0 eight," said Bradfield. "The ones in Mr. Price's pocket were double 0 four and double 0 five."

"Then it is double 0 six that is missing, which would be quite correct. I remember that I put them into Mr. Price's hand one after the other, so reversing the original order. He placed the top one, which would be double 0 six, in his breast pocket, and the others in his hip pocket."

"Many thanks, sir. That's extremely helpful."

"Is there anything further?"

"Did Mr. Price have his walking-stick with him when he left here?"

"Yes. He couldn't get along without it. Next?"

Bradfield stroked his smooth hair, doubtful about whether to raise the matter at this juncture.

"Let's have it," urged Mr. Gault. "I want to get to bed."

"Yes," said Bradfield, making up his mind, "there is just one other thing—more of a general question than about—er—anything in particular. When you were in China with the Downshire Missions, did you come across Mr. Harold Micheldever?"

"I did."

"And did Mr. Price?"

"He did."

Just that and no more. Feeling like one of the team in "Twenty Questions" when the score against them is nineteen, Bradfield hesitated—then hit on a brilliant way out.

"This evening," he said, "Mr. Micheldever was arrested for being drunk and disorderly on licensed premises, and will come before the magistrates tomorrow morning. You might be able to put in a good—"

"I shall most certainly not, inspector. That man was once in Holy Orders. He disgraced himself and his cloth; he brought disrepute on the Church and sorrow to his family. Let him be the sufferer now. A few days in jail might see an improvement, but I gravely doubt it."

"Why did he leave the Church, Mr. Gault?"

"Any answer to that question, inspector, will not come from me. Apart from the fact that I should be betraying a confidence, it has nothing at all to do with your present inquiries." Bradfield rose to his feet. Though Mr. Gault was entitled to his opinions, he himself was not at all sure that he agreed.

Chapter Fifteen

PETTY SESSIONS

I

BY extension of the accepted meaning of the phrase, the Monday saw a series of petty sessions. At ten o'clock in the morning, in Lulverton Police Court, P C. Bristo and Mr. Battle gave evidence, not without a qualm, against Harold Micheldever. He was found guilty of being drunk and disorderly on licensed premises, and, being a first offender—if only as far as the law was concerned—was fined ten shillings for his evening spree. The magistrates ordered that the five-pound note be handed back to him. He received it with a puzzled expression not lost on Inspector Bradfield, who was in court, and paid the fine with it.

Pondering with a muzzy brain on the possibility of Sir Timothy Chatthume being satisfied with four pounds ten shillings instead of the fifteen pounds of vanished rent-money, Harold was leaving the building a few minutes later, when Bradfield stepped up and politely invited him to walk along to the police station for a chat. Harold felt in no condition to do anything more than crawl into some dark corner and quietly die there, so asked to be excused. Bradfield, however, was firm and Harold had to comply, this being less of a painful effort than a flat refusal.

In Bradfield's office on the first floor of the divisional

headquarters of the County Constabulary, a large and handsome building in Lulverton High Street, he provided Harold with a chair. A police stenographer and the coroner's officer, a constable in plain clothes, were in attendance.

"Mr. Micheldever," Bradfield began, "I'm inquiring into the death of the Reverend Dafydd Price, who—"

"What!"

The exclamation started great guns firing in Harold's head. He pressed his hands to his temples, then said in a more subdued tone:

"Say that again."

"Yesterday evening, Mr. Dafydd Price, a clergyman of the Church of England, was found dead in Dark Hollow. I'm going to ask you some questions. You need not answer them, but it is my duty to warn you that anything you say will be taken down in writing and may be given in evidence."

"Price, did you say? I've never heard of him. If he's been killed, I don't know anything about it. I don't know anything about anything. Oh, my head. Ask me later, for God's sake. Ask me this afternoon."

"Very well, Mr. Micheldever—if you wish. Just to give you a general idea of the questions I shall put, I'll tell you now what I've found out so far. I've been told by the landlord of the White Lion at Monk Jewel that at about nine o'clock yesterday evening, you bought a pint bottle of light ale and took it away with you."

"Yes, that's right."

"Don't say anything now if you don't want to."

"Nothing in that. No harm in buying a bottle of beer."

"This morning at the police court I had a word with

Mr. Battle, the licensee of the Seven Stars at Yateham. He said that you went in there at about twenty minutes to ten and has confirmed that you had no bottle with you then."

"I chucked it away. I drank the beer and chucked the bottle away. Where's all this getting us?"

"Mr. Price was drowned. Before he was drowned, he was hit on the head with a beer-bottle. All the evidence suggests that the bottle used was the one you bought in the White Lion. One of the questions I shall ask you this afternoon—"

"Wait. You'd better ask me now. I didn't know I was in such a spot. I'll only make things worse for myself. Ask what you want to know, but don't shout."

"I'm not shouting, sir."

"Then don't start. If you've ever been on a major jag, you'll know exactly how I feel."

"I'll just say again that you're not obliged to—"

"I know. I'm not obliged to answer, but if I don't I'm for the high jump. You carry on, but slowly and quietly, please."

"You've told me that you threw the empty bottle away. Where did you throw it?"

"Well, when it was empty, I couldn't be bothered with it."

"I said where, not why."

"Oh, where Lord only knows. Somewhere on the way back from the White Lion."

"Can you remember which way you went?"

"That's the trouble, old boy. Blasted black-out. Give me time to think."

"All the time you want, sir."

Harold sat with his eyes closed, his elbows on the desk

that separated them, his forehead resting on his hands. After a pause, he said slowly, without altering his position:

"I can remember coming away from the White Lion. I'd run myself out of cash, so I had to walk. . . . After I'd gone some distance, I felt like another drink. ... It would have been bad caught swigging from a bottle on the open road. My guv'nor's the retired rector of Yateham and these things get back. Trouble enough already. So I ... I went down into Dark Hollow. Yes, that's it—I went down into Dark Hollow. . . . And when I got to the millpond, just past old Barlow's cottage ... I nearly knocked old Barlow up, to split the bottle with me. . . . Felt I needed company. ... I decided against it and when I got to the millpond I sat on the parapet of the bridge where the lane goes over and opened the bottle and drank some of the beer, but it gave me hiccups—the gas in it—and I didn't drink much of it. . . . Then . . . No, it's a blank."

In such circumstances, a word or two will often revive a memory. Bradfield said:

"A footpath runs along the side of the pond. Then you come to the mill and—"

Harold sat upright.

"Wait a minute." He closed his eyes again. "The footbridge. . . . Standing on the footbridge, I could see three lights upstairs in Barlow's cottage, which meant three windows and three bedrooms. It took me time to realize that I wasn't seeing three lights, but one light three times, damned fool."

"It was misty in the valley last night, sir."

"Was it? But I saw the light in the Barlows' bedroom."

"I was in the valley myself and it was impossible to see more than about twenty yards."

Harold opened his bleary eyes.

"Then it must have been some other night I couldn't get that light in focus. I go home that way sometimes. I'm pretty sure now, though, that I got as far as the footbridge last night, where I stopped and drank the rest of the beer. I thought it might straighten me up. That's where I must have ditched the bottle."

"You'll understand that the bottle is very important, Mr. Micheldever. If you can tell us what you did with it, it may help you as much as it will us."

"I chucked it in the pond."

"Don't say that if you're not certain."

"I'll stick to it. I threw it in the pond. Let's press on. I want to call in at the nearest chemist for a draught."

"Did you meet the Reverend Dafydd Price during your walk home?"

"I told you I don't know him. I don't remember meeting anybody. I don't remember anything after I drank the beer on the mill bridge."

"You mentioned, sir, that when you left the White Lion, you'd run out of cash. Does that mean that you hadn't enough small change for the bus?"

"Worse, old boy. I was skint. I *know* I was skint. That's why I hadn't a clue in court this morning. Battle and Bristo both said I tried to change a fiver in the Seven Stars. They swore it on oath, so I suppose I must have done, but where the hell I got it from beats me." He laughed, then winced. "The cream of the jest was that it was given back to me this morning. I knew it wasn't mine, but I felt too ill to argue."

Bradfield said very gravely:

"Look, Mr. Micheldever, we want to be absolutely fair

with you. I don't think you realise the seriousness of this case. A witness has testified that shortly before Mr. Price's death last night, he handed Mr. Price three five-pound notes. One of those notes was the one you tried to change in the Seven Stars."

Harold Micheldever looked across the desk at him. He smiled vaguely, as if endeavouring to join in some joke that he did not understand. Then his expression changed, and, thought Bradfield, if ever a person was appalled by sudden, terrible and unexpected news, it was this lank-haired young man with the thick lips, weak chin and trembling hands.

"God Almighty!" he said in a strained whisper. "What have I done?"

II

It was not very long before everyone in Yateham heard about the tragedy in Dark Hollow. The shortcomings of the new rector were forgotten, if only temporarily, and tongues got busy on the far more exciting matter of a real murder in the parish. None doubted that it was murder, even with no more evidence than mere supposition. Oddly enough, the incident in the Seven Stars, though also common knowledge by then, was not connected in the minds of the majority with the death of the Rev. Dafydd Price.

Soon after ten o'clock, at the time of the proceedings in Lulverton Police Court, Sir Timothy Chatthume called at Medlar Cottage. Mr. Micheldever had retired to his study upstairs immediately after breakfast, having given instructions to his wife and Mrs. Smart that he was not at home to callers unless their business was of great moment,

171

so it was Mrs. Micheldever who received Timothy. She took him into the front room, closing the door behind them. He noticed that she had been crying.

"Worried, Aunt Mary?" he asked gently.

"Yes, Timothy, I am. Do sit down, dear."

"I've heard so many wild rumours about goings-on in the local last night that I thought I'd better come along. Harold was a naughty boy, wasn't he?"

Her lips trembled, but she did not answer.

"It's a blow," he went on after a pause, "but don't let it get you down. If it's true that the erring laddie is up before the beaks, it'll probably teach him such a lesson that he'll keep to the straight and narrow from now on."

Though the words were flippant, his voice was full of sympathy, yet it did not seem to comfort her.

"It's not just that, dear," she said at length. "It's— something more dreadful. . . . That poor clergyman who was killed ... I'm sure that when Harold's had a lot to drink, he doesn't know what he's doing."

He bent forward to pat her hand.

"Put it right out of your mind. We must face it that Harold has his faults, but he'd never hit anyone. I'm quite certain of that. Why, he hasn't got the—" He was going to say "guts," but altered it to "temperament."

"Then where did he get that five-pound note?"

"Aunt Mary, do look at it rationally. Is it likely that Harold would go to those lengths for the sake of a miserable fiver?"

"He might have been desperate," said Mrs. Micheldever, then smiled wanly. "But I must try not to think about it. Down in my heart of hearts I'm convinced Harold couldn't do such a thing. . . . Timothy, is he doing well?

Working for you, I mean."

"No complaints at all. He's getting the hang of it and will soon be very useful."

"Is this police summons going to—make any difference?"

"You mean, will he get the push? Good Lord, no. As his stern employer and honorary cousin, I may give him a few pointed words of advice, which he may or may not take, but that's all."

"It means a lot to us, Harold having a post. We're not very well off, you know, and it's bad enough to have another mouth to feed, without having to find pocket-money."

"But doesn't he pay for his keep?"

"We don't expect it—not with Harold only getting two pounds a week."

"Getting how much?"

"Two pounds a week. That's what you allow him, isn't it?"

Should he tell her? He decided against it. There was bother enough already.

"Whatever he gets," he answered evasively, "he ought to give you something. But rest assured about one thing, Aunt Mary: as long as it helps *you*, he'll have a job with me. That's a promise."

He made himself another promise at the same time.

III

Since Inspector Charlton had been granted indefinite sick-leave on account of a diabetic condition brought on by selfless devotion to duty, Peter Bradfield had been in charge of the C I D section attached to the Lulverton division of the County Constabulary. He had under him two plain-clothes men—Detective-Sergeant Hartley, newly promoted, and Detective-Constable Emerson—and could call, if need arose, on the services of the uniformed personnel at divisional headquarters.

Emerson, who had been relieved at the mill by a uniformed constable, arrived soon after Harold, having made and signed a statement, had departed. In making his report before going home for some much-needed sleep, Emerson had little to tell.

"The workmen turned up soon after eight. I told the foreman what you told me to say. When it got light, I had a mosey round for the stick, but didn't find it."

Five minutes later, with Hartley at the wheel, Bradfield was on the way to the mill. Except that he was also young, Hartley was everything that Emerson was not. He was small as policemen go, dark and intelligent. Bradfield had once remarked to Charlton, then his chief:

"If we had a fellow with Emerson's body and Hartley's brains, I'd be out of a job."

"Oh, no, you wouldn't, Peter," Charlton had replied, "and I'm not going to make you swelled-headed by telling you why."

On reaching Dark Hollow, they called at the cottage, where a district nurse was now looking after the bereaved and bedridden Mrs. Barlow. When Bradfield introduced himself, he was allowed to have the ring, with keys attached, that Barlow had kept on a chain in his trouser pocket. These he took with him to the mill, where the workmen were preparing to replace the reciprocating pump on its seating over the sump.

After instructing Hartley to have a look round for the walking-stick of the late Dafydd Price, he held with the engineers' foreman a conversation that he had intended to be brief. The foreman, however, was not of the taciturn kind, and there was so much repetition of "D'you follow my meaning?" that the simple tale of the ailing pump took a long time to tell. The only point of any interest to Bradfield was that the stoppering of the sump with cotton waste had been done some days before by the workmen themselves. Unless it was, as he suspected, that the sump had done office as a combined washbasin and kitchen sink, the reason remained obscure, but the fact was enough: the murderer had taken advantage of the water in the sump, and not filled it to achieve his ends.

"You have a key of the padlock?" Bradfield asked.

"Yes. I got it from the office up at Chatthume Place when we started the job."

"And it hasn't been out of your possession since?"

"No. It'll go back to the office when we're through here."

"Thanks. That's all, I think."

He walked across to the door, and was standing just out in the yard, making sure that one of the keys on Barlow's ring also fitted the padlock, when Hartley came down the steps leading from the footbridge.

"Any luck?"

"I've found one thing that might interest you."

"Lead on."

He followed Hartley up the steps on to the footbridge. On the side nearer the mill-wheel, loosely wedged between the lower rail of the balustrade and the floor-boarding, was a rubber-ringed screw-stopper. Using his handkerchief to prevent obliteration of any finger-prints, Bradfield bent down and withdrew it. On the top of it, in embossed letters, was the word "Trumington."

175

This went to support Harold Micheldever's statement that he had paused on the bridge to finish off the beer. The stopper might easily have fallen or been allowed to drop from his hand and rolled into the crevice where Hartley's sharp eyes had detected it.

"Nice work, Hartley," approved Bradfield. "And the walking-stick?"

"Nothing doing, but with all this undergrowth and what not, it's like looking for a—"

"I know the rest of it. Let's have another shufty."

Together they made an exhaustive search over a considerable area, which took in the yard and the interior of the mill, but without result.

"It must be somewhere around," said Bradfield, pushing his hat to the back of his head. "The old chap was lame. He couldn't have reached here without it."

"He might have been carried."

Bradfield considered this.

"Yes, you've got something there, Hartley. Opens up a new line of thought. The stopper and the broken bottle may be a blind."

He thought for a while before he said:

"While we're in these parts, there's another little point I want to confirm if I can."

They walked along the side of the pond and came out on to the humpbacked bridge over the brook. Here, against the parapet and half trodden into the flinty surface of the lane, Bradfield found what he sought: the top portion of the strip of paper that seals the stopper of a beer-bottle.

Again Harold Micheldever's testimony was supported by the evidence. But it did not exonerate him in any way at all.

Chapter Sixteen

THE SMILE OF THE TIGER

I

THE members of the cast of *The Folly of Polly* were living in a Southmouth boarding-house that catered for stage folk.

No view of the sea was to be had from any of the windows, but its terms were reasonable.

Though it was turned noon, Sabina Danbury was still in bed when Bradfield called, and he had grown tired of the pictures on the walls and the dusty paper flowers in the tall vase in the bay-window, and sickened by the death struggles of the flies on the sticky strip hanging from the central lightfitting, before she joined him in the room that did little to five up to its name of guests' lounge.

It was to be conceded that Sabina had but lately risen and had not had much opportunity for a careful toilet, yet she looked jaded, more of a piece with her drab surroundings than would have been expected of so lovely a lady. It did not take Bradfield long to decide that she had something on her mind, and that she was not at all anxious for him to discover what it was.

"I'm sorry to bother you, Miss Danbury," he began after making himself known, "but last night—"

"I know about it, inspector. I was at Chatthume Place, and Sir Timothy told me when he came back from the mill. Dreadful, wasn't it? I wish I could help you more than I'm afraid I can."

"Perhaps you will. The gentleman who lost his life was the Reverend Dafydd Price. I'm trying to find out what he did and where he went yesterday evening. Mr. Gault, the rector of Yateham, has told me that Mr. Price called on him at the rectory and left there about a quarter past nine. Sir Timothy has told me also of your meeting with Mr. Price."

A frightened look came into her eyes.

"Yes, we did meet him."

"What I want to establish is whether, when you saw him, he was going to Yateham or on the way back."

"I really couldn't say. He was standing on the bridge and we were in the boat. I don't know which way he was going."

"What time did you meet him?"

She gave a helpless little gesture.

"I'm awful with times. Couldn't Sir Timothy tell you?"

"I was hoping you could remember."

"When did you say he came away from the rectory?"

"About a quarter past nine."

"Well, it wasn't as late as that when we saw him. I'd say it was nearer a quarter to—perhaps even earlier."

"Thank you, Miss Danbury. That's very helpful. And after meeting Mr. Price, you and Sir Timothy went back to Chatthume Place, I suppose?"

"Yes. We had some coffee with Lady Chatthume and Mrs. Donaldson. Then one of the servants came in to say that Sir Timothy was wanted on the phone in the office. When he'd taken the call, Sir Timothy popped his head in to tell us that he was going to the mill. Lady Chatthume asked what on earth for, and he said some man whose name I forget wanted him there at once because something peculiar had happened. We didn't think Sir Timothy was going to be gone long, but he was, and we were just beginning to get a little worried when he came back and told us about the—about what had happened." She shot him a quick glance. "I'm sure he'd never dream of—"

She stopped dead.

"Would never dream of what, Miss Danbury? "

"Oh, nothing. I was thinking of something else. Have you any other questions you want to ask me?"

"I gather from Sir Timothy that last night wasn't your first meeting with Mr. Price."

Sabina shuddered.

"No, it wasn't. He was a dreadful little man and he terrified me. He nearly ruined our season at the Empire by stopping the show one night. He jumped up in the middle of one of my dances and began to read out of the Bible in a very loud voice about women having their hair cut off. It was ghastly."

"Yes, very embarrassing for you. Sir Timothy told me about it. And last night "

"It was no business of his, the nosy old creature. We were on private property."

"I don't quite follow you, Miss Danbury."

"Oh!"

It was an ejaculation of horror—the horror of one who has said too much. Bradfield waited for the inevitable evasion. It came.

"The old silly objected to us boating on a Sunday."

"Sir Timothy said Mr. Price called you a woman without shame."

"There you see! That's the sort of man he was. He not only wrecked my act, but wouldn't let me forget it. It was persecution—that's what it was."

"Did Sir Timothy propose to take any steps to—"

He did not say more, for Sabina had burst into tears. Embarrassed, he rose to his feet, and a minute later was walking down the hearthstoned steps from the front door with a thoughtful frown on his face. Some actresses are what is known in the profession as "good off"; Sabina Danbury was evidently not of these.

In the east wing of Chatthume Place was an outer door marked "OFFICE"—the entry to the administrative headquarters of the Chatthume estate and farms, which, under Timothy's guiding hand, had been transformed from a liability into a valuable asset. Through this door, at 12.30 p.m. on that second Monday in September, came Harold Micheldever. A desk had been provided for him in the outer office, where sat also young Miss Nightingale, who was Sir Timothy's secretary, and two clerks: elderly Mr. Forbes and the junior, Stanley Paget.

Few things can be more unnerving for those who work in offices than to be told, almost before they have set foot in the room, that the boss wants them. It always suggests trouble and is in no way ameliorated by the complacent gusto with which the message is delivered. This now happened to Harold. Immediately he entered, Miss Nightingale and Stanley Paget announced simultaneously:

"Sir Timothy wants you."

With age against him, Mr. Forbes did not manage to get in the first two, but came a sporting third with:

"At once."

Harold was not at all dismayed. Stimulated by two

barley wines, he had now decided that he had not murdered the Rev. Dafydd Price and was accordingly much more cheerful than he had been at Lulverton police headquarters. Even the missing fifteen pounds of rent did not alarm him at this juncture.

"Right," he said almost gaily, then hung up his hat, walked to the door of the inner office, tapped on it and entered. As the door closed behind him, Stanley said:

"Hope he gets it 'ot and strong."

"Hot and strong, Stanley," said Mr. Forbes.

"That's two of us," said that young man.

He had his wish, for when Harold came out again ten minutes later, his discomfiture was all too apparent. He snatched up from beside his desk the leather brief-case he used when collecting rents, grabbed his hat down off the peg, and left, slamming the door behind him.

"Whack-oh!" said Stanley.

Before returning to Lulverton, Bradfield visited a firm of harbour contractors and arranged for the Dark Hollow millpond to be dragged for the broken beer-bottle. If it had been used by the murderer, there might be some useful finger-prints on it.

He had been back in his office only a few minutes when Sir Timothy telephoned him. The young baronet was extremely irate.

"What the devil do you mean by making yourself a damned nuisance to Miss Danbury?"

"It was my duty to—"

"Blast your duty! She knows nothing about the murder and she's had quite enough anxiety recently without you making matters worse. If you wanted to know anything, you should ask me instead of crawling round behind my

181

back. You leave her alone."

Bradfield was silent. Timothy said after an appreciable pause:

"Hullo! Are you still there?"

"Yes, sir. I was waiting to make sure you'd said all you wanted to say. When you rang the police last night, where did you phone from?"

It was now Timothy's turn to be silent. He said at length:

"The A.A. box. Why the hell ask that?"

"I just wondered. One other thing, Sir Timothy. Did Mr. Price say he objected to Sunday boating?"

"Of course he didn't! Nobody but a—"

"Miss Danbury told me he did. Good-bye, sir."

II

Janet Micheldever got off the bus at the Seven Stars stop and walked back along Yateham High Street. It was six o'clock in the evening and her day's work was over. When she reached Medlar Cottage, she did not go in, but passed it and continued on until she came to St. Anselm's. As always, the door was unfastened so that those who wished could use the church for meditation or prayer; and, as many troubled souls had done before her over the course of the centuries, she opened the door and went inside.

Ten minutes later, consoled and with her mind more composed, she emerged from the cool dimness into the warm autumn sunshine. At the ancient lych-gate, grey-suited and bare-headed, stood Bruce Gault—whether by accident or design she could only conjecture. As she came down the path, she wished him good evening with a slight inclination of the head. He stood to one side as if to let her pass, but as she did so, he said:

"Miss Micheldever."

She paused and turned back to him.

"Yes, rector?"

"I want to apologize most humbly for my rudeness to you last time we met."

"That's quite all right," she replied, smiling a little. "All of us are bad tempered sometimes and you had plenty of excuse, I'm afraid."

"There was no excuse at all. It was a disgraceful exhibition and I promise you that it will never happen again—never. When you were not in church at either service yesterday, I felt that, through my crass folly, I had lost my only real friend in this very unfriendly little parish. Can I ever be forgiven?"

"Why, of course, rector."

"'For now we see through a glass, darkly; but then face to face.' Why did I take that text? And why did I speak to you like that?"

"Don't let's say any more about it."

"I'm not one man, but two—two men pulling against each other all the time."

Timidly she laid a hand lightly on his arm.

"If there was anything to forgive, you are forgiven."

For the first time since she had known him, he smiled. Janet thought what a difference it made—like a shaft of spring sunshine in a dark, forbidding canyon.

She withdrew her hand.

"Will you come next Sunday?" he asked.

"Yes, and I'll try to bring my mother and father. You must have thought Daddy dreadfully rude, but he's—well, obstinate sometimes."

"Entirely my fault again. In my blundering, inconsiderate

way, I offended him by brushing aside some excellent advice he tried to give me."

"Daddy's always so tactless, but he's a dear really. I do hope you'll become friends. Now I must go."

She smiled again and Bruce Gault smiled too. Then the smile faded from his bearded face and he held her gaze for a long time before he turned and went up the path without a word of farewell or a backward glance.

Janet walked home with her mind in a turmoil. Deep down in those steel-blue eyes she had seen something that had stirred her as nothing had ever stirred her before. Instinctively she quickened her pace as if in flight.

With a man such as the retired rector of Yateham as its head, it was inevitable that the Micheldever household should endure certain periods of distressing silence, when only Janet could find anything to say—and the courage to say it.

Mr. Micheldever's depression hung like a cloud over Medlar Cottage all that day. Ostensibly to prepare a treatise on the authorship of the Fourth Gospel, he kept to his study, refusing even to come down to lunch, and his wife and Mrs. Smart crept quietly about their domestic duties, speaking in hushed tones, as if there were death or grievous sickness in the house.

It was in this constrained atmosphere that Mrs. Micheldever welcomed Janet in the kitchen on her return from the church.

Even Janet's tone was flat as, after kissing her mother, she asked:

"Nothing—nothing except to cheer me up. Timothy's a dear boy and he means much more to me than—"

She broke off and bit her lip. "I hope and pray the

Danbury girl will be a good wife to him. There's always something about the stage..."

Janet tried to smile.

"Mummy, sweet, you're old-fashioned. Some of the highest ladies in the land started in the chorus." She paused a moment before she added: "Don't forget Dick's coming to dinner."

Her mother's expression became even more troubled.

"Do you think it's quite—appropriate, darling?"

"Dick said the same thing this morning. He was all against coming, but I've a stubborn streak, Mummy, and I'm not going to have my arrangements thrown out by that drunken brother of mine."

"Darling, you mustn't. "

"Yesterday evening I agreed to become Dick's wife and I invited him to dinner tonight so that you and Daddy could well, *you* know. I'm going straight down to buy a bottle of champagne from Mr Battle—and that's got its funny side when you think about it, then we'll—".

"Janet, dear, surely it's hardly suitable to—"

"Yes it is! You worry all the time about Harold. What about me and my happiness? Mummy, darling, let's go gay this evening! If we don't I shall explode!"

Mrs. Micheldever gave an impotent gesture.

"But Daddy would disapprove."

"Why should he? Dick's bringing the ring with him. What's there wrong in a little celebration—a glass of champagne to drink our health and wish us luck?"

"Of course, dear—if things were normal. But this trouble over Harold. . . ."

"Harold! I'm beginning to hate the name! It's Harold, Harold, Harold! What happened last night is over and done with. For heaven's sake, let's forget it! In a fortnight, everyone else will have forgotten it too."

For the second time that evening her gaze was caught. Now in these other eyes, which were brown, not steel-blue, there was a different message from the first.

"Mummy, what's the matter?"

Mrs. Micheldever's mouth trembled, then with a little moan, she stumbled forward and hid her head on Janet's shoulder, where she sobbed until the girl was able to pacify her.

"I know what you're frightened about, Mummy," Janet said at length, "and I was frightened too—dreadfully frightened. But now I'm not and you're not to be, either. He didn't do it. Keep on saying that to yourself. It's what I was saying in the church just now—over and over again. He didn't do it. Say it."

"I—I can't."

"Then think it. Harold hasn't a strong character. He runs away from anything he doesn't like. He'll borrow money from anybody if they'll let him—but Mummy, ask yourself this simple question: Would Harold—and you know him as well as I do—would Harold, drunk or sober, hit somebody on the head with a beer-bottle and then cold-bloodedly drown him in a tank? And a clergyman. Can you see Harold doing it? Try to picture it in your mind. Can you?"

"I don't really think I can."

"Remember when we cut or bruised ourselves when we were children? Harold used to cry even when it was only Tim or I who got hurt. People don't change, Mummy. Harold's still as big a coward as he ever was. Look how terrified he is of wasps."

"Yes, dear."

"Then he didn't do last night what you were afraid he did." She turned towards the door. "Now I must get busy."

"What are you going to do, dear?" asked Mrs. Micheldever with apprehension.

"First have a talk with Daddy, then buy the bubbly."

"I'm afraid he won't agree to it."

"Oh, yes, he will, precious. Shall I let you into a secret?"

Her mother looked inquiring. Janet stepped forward a pace and whispered:

"The silly old darling's frightened of me."

Dinner was at seven-thirty, those sitting down to it being Mr. and Mrs. Micheldever, Janet and Dick Farringdon. Mr. Micheldever was grave and thoughtful, but, mindful of Janet's pointed observations in the study on the duties of parents towards newly affianced offspring, he did his best to entertain the visitor. His wife was too occupied with the catering side to give much thought to anything else. Janet laughed and talked gaily, though a forced note made itself evident now and again. Dick smilingly played up to her, so when there was an awkward pause in the conversation, as often there was, one or other of them hastened to fill the gap. No mention was made of Harold, who, understandably enough, was not present at the meal—had not, in fact, been seen by any of them since the evening before. As things were, there was difficulty enough; how the little dinner party would have fared had Harold been there, Janet for one was loath to contemplate.

When the biscuits and cheese had followed the sweet, Mrs. Micheldever and Janet, on the excuse of making the coffee, retired to the kitchen with the tea-trolley laden with crockery. This was Dick's cue and he took it manfully.

Having provided Mr. Micheldever with a cigar, he sought formal permission to marry Janet. It might have been Mr. Micheldever's big moment, but, with his mind filled with other cares, he merely replied:

"I am confident that our dear daughter has chosen well, and wish you every happiness."

After a discreet interval, Mrs. Micheldever returned. On seeing Dick's smiling face she knew that all was well and said:

"Dr. Farringdon, I believe Janet would like you to help her bring in the coffee things."

On the entry of the young couple a few minutes later, Janet displayed the engagement ring on her finger with an expression of pride, mingled with some other emotion that her mother found difficult to analyse.

At a quarter to nine, when the champagne had been drunk and even Mr. Micheldever was more cheerful, outlining to the respectfully attentive Dick the wide implications of the Oecumenical Conferences of 1937, the telephone-bell rang in the hall. Janet went out to take the call and came back with a little frown on her face. She bent over Mrs. Micheldever to murmur without her father hearing:

"It's Tim, Mummy. He wanted Harold, then asked for you."

"Oh, dear. What can have happened now?"

It was told in a few words. Harold, said Sir Timothy, had gone off before one o'clock to collect the weekly rents due from the tenants, and had not since reported back to the office.

"I'll ask him to telephone you, Timothy," she said, trying to keep her voice steady, "as soon as he comes home."

In the front room, Mr. Micheldever was saying as she

returned:

"Even as long before as 1920, there had been a delegation to Lambeth from the Patriarchate of Constantinople, in which we can see the beginnings of a new understanding between the Greek Orthodox Church and the Anglican Communion."

Mrs. Micheldever reseated herself with a repressed sigh. She had not the heart to tell her husband just then.

Chapter Seventeen

WITHOUT AFFECTION OR ILL WILL

"RISE for the coroner, please!"

It was the morning of Friday—a dull, gusty day, with the wind playing havoc among the yellowing leaves—and in an upper room of the Seven Stars in Yateham village, the inquest on Dafydd Price was about to begin. As those present stood, there entered from an inner room Mr. Samuel Trench, a small man dressed in dark grey, wearing gold-rimmed spectacles with very thick lenses on his large nose. He took his seat at the table supplied, together with other necessary furniture, by Mr. Battle and his neighbours, and began to arrange his papers in a manner that stamped him as a meticulous man.

As the court sat, the coroner's officer, a plain-clothes policeman with the voice and presence of a regimental sergeant-major, rattled off:

"Oyea! Oyea! Oyea! All manner of persons who have anything to do at this court before the Queen's coroner for this county, draw near and give your attendance; and ye good men of the jury who have been summoned here this day to inquire for our Sovereign Lady the Queen, when, where, and by what means a man said to be named Dafydd Price came to his death, answer to your names, as ye shall be called, every man at first call, on the pains and penalties that may fall thereon."

Four copies of the New Testament had to suffice for the eight members of the jury, who, having answered to their names, repeated the oath, phrase by phrase, after the coroner's officer.

"I swear by Almighty God that I will diligently inquire and a true presentment make of all such matters and things as are here given me in charge, on behalf of our Sovereign Lady the Queen, touching the death of Dafydd Price, now lying dead. And I will, without fear or favour, affection or ill will, a true verdict give, according to the evidence and to the best of my skill and knowledge."

Young Tony Morris of the Downshire County Herald, who was sitting with the other reporters at the cramped little Press table, here decided that when he could write English such as that, he would give up journalism.

"Be seated, gentlemen," said the coroner's officer to the jury, then stepped across to hand the warrant to Mr. Trench, who then addressed the jury, peering at them through his thick lenses.

"We are here, gentlemen, to inquire into the death of Dafydd Price, a clerk in Holy Orders, whose body was found last Sunday evening in the millhouse in the valley just outside this village that is known as Dark Hollow. I understand that you are all acquainted with the millhouse and its surroundings?"

The foreman rose.

"That is so, sir."

"Then we can proceed." Mr. Trench turned to his officer. "The identification?"

Standing by a small table that did duty as a witness-box, the officer called:

"The Reverend Bruce Gault."

There was a slight stir in the crowded, low-raftered room as the tall, bearded figure rose from among the other witnesses and made his way with long strides to the table, on which lay a card bearing the words of the oath. Without even glancing at this, he took the Testament from the coroner's officer and spoke out in a voice that sounded harsh to many present, and aroused in Janet Micheldever a strange excitement.

Mr. Trench then asked:

"You are Bruce Gault, minister of religion, and you reside at the rectory in this parish?"

"Yes, sir."

"Do you identify the body of the deceased in the mortuary as that of the Reverend Dafydd Price?"

"I do, sir."

"How long have you known him?"

"For nearly twelve years, sir. He and I were missionaries together in China for the greater part of that time."

"Will you now please tell the jury of Mr. Price's call upon you during the evening of Sunday last."

"It was not a long visit—about a quarter of an hour. I can't tell you the exact time he left, but it was approximately nine-fifteen. He told me that he was going to walk back to his lodgings at Lulverton and asked me whether I knew a short cut. I told him about the footpath through Dark Hollow, but strongly advised him not to go that way. He was lame—the result of his terrible experiences in Red China—and I did not think it a safe route for him to take. He obviously disregarded—"

"A moment, Mr. Gault," said the coroner. "You must confine yourself to the facts, without expressing opinions or conjecture."

192

Tight-lipped, the rector bowed apology.

"You did not see which way he went?"

"No, sir. I was standing at the front door of the rectory. Mr. Price walked down the path, opened the gate and went through. As he turned to re-close the gate, I waved good-bye to him, closed the front door and went back to my study."

"Was he carrying his walking-stick?"

"Yes, it was in his left hand, held tight against his leg to give it support."

"Was that the last time you saw him alive?"

"Yes, sir."

Mr. Trench turned to the jury.

"We come now," he told them, "to a matter that may not at first seem apparent, yet may have no small bearing on our inquiry. Mr. Gault, please tell the jury of the reason for Mr. Price's call on you."

"He was badly in need of money to buy new clothes and other necessities, so that he could get employment. As an old friend and fellow missionary, I was glad of the opportunity to help."

"So you lent him fifteen pounds?"

"Not lent, sir," corrected Mr. Gault sharply, taking a small revenge. "It was a gift. I neither suggested nor expected repayment."

"This gift, then, was in five-pound notes, was it not?"

"Yes, sir. I drew five of them on Saturday morning from the Lulverton branch of the Southern Counties Bank, and gave three to Mr. Price."

"You do not know the numbers of them?"

"Not of the ones I gave Mr. Price. I have the other two in my pocket, if the jury wish to see them?"

"Yes, please."

Mr. Gault produced them and handed them to the coroner's officer, who took them to Mr. Trench, then stepped across and passed them over to the foreman. When the jury had examined them and jotted down the numbers, they were returned to the witness. The coroner put his next question.

"In which of his pockets did Mr. Price place the notes?"

One or two of the jury stole glances at each other. This was being a little too thorough, and they were busy men.

"One in his breast pocket, sir, and the other two in the back pocket of his trousers."

Mr. Trench swung round to the jury.

"I shall not ask at this juncture whether you have any questions for this witness. Thank you, Mr. Gault. You may stand down."

Though he had said it over to himself several times in readiness, the name of the next witness to be called gave the officer some trouble.

"Yi Liu-ying."

The neat little man, with the flat, immobile face, gave his evidence in a high-pitched voice, and without hesitation or stumbling.

"You are Yi Liu-ying, a native of China, and are employed with your wife at Yateham rectory, in the service of Mr. Gault?"

"Yes, sir."

"You first became acquainted with Mr. Price in China?"

"Yes, sir—at Haolaofen, in the province of Honan. Together with my widowed father, my sister and my wife, I was servant at the mission there. Mr. Price was a good, kind master, as was also Mr. Gault."

Across the room, Yi Liu-ying caught the eye of his employer, who shook his head almost imperceptibly. Yi Liu-ying said no more.

"We understand," said Mr. Trench, "that you admitted Mr. Price to the rectory last Sunday evening?"

"No, sir."

The court sat up.

"You did not admit him?"

"No, sir, but I observed his entry. It was my wife who opened the door to him."

The court relaxed.

"What time was this?"

"Two or three minutes past nine, sir."

"And you can confirm that Mr. Price left the rectory at approximately nine-fifteen?"

"Yes, sir. I did not see him go, but heard Mr. Gault saying good night to him in the hall."

"So the last time you saw Mr. Price alive was when he was admitted to the rectory?"

"Yes, sir."

"Thank you, Mr. Yi. You may stand down."

The next witness was the young woman cashier who had attended to Mr. Gault on the Saturday morning. She confirmed that she had opened a new packet of five-pound notes and had handed the top five to Mr. Gault. When asked whether she had kept a record of the numbers, she said that she had not, because it was not the bank's custom to do so. She could, however, say that requests for five-pound notes had been few during the past week and that the notes remaining in the packet—or, more exactly, the serially numbered batch that formed part of the packet—were numerically related to those just produced in court.

There was a gap of ten, but their issue to other customers would account for those.

"Where's all this getting us?" one juryman muttered out of the side of his mouth to his neighbour, and was sharply reproved by Mr. Trench, whose ears were keener than his eyes.

Dr. Lorimer, the police surgeon, was next to be called.

"On the evening of Sunday last, you made an examination of the Reverend Dafydd Price?"

"That is so."

"And what was the result of this examination?"

"When I examined him, he had been dead about an hour. I found a lacerated wound on the scalp, and some fragments of glass—brown in colour—both in the wound and in the hair surrounding it. The wound was on the left-hand side of the scalp."

"How do you suggest this occurred?"

"I suggest that the injury was the result of a heavy blow on the head by a right-handed person with some article made of brown glass, which was brought down with such force that it was smashed, leaving fragments in the wound and hair."

"It is not your opinion that the injuries to the head were responsible for this man's death?"

"No, sir. In the post-mortem examination, which I carried out later, I found a depressed compound fracture of the skull. It is possible that this would have led to his death within a few hours, but the post-mortem confirmed my preliminary tests and proved beyond all reasonable doubt that he died from drowning."

"There were no signs of disease?"

"None, sir."

"So you are prepared to say that the deceased met his death by drowning, after having been stunned by an implement manufactured of brown-tinted glass?"

"With respect, sir, not precisely that. However unlikely it would seem to be, there is no definite proof that the blow on the head was delivered before the man was drowned."

Mr. Trench turned to the jury.

"That is a question, gentlemen, that the evidence of other witnesses may enable you to answer for yourselves. Now, before I ask Dr. Lorimer to stand down, have you anything you wish to ask him?"

The man sitting next to the foreman murmured in his ear and the foreman rose to say:

"We should like the witness to tell us, sir, whether the glass implement used was a beer-bottle."

Mr. Trench frowned; the inquiry suggested a foreknowledge that is not desirable in members of a jury.

"Dr. Lorimer?"

"It could have been, but I am not prepared to say that it was. Beer-bottles are not the only articles made of glass of that colour. The question comes more within the province of the technical expert than in mine. All I am prepared to say is that a beer-bottle is of suitable shape and weight to cause the head injuries sustained."

"Thank you, doctor," said Mr. Trench, who was anxious not to prolong the discussion on this point. "If you wish to leave the court, we need no longer detain you."

The divisional surgeon stepped back from the witness-table. Mr. Trench beckoned to his officer, who went round behind him. They held a murmured conversation, at the end of which Mr. Trench said to the jury:

"Doctors have many pressing engagements, gentlemen,

which explains the absence of the next witness. Unfortunately, he has an emergency operation to perform at Lulverton Hospital, but has promised to attend this court as soon as he can. It was he who first found the body of the deceased in Dark Hollow millhouse, and later he will tell you about it. Meanwhile we will hear the evidence of his fiancée, who was with him at the time of the discovery."

"Miss Janet Micheldever," called the officer, now back at his post by the witness-table.

Janet, the only member of her family present at the proceedings, came forward and took the oath, her voice subdued but steady.

"Now, Miss Micheldever," said Mr. Trench in the kindly, almost fatherly tone in which he always addressed witnesses of the other sex, "I am quite certain that I express the feelings of this court when I say how sorry we are that it was necessary to summon you here today."

Tony Morris of the Herald, who had an eye for feminine loveliness, did not whole-heartedly support the coroner in this, but others did and there were general murmurs of sympathy.

"At about a quarter to ten last Sunday evening, Miss Micheldever, you and your fiancé were walking, were you not, past Dark Hollow millhouse?"

"Yes, sir."

"Will you kindly tell the jury just what happened."

"We had arranged to meet on the mill footbridge at half-past nine. I was late getting there, but even then he had not arrived."

"Shame on him!" said a voice from among the members of the public who had been admitted.

The laughter that followed was swiftly quelled by the coroner's officer.

"Please continue, Miss Micheldever," said Mr. Trench.

"I waited on the footbridge for a little while, then decided to go on, which I did. I met my fiancé, who'd been detained at the hospital, and we walked back together to the bridge, where we stood for a few minutes, then started off back to my home. We were just—"

"Before we come to that, Miss Micheldever, I would like you to tell the jury, please, what you found on the floor of the footbridge when you reached it."

Janet would have preferred to make no mention of this, and her voice was not so steady as she answered:

"A piece of broken beer-bottle."

There were murmurings in the court. They swiftly died down when Janet spoke again.

"It was my fiancé who noticed it. Because it was dangerous where it was, he picked it up and threw it in the pond."

"Will you describe it, please?"

"Well, it was really the bottle without the neck, which sloped in—not like a bottle with sort of shoulders."

"You did not find the neck portion?"

"No."

"Thank you," smiled Mr. Trench, then looked towards the back of the court. "Detective-Inspector Bradfield, exhibit number one, please."

Bradfield, who had received his instructions before the opening of the inquiry, stepped forward from his standing position alongside Hartley and came up to the witness-table carrying something loosely wrapped in brown paper. He set this down on the table and pulled back the paper to reveal the exhibit.

"Miss Micheldever," said Mr. Trench, "do you recognize that as the portion of bottle you found on the footbridge?"

Janet bent forward to examine it.

"Yes, I think so."

"Can you be more positive?"

"Well, this jagged piece sticking up above the rest of it. It was the same on the other one."

"Thank you, Miss Micheldever."

At a signal from Mr. Trench, Bradfield retired to his place against the wall. Mr. Trench addressed the jury.

"Inspector Bradfield will give his evidence later, when you will learn how exhibit number one was retrieved from the millpond." He turned to Janet. "On leaving the footbridge, you did not keep to the footpath, I believe?"

"No, we didn't. We were in rather a hurry because my fiancé had to get back to Lulverton after seeing me home, so we took a short cut by going down the stone steps at the side—or I suppose you'd call it the front—of the millhouse. Just as we were walking past the door, we saw the brim of a hat sticking from under it."

With an occasional question from the coroner, Janet went on to repeat the evidence she had given to Bradfield on the night of the murder. When she had finished, Mr. Trench asked the jury whether they had any questions. They conferred, then the foreman stood.

"Will the witness please give the reason for their appointment on the footbridge?"

The same voice as had spoken before now threw in:

"Use your loaf!"

There was laughter. Mr. Trench passed a hand across his mouth before he said with convincing sternness:

"If there are any further interruptions, I shall have to clear the court. Gentlemen of the jury, I know of no law that prohibits affianced couples from meeting wheresoever they please. Have you any other questions?

The stress was slight, but deliberate.

"Yes, sir," replied the foreman stiffly. "Did the witness meet anyone besides her fiancé, either while on her way to keep the appointment, or during the time they were at the mill?"

Janet began: "Sir Timothy—"

"We've heard about him already, sir," persisted the foreman. "Did the witness meet anyone else?"

The girl looked appealingly at Mr. Trench.

"Must I answer that?"

"It is a relevant question, Miss Micheldever."

"Well, I met my brother."

This took Mr. Trench by surprise; it was mentioned nowhere in the statements before him on the table.

"Mr. Harold Micheldever?"

"Yes."

"Where did you meet him?"

"At the stile in Church Lane."

"That is to say, the stile at the end of the footpath leading westward from the mill?"

"Yes. He was trying to—he was getting across it when I got there."

"He having come, I take it, from the direction of the mill? "

"I don't know. I suppose so. He didn't tell me—except he said he'd been talking to a friend."

"Did he mention the name of the friend?"

"No. I was in a hurry to keep my appointment, so I got

over the stile and left him."

"Thank you, Miss Micheldever. That is all for the moment, but I may have to recall you."

Janet went back to her place. As she made her way between the rows of chairs, her eyes met Bruce Gault's. She gave him a little smile, but he turned his head away and spoke to Yi Liu-ying at his side.

Chapter Eighteen

CORONER'S WARRANT

MR. TRENCH said to the jury:

"As you have heard, soon after the discovery of the body, Sir Timothy Chatthume arrived at the mill. I propose, therefore, to call Sir Timothy."

Those in court who were not acquainted with the twelfth baronet, expecting to see the conventional lord of the manor—portly, at least fifty years of age and bald, maybe—were surprised when there rose from his chair a slim, fair-haired young man, fine-drawn in features and physique. One woman present, who remembered that accomplished actor, whispered to her neighbour:

"Isn't he like Leslie Howard? "

When the oath had been administered, the coroner said:

"At about half past nine last Sunday evening, you were telephoned, were you not, by your employee, Frederick Barlow, from the cottage in Dark Hollow where he lived?"

"Yes, sir."

"Please tell the jury the reason for this call."

"It was Barlow's job to look after the mill and water wheel, which supplies fresh water to various parts of the estate, including his cottage. We've had the engineers there recently, attending to the pumping arrangements, which meant that Barlow, with his usual supply cut off, had to make periodical trips with a bucket to the millhouse, where a temporary hand-pump had been fixed. Barlow told me on the phone that he'd just been to the millhouse for that purpose, and while he was filling his bucket inside the building, somebody took the padlock off the staple, so that when he came to lock up again, it wasn't there."

"Can we take it, Sir Timothy, that Barlow was dependable—that he was not mistaken?"

"He was an old man, but he still had all his wits about him. I'd say that if Barlow said the padlock was pinch—was removed, there's no doubt that it was. But I can tell you this: when I got to the mill and had a look, the padlock was back where it ought to be—hanging from the staple by its loose shackle, just as Barlow would have left it while he filled the bucket. Somebody must have taken it off while Barlow was in the millhouse, then put it back again after he'd gone off to telephone me."

"That is a rational assumption, Sir Timothy," said Mr. Trench in a very kindly tone, "but I want you, please, to confine yourself to such direct evidence as you are able to give the jury."

Timothy grimaced like a reproved schoolboy.

"Sorry."

"When you received this telephone-call from Barlow, you went at once to the mill?"

"Yes. I thought I'd better; it sounded as if something funny was going on there. You can't take a car right round to the millhouse. In the old days, there used to be a cart-track, but it's disappeared. So I got out the skiff, rowed up-stream and moored just below the mill. When I came round into the yard, Miss Micheldever was standing just outside the open door."

"You saw nobody on the other side of the mill?"

"No. In the millhouse, the doctor was bending over the sump and he asked me to come in, which I did, and saw the poor old padre's body lying in the water. I at once went off and phoned the police."

"I understand, Sir Timothy, that you had met Mr. Price earlier in the evening?"

"Quite true. About a quarter to nine, I suppose it was, though I can't be sure to the minute. My fiancée and I were rowing in the skiff and he—er—had a chat with us from the bridge that runs over the stream. Then he went his way and we went ours."

Mr. Trench seemed not disposed to pursue this matter.

"Thank you, Sir Timothy." He turned to the jury. "Our inquiry today concerns the death of the Reverend Dafydd Price and no other. It is, however, necessary for me to tell you at this point that on the same evening Frederick Barlow died also—from natural causes. The telephone call to Sir Timothy was, as far as can be ascertained, his last act. His widow, who is a confirmed invalid and cannot leave her bed, has been interviewed by the police. She has told them that she heard no sounds downstairs and may have been asleep when Barlow returned with the bucket of water. There seems little doubt that, having made the telephone call, he collapsed and died. So we are not able to hear from his lips a fuller account of what occurred at the millhouse. Having telephoned the police, Sir Timothy returned to the mill. That was so, I believe?"

"Yes. I waited until Inspector Bradfield arrived with his assistant, then I began to get anxious about Barlow, who'd told me on the phone that he was going back to the mill and would meet me there. He hadn't turned up, so I suggested to Inspector Bradfield that I popped over to the cottage to see what had happened. The front door was locked, but the back one was open and I went in. Barlow was slumped in a chair in the parlour. He looked dead to me. I fetched Dr. Lorimer."

That was the end of his interrogation as far as the coroner was concerned. The jury, however, had another question to put.

"Why did the witness wait so long before going to Barlow's cottage?"

Mr. Trench said: "That is beyond the scope of this inquiry. Nevertheless, Sir Timothy may wish to answer it."

"Yes, of course. I can answer it best by inviting the gentlemen of the jury to put themselves in my position. I was suddenly confronted with a corpse and—well, quite frankly, poor old Barlow went right out of my mind."

This gave rise to a further question from the jury.

"Did not the witness telephone the police from Barlow's cottage?"

Timothy shook his head.

"Oh, no. He wasn't on the phone. The one he talked to me on was a private line. No, I phoned from the A.A. box at the top of the hill."

The foreman of the jury, still smarting from Mr. Trench's rebuff, now said in a no-hanky-panky tone:

"I know that box, sir, and I know the mill. To reach the box, the witness would have had to pass Barlow's cottage, and he would have had to pass it again on his way back. We would like him to tell us why he did not call in at the cottage after making his telephone call."

Timothy shrugged his shoulders.

"I can only say what I said before: I was too concerned about the body in my millhouse to worry about Barlow just then. After all, I did think of it very shortly afterwards and dashed off to see what had happened to him."

"Thank you, sir," said the foreman to Mr. Trench. "We have no more questions for this witness."

Bradfield was called to give evidence. He brought with him to the witness-table the parcel containing exhibit number one, and a smaller package. Having told the court of his interviews with Janet, Timothy and Dick, he went on:

"I examined the sump in which the body was found. The inside dimensions are seven feet long, two feet wide and two feet deep. The top of it, on which the reciprocating pump normally rests, is eight inches above the level of the floor, the rest of it being sunk in the ground. There was water in the sump to the depth of about a foot. The outlet pipe, through which surplus water can drain away, was blocked up with a piece of cotton waste. On Monday morning I had a word with the engineers' foreman, and he told me that this had been done by them."

"You then searched the clothing of the deceased?"

"Yes, sir. There was nothing to suggest that he had been drowned in the pond and then put in the sump. The pond is stagnant round the edges, but there were no traces of blanket weed on his clothing. In the pockets I found a few personal belongings, a flashlamp and, in the hip pocket, two five-pound notes."

Mr. Trench said to the jury:

"You have the numbers of the two notes retained by Mr. Gault. All four notes bear the same serial number, with the exception, of course, of the last figure. Those retained by Mr. Gault were seven and eight. Inspector Bradfield will now tell you the last figures of the two found by him on the body of the deceased."

"Four and five, sir."

"We are aware, gentlemen, that the Bank of England does not guarantee that new notes are issued in strict numerical order. Nevertheless, we have here four notes—four, five, seven and eight—leaving us with the strong supposition that the fifth note drawn by Mr. Gault from the bank was number six in the series. Please do not misunderstand me: there is no proof—only, as I said, a strong supposition. Inspector Bradfield, we have heard from Mr. Gault that he handed Mr. Price three five-pound notes, and that Mr. Price placed one in his breast pocket and the other two in his hip pocket. Did you find the one in his breast pocket when you came to search him?"

"No, sir. I made a thorough search and listed everything I found. There were only two notes on him, both in his hip pocket."

"Thank you, inspector. We come now, gentlemen, to two remarkable details in this singular case. Miss Micheldever has told us about the hat-brim projecting below the door of the millhouse. We know that this hat belonged to the deceased; it had his name inside it. By its position under the door, it would seem—I say seem—that it had fallen or been thrown there, and that the door was not subsequently reopened until the arrival of Miss Micheldever and the doctor. If that was so—and it is for you to decide—whoever it was drowned Mr. Price by placing him in the sump was either still in the building when thus surprised, or had left by some means other than the door. I should add that the millhouse has but one door. The doctor will tell you that, on entering the millhouse, he thought he heard some person moving about upstairs, but that when he went up to investigate, found nobody there. Inspector Bradfield, please now tell the jury of your own investigations."

"One of the first steps I took, sir, was to send my assistant upstairs to have a look round. He found nothing suspicious—except that a window was open, with the casement-stay hanging loose. I went up myself a little later and made a close examination of the window and frame. I found nothing to suggest that anyone had climbed out. It would be very easy to escape through the window, but there was no evidence to show that it had been so used."

"The second remarkable detail, gentlemen, concerns the walking-stick used by Mr. Price. We have witnesses to testify that he was never without it—that, in fact, he could not walk unless he had the stick to support him. Mr. Gault has told us that when Mr. Price left the rectory he had the stick with him. Please tell the jury, inspector, of your search for it."

"We didn't find it, sir. As soon as it grew light on Monday morning, one of my assistants made a search. This we followed up with another search, over a wider area. There's a great deal of undergrowth and rubble around the building, and the stick may still be somewhere there, but we went over the ground very thoroughly, sir, and I think we should have found it if it had been there."

"Could it have fallen into the brook and been carried downstream?"

"May I have your permission, sir, to come back to that in a moment or two?"

"By all means."

"After I had carried out my examination of the upper floor of the millhouse, I climbed through the window in search of traces of someone else having gone that way. I found none."

"Nevertheless, inspector, you say it is a simple matter to leave the millhouse through that window?"

"Very simple, sir, for any normal person. The ground there is at two levels. The millhouse is built on the lower level, so its upper floor is more or less horizontal with the pond and the footbridge. A ledge runs along under the window, and it's quite easy to get from the window to the footbridge."

"This you did—and made certain discoveries. Please tell the court about them."

Bradfield described the finding of the beer-bottle fragments, the stopper, and the label caught by the trash-rack.

"Since then, sir," he went on, "the pond has been dragged, under police supervision, and two parts of a beer-bottle recovered."

"The first of these," said Mr. Trench to the jury, "has already been produced in this court. Inspector Bradfield will now show you exhibit number two."

Bradfield unwrapped the smaller parcel and brought out the neck portion of the bottle.

"This, you will remember, gentlemen," said Mr. Trench, "was not found by Miss Micheldever and her fiancé, from which you may wish to deduce that it was thrown into the pond by some other hand."

While this was being said, Bradfield had unwrapped the larger parcel. Mr. Trench motioned to his officer, who gingerly picked up the two parts.

"They can now be handled freely," Mr. Trench told the jury, "for they have been tested by the Central Fingerprint Bureau at New Scotland Yard."

The officer stepped first up to Mr. Trench, then across to the jury.

"You will see," Mr. Trench went on as the officer brought the two parts together for their inspection, "that they once formed a single bottle. Naturally, it is not absolutely complete, and I need not remind you of the fragments that Inspector Bradfield and Dr. Lorimer, the police surgeon, found elsewhere. Now, gentlemen, Inspector Bradfield will give you some information about the finger-prints."

"The report from the Bureau, sir, refers to finger-prints left by three persons. They are all on exhibit number one—the lower part of the bottle. No prints at all were found on exhibit number two. Two of these persons are the doctor who picked up exhibit number one and threw it in the pond, and Mr. Taske, the licensee of the White Lion at Monk Jewel."

Mr. Trench interpolated here: "Mr. Taske will be the next witness called. Please proceed, inspector."

"The Bureau were supplied with full sets of the prints of the two gentlemen I have just mentioned. On exhibit number one, there were prints left by some person who has not yet been identified. I'd like to mention now, sir, the clergyman's hat found in the millhouse. When I examined it, I noticed that it smelt of creosote. I had it analysed, and the report confirms the presence of creosote on the hat. The only newly creosoted woodwork in or around the millhouse was the floor-boarding of the footbridge. Mrs. Barlow has told me that her husband did it on Sunday afternoon, then took the can and brush back to the cottage."

"Have the police drawn any conclusions from this?"

"If we accept the evidence of Miss Micheldever, sir, that they found exhibit number one on the footbridge, and if we add to that the fragments of glass found by myself, and if we take it that the creosote on the hat was transferred from the floor of the bridge, there is strong circumstantial evidence that the attack on Mr. Price took place on the footbridge."

"The theory being, I assume, that Mr. Price's hat was knocked off or otherwise removed before or during the attack?"

"Yes, sir. There's no doubt, from the medical evidence given by Dr. Lorimer, that Mr. Price was bare-headed when the blow fell."

"Thank you, inspector. Now you have something to tell us about the walking-stick."

"Mrs. Steadley, the proprietress of the boarding-house in Lulverton where Mr. Price was staying up to the time of his death, has given me a description of it. It is made of ebony and has a bent ivory handle." He smiled. "I think the technical term is a C-hook. Where the handle joins the shaft there is a silver band with Chinese characters engraved on it, and at the other end is a large rubber ferrule. You asked me, sir, whether I thought it had floated down-stream. I suggest not. If it had fallen or been thrown into the pond, it would have been held back by the trash-rack. The only way it could have got into the lower stream would have been over the water-wheel—unless, of course, it was diverted into the spillway, which is unlikely."

"I hope," said Mr. Trench with a smile, "that the members of the jury follow these technicalities?"

There were murmurs of assent; they were all country folk.

Bradfield went on: "To pass over the wheel, the stick would have had to fall or be thrown into the gut. From the position of the glass fragment on the floor-boards, the attack was made more to the middle of the bridge, and it's highly unlikely—or so it seems to the police—that the stick fell by accident into the gut. One last point, sir: we've no proof that the stick was light enough to float."

"Then I think we should leave it at that. For the moment, gentlemen, the walking-stick remains untraced. Please stand down, inspector. I may have to recall you."

Bradfield obeyed, and Mr. Trench continued to the jury:

"You have heard about the beer-bottle label and how it bore the name of Messrs. Trumington's. The nearest Trumington's house to the scene of the tragedy is the White Lion at Monk Jewel." He turned to add to his officer: "Call the next witness."

"Mr. Horace Taske."

This unimpressive little man with the long moustache much stained by tobacco took his place at the witness-table and repeated the oath.

"On Sunday night, Mr. Taske, you received a call from Inspector Bradfield?"

"Yes, sir. Oh, yes."

"And he showed you the label from a beer-bottle? "

"He did, yes."

"You identified it as one attached to a bottle sold by yourself earlier in the evening?"

"Oh, yes. Yes. Undoubtedly yes."

"One affirmative is sufficient, Mr. Taske."

"Yes, oh, yes. Quite sufficient, yes."

"Please tell the jury why you are so certain about the label."

"Because of the two deposit stamps. Yes, the two deposit stamps. I stamped it twice, yes. Yes, the first was a bad impression, so I inked the stamp and did it again. Yes."

"So, gentlemen, certain points have now been established. Finger-prints confirm that this witness handled exhibit number one. He has identified the label retrieved from the pond. Whether it can be properly assumed that the label was attached to exhibit number one prior to being loosened by the water in the pond, is for you to decide. One other interesting point—and a very significant one— emerges from Mr. Taske's evidence. You can tell the court, Mr. Taske, I believe, where the stock of bottled light ale is kept for counter use in your bar."

"Yes: on a shelf at the back."

"And this shelf is sufficiently low for you to bend down when taking a bottle from it?"

"That's it, yes."

"It is also a natural movement, on picking up a bottle from that shelf, for you to take it by the neck?"

"Yes, oh, yes."

"This bottle with which we are now concerned. Did you remove it from the shelf in that manner?"

"Yes. I never bend down any further than I can help. Lumbago. It gives me gyp—real gyp. Yes."

"Thank you, Mr. Taske. Gentlemen, we have to ask ourselves this question: Why were Mr. Taske's finger-prints not found on exhibit number two? We can well imagine that his prints were made on exhibit number one while he was rubber-stamping the bottle, but why not on exhibit number two when he took the bottle from the shelf? You may well be satisfied with the suggestion that they were removed in the process of removing other prints more damning to some person as yet unidentified. Now, Mr. Taske, I should like you to tell the jury the name of the person to whom you sold a bottle of light ale bearing the label that was brought to you for identification."

Janet, her screwed-up handkerchief pressed to her mouth, had to repress a natural instinct to jump up and prevent a reply.

"Yes," said Mr. Taske. "It was Mr. Micheldever."

"Mr. Harold Micheldever?"

"The son, yes. Son of the rector of Yateham as was."

"It was an off-licence sale, was it not?"

"Yes, he took it away with him Sunday evening."

"At what time?"

"Round nine o'clock. Yes, nine o'clock, more or less."

"Gentlemen, have you any questions for this witness?"

They had not, and his place at the witness-table was taken first by Mr. Battle of the Seven Stars, Yateham, and then by P.C. Bristo. Mr. Battle was called upon to confirm that Harold Micheldever had attempted to change a five-pound note on the Sunday evening; Bristo to tell the court that the number of the note, as officially recorded by him, was Bc/8 184 271006. They both stated that Harold had no bottle in his possession at the time. When Bristo had been told to stand down, Mr. Trench said to the jury:

"As I informed you earlier in this inquiry, gentlemen, there is a strong supposition that the fifth bank-note drawn by Mr. Gault from his bank last Saturday was number six in the sequence: four, five, six, seven, eight. You have been told the numbers of the other four, two of which were found on the deceased, and the other two of which have been produced by Mr. Gault in this court. Here, now, is evidence concerning the fifth, making a complete sequence. I must leave you to judge whether the five-pound note offered by Mr. Harold Micheldever to Mr. Battle on Sunday evening was one of the five drawn by Mr. Gault from the bank, and, further, one of the three handed by Mr. Gault to Mr. Price a short time before Mr. Price's death."

Janet was here recalled and required to confirm that, when she had met her brother at the stile, he had, as far as she could observe, no beer-bottle on his person. This she did. When she had gone back to her chair, Mr. Trench turned over the sheets lying before him on the table.

"An important witness in this inquiry—and one, gentlemen, who might have helped you to reach a verdict—is, unfortunately, not available. I refer to Mr. Harold Micheldever. Inspector Bradfield, please."

Bradfield took the stand. In answer to Mr. Trench's question, he said:

"He left this neighbourhood on Monday afternoon, sir, or during the early evening, and has not been seen since, either at his home or at his place of business. On Monday morning, I questioned him and he subsequently made a statement, which was written down, signed by him, and witnessed by your officer and myself."

"What efforts have been made to trace him, inspector?"

"We've made extensive inquiries, sir, over a wide area, and there seems no hope of tracing him yet. The search is being continued."

"Then I think we can allow the statement to be read."

Bradfield left the witness-table, and, while the court waited expectantly, Mr. Trench removed his spectacles, polished them carefully with his handkerchief, resettled them on his big nose, then picked up the document.

"It runs as follows: 'I, Harold Bagehot Micheldever, aged thirty-two, am employed as a rent collector and reside with my parents at Medlar Cottage, Yateham, Downshire. At approximately 9 p.m. in the evening of Sunday, 7th September, 1952, I purchased a pint bottle of light ale at the White Lion public house, Monk Jewel, Downshire, and took it away with me, intending to walk back to my home in Yateham, not having enough money in my possession to pay for the omnibus fare. On the way I felt thirsty and, not wishing to be seen drinking from a bottle on a public thoroughfare, I left the road and went down the lane into Dark Hollow. On reaching the millpond, I sat down on the parapet of the bridge that spans Snare Brook at that point, where I opened the bottle and drank some of the beer. It gave me hiccups—'"

An undercurrent of laughter ran through the court.

" '—and I did not drink much of it. I had already had a good deal to drink, and do not remember walking along the footpath to the mill. I am subject to forgetfulness when I have been drinking. I can, however, recollect standing on the mill footbridge and drinking the rest of the beer from the bottle, which I then threw in the pond. I have no recollection of anything else until I awoke this morning. I cannot explain how I came into possession of the five-pound note. I do not remember trying to change it in the Seven Stars public-house in Yateham. I do not remember meeting any person at any point between the White Lion and the Seven Stars. I am not acquainted with the Reverend Dafydd Price. I did not meet him last night or on any previous—'"

"That is not the truth!"

Yi Liu-ying was on his feet.

"That is not the truth!" he repeated. "In China, at Haolaofen, Mr. Micheldever and Mr. Price worked together as missionaries."

Bruce Gault caught his arm and tried to pull him down in his seat, but the grip was thrown off.

"Mr. Micheldever was unfrocked by the Bishop of Shungchow and forbidden to exercise his Orders. He had stolen much money from the Chinese Christians, and it was Mr. Price who laid the charge against—"

"Be silent!"

Gault had jumped up and was towering over him. For a moment it seemed that Yi Liu-ying would defy his master. Then he meekly reseated himself. Gault turned towards the coroner and bowed stiffly.

"I must apologize for my servant, sir. He does not understand our legal procedure. With your permission, I will take him from the court."

Most of those present would have liked to hear more on this intriguing theme. Mr. Trench, however, thought differently.

"Please do, rector. We shall not need either of you again."

The two men afforded a sharp contrast as the tall one, looking neither to right nor left, stalked out of the room followed by the short one, who held his sleek head high because he had spoken out against falsehood—forgetful, perhaps, that in that court he himself had committed perjury.

"Quiet, please!" called the coroner's officer, for general excited conversation had followed the departure of this strange and, thought some, sinister pair.

Mr. Trench addressed the jury.

"That was a regrettable interruption, gentlemen. You

218

may be thinking that this court should take cognisance of the statements just made by—er—Mr.Yi. As, however, Mr. Micheldever is not present to rebut or to confirm them, I ask you, please, to disregard them when considering your verdict. Your duty is to decide when, where, and by what means Mr. Price met his death—just that and nothing more."

He picked up Harold Micheldever's statement and glanced through it before he continued:

"Yes, I had reached the end when the interruption came. Two points emerge, so I shall recall the police witness."

Bradfield came forward to the table.

"Mr. Micheldever states here," said Mr. Trench, then read out: "'On reaching the millpond, I sat down on the parapet of the bridge that spans Snare Brook at that point, where I opened the bottle and drank some of the beer.' Inspector, please tell the court what you found on this bridge on Monday morning—and, gentlemen, please remember that the bridge referred to is the one near the Barlows' cottage, not the footbridge by the mill."

"I found there, sir," said Bradfield, "at the foot of the parapet, part of the paper label from the stopper of a beer bottle. The name printed on it was 'Trumington.' Any paper left on the neck of the bottle when the stopper was unscrewed had been washed off in the pond, so I wasn't able to identify the stopper-label with exhibit number two."

"That, gentlemen, goes far to confirm Mr. Micheldever's statement that he opened the bottle on that bridge. Notwithstanding this, there seems a serious discrepancy in his later evidence." He read aloud once more: "'I can, however, recollect standing on the mill footbridge and drinking the rest of the beer from the bottle, which I then threw in the pond.'" He looked across at the jury and repeated: " '... which I then threw in the pond.' You must judge for yourselves the validity of that statement, but first I would like Inspector Bradfield to tell of the manner in which this statement was made by Mr. Micheldever."

"He was very uncertain, sir. I reached the conclusion that he was not at all clear in his mind about anything that happened after he left the bridge over the stream. I urged him not to say anything he wasn't quite sure about, but he stuck to his statement that he threw the bottle in the pond. May I express an opinion, sir?"

"Proceed."

"I believe—in fact, I'm convinced—that he made that statement because it was the easiest way out; that he didn't remember what he'd done with the bottle, and decided it was safest to say that he'd thrown it in the pond."

At this juncture, Dr. Dick Farringdon came into the court. As the jury had no further questions for Bradfield, Dick was called up to give his evidence, which was little more than a confirmation of the details already supplied by Janet. Of his entry into the millhouse, he said:

"I thought I heard someone moving about upstairs and called out. I went up the staircase to investigate, but all I found was the open window. There was no sign of anyone, either inside or out. I looked through the window and saw no one."

"Are you still of the opinion, doctor, that you heard these suspicious sounds?"

"I must confess, sir, that I'm not sure. That old building could never be completely silent—the running water and the creaking of the wheel. All I would like to state definitely and on oath is that I received the impression at the time that someone was upstairs."

"Thank you, Dr. Farringdon. Any questions, gentlemen? ... No? Then you may stand down, doctor."

Mr. Trench tapped the papers on the table into a tidy pile, informed the jury that all the available evidence had now been heard, then proceeded to sum up. He concluded:

"It is far from customary in inquiries of this nature for statements to be read in the absence of those who have made them. It gives them no opportunity to explain or enlarge upon them, to confute or to disprove. I was at first undecided whether or not to lay before you today the statement made to the police by Harold Micheldever. After deliberation—and after, as you have heard, sustained efforts by the police to trace Mr. Micheldever, so that he could be summoned to appear at this inquiry—I arrived at the conclusion that it would be fairer to him that his statement should be read out in this court. In asking you now to consider your verdict, I strongly urge upon you that, bearing in mind the circumstances and that the inquiries of the police are not yet complete, your verdict should be one of murder against some person or persons unknown."

The jury retired and returned within a very few minutes. They filed back to their seats, and the coroner's officer called for silence.

"Well, gentlemen," said Mr. Trench. "Have you arrived at a verdict?"

The foreman stood.

"Yes, sir."

"What is your verdict?"

A deep hush fell on the crowded little court.

"Murder by Harold Bagehot Micheldever."

Dick, who had taken a chair behind Janet, put a comforting hand on her shoulder. She covered it with her own.

Mr. Trench kept his feelings in check.

"The cause of death, on the medical evidence," he said evenly, "was drowning, and your verdict is murder against Harold Bagehot Micheldever."

In the centre of the court, between the jury and the witness stand, was a small table. To this the jurymen were called one by one by the coroner's officer, in order to sign the inquisition. This document was then handed by the officer to Mr. Trench, who punctiliously checked off the names with the list in his possession. Before appending his own signature, he said sternly to the jury:

"I have no alternative but to sign this inquisition. You must understand, though, that I entirely disagree with your verdict and sign under protest."

The jury looked embarrassed—all save the foreman, who considered that he had won his match with Mr. Trench on points.

The witnesses were then called back to the witness-table one by one. There evidence was read over to them by Mr. Trench and they were then asked to sign the deposition. Before leaving the table, they were bound over to attend the trial. Mr. Trench gave instructions to his officer to send for Mr. Gault, so that he too could be treated in the same way, then issued a warrant for the committal of Harold Micheldever, which he handed to Bradfield.

There were general preparations for departure—the clatter of chairs and the hum of conversation. Some were already scrimmaging round the door. Suddenly the whole court became stationary and silent, for a resounding voice had proclaimed:

"Oyea! Oyea! Oyea!"

The coroner's officer was making it clear that the last word was his.

"All ye good men of this county, who have been sworn of this jury, to inquire on behalf of our Sovereign Lady the Queen, when, where, and by what means Dafydd Price came to his death, having discharged your duty, may depart hence and take your ease. God save the Queen!"

Not a few of those so enjoined, having departed thence, speedily took their ease in the bars downstairs.

Chapter Nineteen

EMERGENCY EXIT

I

MISS MAISIE BROWN was not one who could keep a secret for long, especially from her bosom friend, Sabina Danbury. After breakfast on the Friday morning, an hour before the opening of the inquest at Yateham, when they were walking from the boarding-house to the Empire to hear Jake Harris's plans for the winter season, she told her that she had that morning received a letter from Harold Micheldever.

The immediate eager concern shown by Sabina rather surprised Maisie, for Sabina had told her in forthright terms on more than one occasion that Maisie, with her looks, could do better than Harold Micheldever—much better. In fact, Sabina had expressed great satisfaction when Maisie had told her that she had sent him packing. Now she seemed so keen to know how he was, where he was and what he was doing—and asked with such smiling and friendly interest—that Maisie was taken aback. She, however, did not know what Sabina knew: that a number of persons were anxious to learn the present whereabouts of that young man. Even Sabina did not know the whole story, though she had her suspicions—and some of these were not pleasant ones.

"It's ever such a funny letter," Maisie confided under

this pressure. "He says he's safe and well, but I'm not to tell anybody where he is. Anyway, I've never heard of Graystoke. Why doesn't he want anybody to know? Do you think he's done something he shouldn't?"

"Actually it wouldn't surprise me, darling. But it isn't your worry, is it? You've given him"—she was going to say "the brush-off," but decided that it was not a phrase suited to the lips of the future Lady Chatthume, and altered it to "his congé."

Maisie looked unhappy.

"I'd still not like anything—sort of nasty. You see, Bi— well, I know it's ever so silly, but I still love him."

"Maisie, you're crazy! Don't be a little fool!"

They were passing the entrance to the fairground where Maisie and Harold had disported themselves on the night of their first meeting. She now paused at the gaudily painted gateway and surveyed the Great Dipper, the roundabouts, the swing-boats and side-shows, none of which was doing much business.

"He's ever so brave, really—brave because he's frightened. That night when Tim went off and left him, he and me came along here, and you could see he was scared stiff on the switch-back and things. But when we got in the swing-boat, he showed he could be brave and wouldn't come off for ever so long, just making himself do it. I thought he was mad when he wouldn't stop, and it wasn't till afterwards that I guessed the real reason."

This ingenuous essay at *a posteriori* deduction would have interested Harold, even if it would not have amused him.

They resumed their way to the Empire, and by the time they reached it Sabina had extracted from Maisie the address where Harold was to be found in Graystoke.

After the inquest, Janet and Dick went back to Medlar Cottage, where they found Mrs. Micheldever in a condition of great nervous suspense.

"What happened?" she asked, almost before they had stepped into the hall.

"Mummy, darling, you must prepare yourself for bad news."

Janet put an arm round her mother's shoulder, guided her into the front room and persuaded her to sit down.

"The coroner," she then told her, "didn't agree with the jury and said so very forcibly, but they decided that Harold did it, which is ridiculous."

"Does that mean that he'll be—punished?"

Janet looked at Dick, who said, his deep voice full of reassurance:

"Oh, no—not till they can prove it. The verdict of a coroner's jury, if it's against any particular person, doesn't carry much weight. We have to face the fact that, as soon as he's traced, he'll be arrested on what's known as a coroner's warrant, but he'll still have the chance of a fair trial—and learned counsel will make short work of some of the evidence Janet tells me was brought against him this morning."

Mrs. Micheldever's expression showed plainly that she did not share this belief.

"Haven't they found him?" she asked.

Janet replied: "Not yet, dear."

"I do wish he hadn't run away. It makes everything look so black against him."

She rose to her feet.

"I must go up and tell your father."

"Let me do it, Mummy."

"No, dear. It should come from me."

"Don't forget to say," said Dick, "that the coroner disagreed with the verdict."

"I'm afraid," was Mrs. Micheldever's reply, "that my husband thinks the same as the jury."

II

"One thing I've got to know," said Jake Harris to his company, assembled in the greenroom of the Empire, "is whether Bi's carrying on or not."

"You know I won't want to leave you, Jake," replied Sabina. "You're all such pets."

"That don't get us no—doesn't get us anywhere. Musgroves say I can have Lucille Armitage, but they must know one way or the other before the end of the week. She can play lead, dances, sings and does male impersonations."

"So does her husband," said Beverley Bott.

"Cut it out, Bev," pleaded Jake. "This is dead serious. Come on, Bi—yes or no?"

"It all depends on when we get married."

"If, more like it," added Bott in a very audible aside.

Just then a member of the staff poked in his head to say that Miss Danbury was wanted on the telephone by Sir Timothy Chatthume. Sabina hastened out to take the call. Timothy was speaking from his office in Chatthume Place.

"I thought you'd like to know the verdict," he said. "Harold Micheldever's been charged with the murder."

"Darling, that's splendid! I'm so relieved."

"There's something wrong with this line. It sounded as if you said it was splendid."

Sabina thought quickly.

"No. I said, 'So that's how it ended?'"

"We're all badly shaken here, of course, trying to think what to do for the best. Trouble is the silly idiot's skedaddled."

She dropped her voice as she asked:

"Can you still hear me?"

"Yes. Carry on."

"Would it help if you knew where he was?"

"It would—most certainly."

"He's at Pinehurst, Liphook Road, Graystoke, Surrey. Maisie's had a letter from him, but don't tell her I told you."

Sabina went back to the greenroom with a happy smile on her face.

"Jake, darling," she said as she entered, "you can sign up Lucille Armitage right away."

III

The Bug was brought to a stop outside Medlar Cottage, then, to the relief of Yateham residents, silenced by the turn of a switch—a mitigation that did not prevent this rakish, resting monster from occupying more than its proper share of the roadway.

Mrs. Micheldever was still up in the study with her husband. Downstairs in the front room, Janet and Dick saw Timothy come up the garden path. Janet went out to let him in, and the three of them discussed the situation.

"Don't you think," suggested Timothy, "that Harold would stand a better chance if he came forward and faced the music like a man?"

"Far better," Dick at once agreed, and Janet added:

"Running away's the sort of fat-headed thing he would do."

"Could we persuade him to give himself up?"

"We might," nodded Janet, "if we knew where he was."

"We do," answered Timothy, and told them the address.

The outcome of their deliberations was the decision that, after lunch, Timothy and Dick, who was not expected back at the hospital until the morrow, should journey to Graystoke in the Bug and bring back Harold, as Timothy put it, willy-nilly.

At about this same time, Sabina was saying to Maisie as they walked back to their boarding-house:

"I didn't want to tell you in front of the others, darling, but there's bad news about Harold."

"Tell me quick!" demanded Maisie.

"Tim said on the phone that Harold's been charged with murder. The old clergyman, you know."

Maisie received this in frightened silence. She said after they had gone several paces:

"Are the police looking for him?"

"I should think so. Tim didn't say on the phone."

"What happens if they find him?"

"I suppose," replied Sabina, not without a certain relish, "that he'll be tried, found guilty and hanged."

"Bi!" protested poor Maisie. "Don't be so brutal!"

Half an hour later, having confided in nobody, Maisie was in the booking-office at Southmouth station, asking how to get to Graystoke. On being told that it was fifty minutes' run on the main line to London, she bought a return ticket.

Her place at the window was taken by another traveller, who, having taken care to overhear her remarks, booked for the same destination. This was that slim, dark, earnest young man, Detective-Sergeant Hartley.

IV

Had Mr. Theodore Allen not left his wife in charge of his establishment and attended the inquest as a member of the general public, the investigations of the police might have proceeded more slowly.

Mr. Allen was the proprietor of Yateham's curio and art shop, which passers-by referred to by a harsher name. Early in the afternoon of that same day, he was called upon by a gentleman in the same line of business, though more peripatetically conducted, for in place of premises of bricks and mortar, Mr. Bert Clarke—"Nobby" to his friends—had a horse and cart.

Nobby's present mission was to interest Mr. Allen in some of the purchases he had made while hawking the streets of Yateham, Monk Jewel, Lulverton and beyond. Of the miscellaneous haul in the cart, one item in particular caught the eye of Mr. Allen. He took it up and examined it with such close attention that Nobby felt sure of a sale. In this he was to be disappointed; instead of buying it, Mr. Allen immediately telephoned the police.

V

The little town of Graystoke lies just inside the south-west boundary of Surrey—a lovely region of high pine woods, with long slopes of heather and gorse. Not far away is Highcombe Bottom, that great wooded glen better known as the Devil's Punch Bowl.

Maisie Brown stepped out of the train at Graystoke station. The porter at the ticket barrier said, in answer to her inquiry, that Liphook Road was part of the London-to-Portsmouth road, that it was two miles long and uphill most of the way, and that she would do well to take a taxi. Maisie, who was prudent with her own money, however prodigal she was with the financial resources of her cavaliers, asked about buses. The porter advised against this: buses were slow and infrequent, in addition to which, though he did not mention this to Maisie, he drew a small but welcome commission on all taxi-rides arranged.

She thanked him and went out into the yard, where a vehicle stood waiting.

"Liphook Road, please," she said to the driver. "A house called Pinehurst."

He drove down the short approach, turned to the right, proceeded for fifty yards, then stopped.

"'Ere we are, miss. Two bob, please."

She gave him half a crown, having learnt, at some expense to herself, that, though a road be two miles long, one's objective may not be at the far extremity.

Meanwhile Sergeant Hartley waited in the station yard for the taxi to return to base.

From a top-floor window of the unpretentious little guesthouse, Harold observed the arrival of Maisie and hastened down to intercept her before she asked for him by name. Having avoided the necessity of producing a ration book by having all his meals out, he had described himself in the visitors' book as John Lawrence of Brighton. A ruthless haircut, the purchase of a pair of tinted spectacles, and a five-days'-old moustache had changed his appearance enough for Maisie to wonder for a moment whether this was the man she sought, when he met her in the hall.

"Come up to my room," he murmured.

He led her upstairs and into the little bedroom, furnished

very simply, and with a small gas-fire in the grate. After closing the door behind them, he said in the same low tone:

"You shouldn't have come. It's a hell of a risk."

"I had to, darling."

"Darling? I thought I'd been thrown over."

"I've changed my mind. Anyway, I always call everybody darling. Everybody does."

She sat down on the bed.

"You know what's happened, don't you?"

"No; I've been lying low."

"They had the inquest this morning and the jury said you did it. The police are looking for you and when they find you, you'll be charged with murder."

Harold dropped down beside her on the bed and sat with bent head, his eyes on the patterned linoleum.

"I suppose it was bound to happen," he said after a pause. "I only made it worse by skipping out. If I'd been at the inquest, I could have pitched them some sort of yarn. It's nice of you to come, Maisie, but it's done no good."

"Yes, it has! I came here to warn you, and now you've got to be extra careful not to be seen. That'll give the police time to find the real murderer."

"Sorry, old dear, but you're too optimistic. I killed old Price and that's an end of it."

"Darling, you didn't. Don't be stupid."

"I must have done." He laughed shortly before he added. "Funny I didn't send myself a memo."

"What do you mean? I don't understand."

"After the odd sherbet or two, I get a sort of black-out, so I jot down anything I may want to remember afterwards."

232

Maisie jumped up from the bed.

"Turn out your pockets!"

"What do you expect to find?" he asked with a twisted smile.

"'Slugged Rev. D. Price with a bottle'?"

"There may be something else."

They found nothing among his papers.

"What else might you have used?"

"Cigarette-packet? If I did, I must have chucked it away. No, Maisie, I've got to face up to the fact that I killed Price—and I can guess why."

Maisie plied him for an explanation, but he would say no more on the matter. Instead he urged her to return at once to Southmouth.

"I'll go on lying low here," he said, "as long as the money lasts. If there's any news for me, drop me a line—and don't forget the name's John Lawrence."

He did not accompany her downstairs. As soon as she had left the house and turned into the road on her way back to the station, he locked the door and closed the window, then pulled the mattress off the bed on to the floor near the fireplace and arranged the pillow on it. Next he felt in his trouser pocket and brought out a shilling, which he pressed in the check-meter before turning on the gas.

This morning at the inquest, the jury returned a verdict against Harold Micheldever and he is to be charged with a murder committed by me. By a combination of coincidences in the purest traditions of stage farce, he became involved in the events in Dark

Hollow last Sunday evening, and now he is to be charged with a murder committed by me.

If he is condemned to death, shall I stand by and let them hang him? Shall I deliberately bring grief upon his parents—and Janet? What is the alternative? Full confession? . . . Suicide? . . . Surely there is another way? I do not want him to suffer for my crime, useless wastrel though he is. Could I ensure that he is proved innocent without implicating myself? That stupid fool, Yi Lui-ying, made matters worse by shouting accusations at the inquest.

What happened on the footbridge of the mill? One thought was uppermost in my mind: Dafydd must be silenced. The bottle stood on the top rail, where Harold Micheldever must have placed it after finishing the beer. I snatched it up, whipped off Dafydd's hat with my left hand, and brought the bottle down on his head with such force that it smashed it, leaving me with the neck in my hand. He fell like a pole-axed sheep.

Finger-prints ... I carefully polished the glass with my handkerchief, then threw the neck into the pond. I was about to do the same with the rest of the bottle, when I saw a light looming out of the mist. Someone with a hurricane-lamp was approaching along the footpath.

Dafydd was unconscious. Luckily he was small and light. I picked up his hat, then lifted him, got him across my shoulder and carried him down the steps. I laid him behind some bushes near the wall of the yard, then crouched down myself, waiting for the person with the lamp to go on his or her way along the footpath above us. But I heard feet descending the steps.

It was old Barlow. In his left hand was a bucket, and the sound as it struck the stonework on the way down spoke of its emptiness. He went along the front of the building to the door, where he set down lamp and bucket, fumbled in his pocket for a key and undid *the padlock. Then he went inside.*

Soon I heard a rhythmic clanking sound. Acting on an impulse, I left my hiding-place and, keeping to the wall, stole swiftly along until I reached the open doorway. On peeping round the jamb, I saw Barlow pumping water into the bucket. There was noise enough from this, and from the water-wheel, to cover any small sound I made. Then, as I stood there, the high-pitched buzz of a gnat impinged on my left ear. Instinctively I raised my hand to ward it off—and my coat-cuff caught the padlock and dislodged it from its staple.

The padlock fell to the ground and inside the mill the pumping stopped. I bent down and had just picked up the padlock, when my ears told me that Barlow had picked up the full bucket and the lamp and was shuffling towards the door. With no thought but to hide myself, I withdrew swiftly, the padlock still in my hand.

I had no time or opportunity to observe Barlow's reactions when he found the padlock missing. I waited under cover as he came along with his two burdens, leaving the door open. While he was going up the steps, Dafydd groaned faintly, but Barlow did not hear.

After his footsteps had died away in the mist, I came out again from behind the bushes, went forward and rehung the padlock on the staple. Then, taking out my torch, I slipped into the building, an idea taking shape in my mind.

There was some depth of water in the concrete tank. When Dafydd recovered consciousness, he would talk … he would talk … he would talk … I could not bring myself to hit him again, whatever implement I might find, for the purpose. I went out to him, lifted him from behind the bushes and brought him into the millhouse. As I pushed the door to behind me with my foot, his hat fell to the floor.

He was just coming round when I laid him in the tank. I kept his head under the water until the life went out of him.

Then some sixth sense flashed a danger signal. Someone was approaching.

To leave by the door might be dangerous. As quietly and swiftly as I could, I went up the wooden staircase. I opened the window and looked out. Yes, I could escape that way. I swung a leg over the sill...

Now what of Harold Micheldever? At this morning's inquest, they heard about the gift of fifteen pounds. It was providential for me that it happened so, yet how did one of those notes get into the possession of Harold Micheldever? Did he fall in with Dafydd before meeting Janet at the stile? Did Dafydd give him five pounds—or did Micheldever force it from him by threats? No, Dafydd could never be intimidated by a weakling like Micheldever. Dafydd, who stood up to the Red Asiatics and, in Chinese with a Welsh accent, threatened them with the fires of everlasting Hell— no drunken lout could frighten Dafydd. Micheldever must have told him some hard-luck story and softened his heart. . . . Five pounds . . . Five pounds intended for cretonne curtains in the rectory—an ironical twist.

The problem remains—and the heavy burden of guilt. It will be with me day and night. Till when? Till Micheldever is hanged and the police dossier on The Case of Dafydd Price is filed away and the Public Prosecutor turns his mind to other things? Or after?

One other anxiety haunts me: Dafydd's walking-stick—a gift from the Chinese Christians at Haolaofen after those despicable curs had lamed him for life. . . . Despicable? They despicable? They lamed him, they flogged him, they subjected him to the mental torture of hour after hour of questioning, but they did not kill him. No, that was reserved for me.

The walking-stick ... I can but hope ... Hope what? ... My soul, my whole being, feels like the string of a violin, tightened, tightened, tightened—until it snaps. When shall I snap?

Identification? The beard may save me. . . . But Dafydd was not deceived.

At all costs, I must have the girl.

Chapter Twenty

EAST MEETS WEST

I

FROM his appearance and mode of life, there was reason to think that Nobby Clarke had gipsy blood in his veins; from his accent, that he was not country bred. About fifty years of age, he was not very clean, nor was he very honest. It can be well imagined, therefore, that he was not at all pleased when Mr. Allen—tall, solemn, long-featured and a churchwarden of St. Anselm's—insisted on calling in the police on the matter of the article Nobby had offered for sale—an ivory-handled ebony walking-stick with a silver band engraved in Chinese.

Bradfield came at once and interviewed Nobby in the little room behind the congested shop.

"I ain't done no wrong," protested Nobby. "All above board, that's me. Sem bob I give fer ver lot—an' most er vit junk. Sem bob's not aht er ver wy fer—"

"Look," said Bradfield, "I'm only interested in one thing: where did you get this walking-stick?"

"It was wiv ver uvver stuff in a box in ver garridge. 'What charskin'?' I says to 'er, not as I like doin' dills wiv Chinks. "Ow much yer gimme?' she says. 'Sem bob,' I says, 'not as what I ain't doin' yer a fiver takin' it orf yer 'ands,' I says."

Guessing now what the answer would be, Bradfield repeated his question. Nobby replied in forty words, which can be reduced to two: Yateham rectory.

Timothy and Dick arrived at Pinehurst very shortly after the departure of Maisie Brown, and at the very moment when Sergeant Hartley was about to cross the road to make a call on Harold. When he saw the Bug pull up outside Pinehurst, and noted the driver and passenger, he turned casually away and inspected the layettes and baby-linen in a shop window with a show of interest that was, for a bachelor, most convincing.

Met in the hall by Miss Maybank, the proprietress, Timothy asked to see Mr. Micheldever, and was informed that no gentleman of that name was staying at Pinehurst.

"Perhaps I've got the name wrong," said Timothy. "He's by himself, I believe."

"The only single gentleman we have is Mr. Lawrence." Timothy took a chance.

"Yes, of course. I got the two names confused. It's Mr. Lawrence we want."

"Then if you'll kindly wait, I'll go up and tell him. Can I take your name?"

"Sir Timothy Chatthume."

Miss Maybank's expression suggested that she was not quite sure whether she believed this. She ascended the stairs with the dignity of an angular empress—and fifty seconds later they heard her screams for help.

Timothy was the first to reach her. She was standing outside a door, wringing her hands. The narrow landing smelt strongly of gas.

"He's gassed himself!" she wailed.

Timothy stepped past her, turned the knob and shook the door. Dick came up.

"Locked," said Timothy, then thumped on the panel.

"Badger, you damned idiot, open the door!"

There was no reply or sound of movement within the room.

"Better burst it open," suggested Dick.

Timothy was about to get his shoulder to the door, when the key was turned in the lock. The door was then opened and Harold Micheldever stood there swaying, his face a bright pink from the carbon monoxide he had absorbed.

"Tactless moment to call," he complained, "just as a fellow's committing suicide."

Whereupon, after the exertion of standing up and going into a stronger concentration of gas nearer the low ceiling, he collapsed.

"Pull him out," said Dick. "I'll get the room clear."

Knowing that a handkerchief over the mouth and nose will not keep out CO, he merely held his breath as he went into the room, turned off the gas-fire, then ran to open the window. There he drew another breath before going back to the door, by which time Timothy had got hold of Harold and dragged him on to the landing.

Other residents were coming up to see what all the excitement was about. Miss Maybank, who, with the prospect of a suicide on the premises receding, had got her nerve back, called down over the banisters:

"It's quite all right. There's nothing to worry about. Mr. Lawrence has had a slight accident with the gas-fire."

They managed to get the only half-conscious patient downstairs and laid him on a settee near an open window.

"I think we'd better run him round to the hospital," Dick said. "The B.L.B. mask is called for."

Miss Maybank was consulted and, when she had told

them where the hospital was situated, the three of them left Pinehurst, Harold supported by the other two. Their sudden appearance did not take Sergeant Hartley by surprise, but this was the main London road and traffic was heavy, so that before he could get across to them, they had piled into the Bug and roared off to the hospital.

On a couch in one of the examination rooms, Harold was made to inhale a mixture of oxygen and carbon dioxide. The casualty officer was busy and, on learning that Dick was a doctor, left Harold in his care. After ten minutes or so, the treatment had its effect; Harold's colour returned to something nearer normal and eventually Dick considered him sufficiently recovered to remove the mask.

Timothy, who had sat in silence, bottling up his exasperation, now burst out:

"You crazy loon! Why try damfool games like that?"

"It's no business of yours," retorted Harold.

"That's where you're wrong. You've caused enough trouble already, without causing any more. It's not you I'm concerned about. Don't think that. I'd let you go to hell in your own way if it wasn't for your mother."

"Sometimes," sneered Harold, "I've a suspicion she's your mother too."

"We'll let that pass for the moment. Farringdon, you'd better do the talking."

Dick explained the position, trying to convince Harold that the evidence against him was so circumstantial that he stood a very good chance of acquittal. But Harold was not to be easily convinced, being, by this time, quite persuaded that he had murdered Dafydd Price. Dick, however, persisted and finally prevailed upon Harold to agree that, on leaving the hospital, he would go straight along to Graystoke police station and give himself up.

"But," said Harold, "you fellows keep out of it. I'm not having you as an unofficial guard of honour to escort me to clink. If I go, I go by myself."

"Give us your word on it," said Timothy, "and Farringdon and I will stay here until you've had time to get to the police station."

"Right—word of honour."

Dick went out to speak to the casualty officer, assured him that Harold was now well enough to go home, then came to tell Harold that he could depart. With no more than a grunt of thanks, Harold slouched out—and caught the first bus at the nearest stop.

He had just alighted at Godalming, when Detective-Sergeant Hartley tapped him on the shoulder.

Early that evening, under a grey and stormy sky, with the complaining trees writhing under the lash of constant squalls of wind and rain, the Reverend Bruce Gault, bare-headed and with his raincoat buttoned up to the neck, brought his old and shabby little car to a stop outside Medlar Cottage and, extricating his long legs and bending low to avoid the roof, alighted.

He turned to say to Yi Liu-ying:

"I shan't be long."

Janet opened the door to him and said when she saw him:

"Oh!"

"Good evening," he said coldly. "Is your father at home, please?"

"Yes, rector." She smiled bravely. "Do come in."

She took him into the front room, then went up to inform Mr. Micheldever, who was loath to receive this visitor, yet could find no polite excuse to send him away.

"I will see him here, Janet," he decided. "Be good enough to show him up."

This she did, and left them alone together.

"I've ventured to call," said Gault as he took the offered chair, "because I want you to know, sir, how deeply I feel for you and your wife."

"Thank you," replied Mr. Micheldever, trying to keep his voice steady. "It is indeed a calamitous blow. While confessing that our son has always been of a—ah—wayward disposition, never till now have I thought for a moment that he would do—what he has done."

Gault leant forward.

"I urge you, sir, to put that idea out of your mind. If I am convinced of anything in this world, it is that your son was the victim of circumstances—innocently involved. I refuse to believe that he murdered my old friend."

"It has come to my ears, Mr. Gault, that during this morning's proceedings, your Chinese servant made certain charges against my son. Were they true?"

"May I ask you not to press that question? Your son must be the one to answer. I've already rebuked Yi Liu-ying severely, but the damage has been done. If he hadn't spoken, the jury might have hesitated. I hope you'll believe me when I say that if there's anything I can do to clear him, I'll do it, even if—"

He broke off and chewed his lip. Then, with a sudden movement, he rose to his feet.

"That's all I have to say, sir."

Mr. Micheldever tried to smile as he too stood up.

"It is most kind and thoughtful of you to call. I shall give myself the pleasure of attending divine service at St. Anselm's on Sunday. Our united prayers will surely—"

But Bruce Gault was no longer there.

Janet emerged from the front room as he came down the stairs. He passed her with a curt "Good night," but as he reached for the catch on the front door, she made him pause by saying softly:

"I'd like to talk to you before you go."

With a little gesture, she invited him into the front room. He followed her.

"Please close the door," she said, "and sit down."

He obeyed, then said, his face stern:

"What do you wish to say to me?"

"Last Monday evening you made me a promise. Do you remember?"

"I remember."

"You promised you'd never be bad-tempered with me again—never be unkind." Her voice did not rise, but took on another quality as she added, every word as clear and sparkling as a cut diamond: "Ever since you've been an utter beast. Why?"

He looked at her for a long time in silence.

"Why?" he said finally, his voice no less harsh than before. "Your own intelligence, your own heart should tell you why."

He got up and walked to the window. Outside, the leaves, not ready to fall, were being wrenched from the reluctant trees. He turned back to her.

"I've no talent for small talk, for smirking civilities. How can I laugh and chat with you when ..."

"Please say it."

"No, it's better left unsaid. Yi Liu-ying is waiting for me in the car. I must go."

He strode to the door, opened it and went out into the hall.

"Bruce!" she called after him in a little pleading voice, but the only reply was the slam of the front door.

Confident that Harold would keep his word, Timothy and Dick gave him five minutes to reach the police station, then left the hospital themselves and started off for Yateham.

Dick had promised Janet that he would report back to her before he went home to Lulverton, and Timothy wanted to take him all the way to Medlar Cottage. Dick, however, insisted on being dropped at the gates of Chatthume Place, and finished the journey on foot.

He had his hand on the front gate of Medlar Cottage when Bruce Gault came out of the door. Janet, who had run to the window to watch Gault depart, saw them meet—one on each side of the closed gate.

"Good evening," Dick said with a smile.

"Are you Farringdon?"

"Yes."

"Then I want a word with you."

Dick was not pleased or impressed by the man's arrogance, but he managed to ask politely:

"You're Mr. Gault, aren't you?"

"That is my name. Farringdon, I've heard of your engagement to Miss Micheldever and I advise you to break it off."

"What the devil's that to do with you?"

"Shall I tell you quite frankly?"

"Do."

"I am a man as well as a minister of religion. I don't want to see her married to you. I've not told her, nor do I intend to."

"I must say," said Dick with a half-humorous grunt,

"that you're being very gentlemanly about it, but she was free to choose, you know."

"Will you do as I ask?"

"Would you—in my place?"

"Then I'll fight you, Farringdon."

Dick raised his eyebrows.

"Really? Swords, pistols or bare fists?"

"Comedian," rasped Gault.

He pulled open the gate, pushed past Dick and entered his car. Dick watched them drive away before, with a shrug of his shoulders, he went in to the anxiously waiting Janet.

II

If the most serious, the murder of Dafydd Price was by no means the only criminal investigation upon which Inspector Peter Bradfield was engaged, so it was not until the evening that he was able to pursue his inquiries concerning the walking-stick. He called first on Mrs. Steadley, who immediately and with certainty identified it, then drove with Emerson to Yateham rectory.

Leaving the stick with Emerson in the car, he walked up the short drive. The door was opened by Mrs. Yi.

"Good evening," he smiled, raising his hat. "Is Mr. Gault at home, please?"

She shook her head.

"No, he is out in the motor-car with my husband. They have gone into Southmouth to buy some furniture."

This suited Bradfield very well. He said:

"Then perhaps you can help me. Did a hawker call here today? You know a hawker?—a man with a cart, who—"

Mrs. Yi smiled kindly upon him.

"I speak English. Yes, this morning."

"Did he buy anything from you?"

"Yes, some articles which were useless to us. They belonged to Mrs. Donaldson. Mr. Gault asked her to take them away because they were not convenient in the garage. She asked him to throw them in the dustbin, but the men would not take them away. Before Mr. Gault went with my husband to the legal sitting this morning, he told me to sell them to a hawker if one came along. When I was returning from the village with the food for luncheon, I saw this man and invited him to call here. This he did and paid me seven shillings, which was two shillings in excess of the sum which Mr. Gault informed me to accept."

"The things were in a box, weren't they?"

"A large wooden packing-case. The man took the articles away in it."

"Can you tell me what they were?"

"China and glass, old kitchen utensils. I did not examine them all. When the man came to the house, I sent him to the garage, which is along there, while I continued with my duties. Then he returned to the front door and made me the offer of seven shillings, which I accepted. He handed me the coins, then removed the packing-case from the garage and carried it on his shoulders out to his cart."

She stood in the doorway, an amiable smile on her round, flat, yet attractive little face, waiting for him to continue. He turned and beckoned to Emerson, who got out of the car and lumbered up the drive with the walking-stick, which seemed a flimsy trifle in his great hand. Bradfield took it from him and, extending it on his flat palms, asked Mrs. Yi:

"Do you recognize this?"

The smile had vanished from her face.

"It was the property of Mr. Price. We of the mission of Haolaofen gave it to him. On the silver band is his name in Chinese."

"Was it one of the things sold to the hawker?"

The question seemed to horrify her.

"No, no, no! We would never dispose of it so."

"When did you last see it?"

"Mr. Price carried it with him when he went from here on the last Sunday evening."

"You saw him leave with it?"

"No, it was Mr. Gault who came with him to the door. My husband and I were in the kitchen. But Mr. Price was with the stick when he arrived. That I saw."

Bradfield was about to put another question, when Bruce Gault came through the gateway, followed by Yi Liu-ying. The police car had prevented them from driving straight into the garage.

"What is it now, inspector?" demanded the rector tartly as they approached the little group at the front door.

"This stick, sir. I understand it belonged to Mr. Price."

"That is so. Where was it found?"

"A hawker offered it for sale today in the second-hand shop in the village. He said it was included in a box of odds and ends he bought here this morning."

"Nonsense!"

Gault turned to Mrs. Yi, who repeated the explanation she had already given Bradfield.

"The man's lying," said Gault. "How could it have been in that box? He probably picked it up somewhere. Yi, do you know anything about this?"

"No, master."

Gault swung round to Bradfield.

248

"I suggest you see this man again and question him more closely. Is there anything else?"

"Is the garage kept locked?"

"Not during the day. I lock it at night before I go to bed—or my servant does."

"Thank you, sir. Good evening."

As the two detectives were moving away from the house, Yi Liu-ying jumped forward with outstretched hand.

"Do not take it away! Let us have it—a precious relic of our dead master and friend!"

"Stand away, Yi!" rapped out Gault, and with bowed head, the young Chinaman stepped back, his hands across his chest.

Bradfield and Emerson went down the drive. As they got back into the Wolseley, Emerson made one of his rare excursions into informed comment.

"Funny old carry on, eh, sarge?"

Night fell and the gale did not abate. Dinner at Medlar Cottage was another of those silent meals that were becoming more frequent than ever in that stricken home. When the dishes had been cleared away and mother and daughter had done the washing up while Mr. Micheldever and Dick carried on a desultory conversation, the young couple were left alone in the front room.

They sat side by side on the settee, Janet mute and abstracted, Dick humming tunelessly. There were no other sounds, save those caused by the wind. A savage gust rattled the windows and somewhere near, a branch fell with a splintering crash. Janet gave a little sigh, and, as if to break a baneful spell, Dick began to recite in the voice that never failed to send a quiver of delight through her—delight in lovely words said perfectly:

" 'O wild West Wind, thou breath of Autumn's
    being,
    Thou, from whose unseen presence the leaves
    dead
    Are driven, like ghosts from an enchanter fleeing,
    Yellow, and black, and pale, and hectic red,
    Pestilence-stricken multitudes! . . .'

"More!" said Janet. "'If I were a dead leaf . .

" 'If I were a dead leaf thou mightest bear;
    If I were a swift cloud to fly with thee;
    A wave to pant beneath thy power, and share
    The impulse of thy strength, only less free
    Than Thou, O uncontrollable! . ."

He went through it to the end.

"Yes," breathed Janet, and repeated after him: " 'If Winter
comes, can Spring be far behind?' When you say poetry
like that, it does things to me. If only . .."

Dick laughed softly.

"You've a disconcerting trick of leaving your sentences
unfinished. They hang suspended by a hair—like the sword
of Damocles—while I sit tormented below."

Janet swung round towards him.

"Dick, I can't go on like this. There's something I've got
to say to you. Do you remember what I said last Sunday
on the mill bridge—that love's a thing that suddenly
overwhelms you? That's what's happened to me—like a
flood that I can't struggle against."

He looked puzzled.

"I don't get it. What are you trying to tell me?"

"That there's someone else. I think you're quite the nicest and most charming man I've ever met and I've tried so hard to—be what you want me to be. But I can't, Dick—I can't. Something's happened to me and I'm frightened—frightened of myself. I'm like a bird hypnotized by a—"

"Snake?"

"I love him more than I thought I ever could anyone—and I had to tell you. He's so hard and stern and cold, but he needs me and I must go to him."

"Who is it—Gault?"

"Yes—and he's in a terrible state of nerves. He says what he doesn't want to say, and he's got to be untangled. I'm the only one who can do it. If I don't. . ."

Dick made a wry face.

"In one breath you say you love him violently; in the next he's a psychiatry case. Jan, darling, aren't you rather wasting your sympathy on him? I know it's second nature for you to rush to the rescue of the underdog and that he's having a thin time in the parish, but don't let yourself be blinded by sentiment." He laid his hand on hers. "Don't leave me, Jan."

"I must, Dick. He wants me—everything tells me so."

"Look, dear, this has come as a nasty blow, but let's both try to be sensible and not go into hysterics. I think the real trouble is that you're worked up over—other things, and not quite your own sweet, sane little self. You're too transparently honest not to tell me straight out, and I'm optimistic enough to think that you'll change your mind in a day or two. I'll go home now, shall I? A good eight hours' shut-eye may make all the difference to you."

"No, Dick, that's just putting it off—shelving it, not facing the facts. You must understand now. I don't love you as I love him—and never will. Oh, how I hate myself for hurting you."

She drew her hand from beneath his, slipped the engagement ring from her finger and held it out to him. He took it, then stood up.

"When you want me back," he said quietly, looking down at her bent head, "I'll come. Good night, little friend—not even a regular now."

She did not accompany him to the hall. He put on his hat and raincoat and went out to battle with the weather in the streets.

III

After the departure from the rectory of Bradfield and Emerson, Bruce Gault went into his study. Later he summoned Yi Liu-ying. They talked in there together a long time, and when at length Yi Liu-ying came out again, there was, though his face was as inscrutable as ever, a purposeful air about him as he went into the kitchen and pulled open the dresser drawer.

Only a miracle saved Dick Farringdon's life. Fighting his way against the wind on his way to the bus-stop opposite the Seven Stars, he was passing a narrow, fenced footpath between two front gardens, when a low and urgent voice called:

"Dr. Farringdon."

He paused and stepped into the dark passage. As he did so, the assassin leapt forward with knife raised, but before the blade could reach its mark, an ancient tree in one of the gardens came crashing down, bringing the fence with it.

Dick jumped backwards just in time to avoid more than

a glancing blow from a branch, and by the time he had recovered his wits, Yi Liu-ying had disappeared into the boisterous night.

Chapter Twenty-one

THREE QUESTIONS FOR SIR TIMOTHY

HAROLD MICHELDEVER, who had missed the opportunity of gaining a good mark by voluntarily surrendering himself to the police, was brought back from Godalming to Lulverton on Friday evening in a police car placed at Hartley's disposal by the Surrey police.

Formally charged with the murder of Dafydd Price, he was examined by Dr. Lorimer to ensure that he was not still suffering from gas poisoning, then placed in a cell, instructions being given that, as he had already tried to take his own life—Hartley had seen and questioned Miss Maybank—he was to be kept under constant observation throughout the night.

On Saturday morning, there was convened what is known as an occasional court, which lasted but a few minutes. The only witness called was Sergeant Hartley, who gave evidence of arrest on the coroner's warrant, and Harold was remanded in custody until the Monday week, pending further police inquiries.

By one of those happy coincidences that lighten all too seldom the load of a hard-working police officer, Tony Morris of the *Downshire County Herald* was in Bradfield's office at Lulverton police headquarters when Maisie Brown telephoned. He had been chatting with Bradfield on other matters and, though some feet away from the instrument, could not help hearing Maisie's high, anxious voice. She wanted news of Harold. Bradfield saw no harm in telling her the bare facts of his arrest and detention. Then she said:

"Don't believe anything he tells you. When he's had a lot to drink, he can't remember afterwards what he's done and what he hasn't. If he says he did the murder, don't believe him, 'cause he doesn't know. Please don't believe what he says—and *please* get him off. It means ever such a lot to me."

"We're doing what we can, Miss Brown, to find out what actually happened."

"I know you are. I know you won't hang him if he didn't do it, but everything's ever so black against him, isn't it? If only he'd written a little note."

"Will you say that last bit again, please?"

"I said, if only he'd written a little note—you know, scribbled it down."

"Scribbled what down, Miss Brown?"

"Why, that he didn't do it, of course. When Harold knows he's had too much to drink, he always writes things down he wants to remember. If he didn't do the murder, he might have written it down."

"He couldn't very well do that, could he?"

"No, but he might have written something else down—something that will prove he didn't do it. Yesterday I made him turn out his—"

She broke off. This was admitting too much.

"Please go on. We know you called on him at Pinehurst, if that's what's worrying you."

"There was nothing in his pockets to help, but he said he sometimes used cigarette-packets for writing on, and

255

he might have thrown it away, mightn't he?"

Across the desk, Tony Morris was signalling for attention. Bradfield placed his hand over the transmitter.

"Get rid of her," said Tony. "I can tell you something."

Bradfield removed his hand to say:

"Many thanks for the suggestion, Miss Brown. We'll certainly look into it. Good-bye. ... Yes, he's quite fit and comfortable. Good-bye."

He replaced the hand-microphone.

"What's the excitement, Tony?"

"I was in the Seven Stars at Yateham when Micheldever came in on the night of the murder. He was bottled up to the eyebrows and—"

"It's something new I'm after."

"Wait, impatient one. While Mrs. Battle was conferring in the back parlour, Micheldever pulled out a packet. There was only one smoke in it, and he chucked the packet on the floor."

Bradfield considered this.

"May be worth following up. Thanks for the tip, Tony."

"Not at all. Now what about giving me some pucka gen about the bacon racket. The guv'nor wants a leader on it."

Tony was given enough information to send him away happy, then Bradfield drove to the Seven Stars. Fate continued to smile upon him, for a careful search through the contents of the bulging salvage-sack in the shed produced the slide—that is, the inner part—of a cigarette-packet, on the folding flap of which had been scribbled with a pencil these words:

"Met Price Gave me 5£ Send him letter"

Besides this vital piece of evidence, he brought away

with him another empty packet of the same brand, and with these he proceeded at once to the cell in which Harold was confined, taking Sergeant Hartley with him.

Harold, deeply despondent, was sitting limply on a chair of such hardness that it did not add to his comfort. He looked up as they entered and regarded them with lack-lustre eyes.

"I suppose you're happy now?" he sneered. "Another feather in your blasted cap."

"The coroner's jury put you here, not I," replied Bradfield, then went on briskly: "Look, Micheldever, you've got to take my word for it that I'm not putting over a fast one. This may get you out of big trouble, so do as I ask, for your own sake. Stand up."

As Harold obeyed, Bradfield produced a pencil and the spare empty packet with which he had supplied himself from the salvage-sack. These he handed to Harold.

"Now write on that as I dictate."

"Which part?"

"I leave that to you."

Harold paused uncertainly, turning the packet over. Then, with his thumb, he pushed the slide out about an inch and flattened the double-creased flap. He looked round for something on which to rest it as he wrote.

"No," said Bradfield, "I want you to do it standing up."

"Carry on, then," said Harold, with pencil ready.

"Write this: 'Met Price

They waited while he wrote this down. With the second word finished, Bradfield started on the next phrase, but had got no farther than "Gave" before Harold stopped him.

"Just a tick. You've put me on to something. Please keep quiet."

No one spoke in the little cell while he stood with his eyes closed, the packet in one hand, the reversed pencil in the other, tapping with the end of it on the shell of the packet. After a silence of almost half a minute, he opened his eyes and said in a voice quivering with suppressed excitement:

"I've got it now! Don't speak."

He wrote again on the slide, then handed the packet and pencil back to Bradfield. The wording on the slide read:

"Met Price Gave me 5£ Write to thank him"

Bradfield compared it with the memo on the other slide.

"Do you always," he inquired, "put the pound sign after the figures?"

Harold Micheldever smiled for the first time that morning.

"You ask Tim Chatthume," he said.

Soon after this, P.C. Bristo called on Bradfield at police headquarters, having cycled in from Yateham. As Sergeant Hartley was present, Bristo was most respectful.

"I just missed yer at Yateham earlier on, sir," he told Bradfield. "I wanted to tell yer there's some funny talk goin' rahnd the village this mornin'."

"What are they saying?"

"Miss Frost it was what seems to 'ave started it—'er that keeps the sweet-shop. Last night there was a tree blown dahn in one of the gardens in the 'Igh Street. Mr. Jackson's it was, 'longside what's known as Elms Walk, which is dead opposite Miss Frost's place. When she 'ears the crash, Miss Frost runs to the upstairs window—and there was Mr. Jackson's tree lay in' right acrorst the Walk and the fence dahn with it. Next thing Miss Frost seen was Dr. What's-'is-name—Miss Micheldever's intended."

"Dr. Farringdon?"

"That's the chap. It looked to Miss Frost as if 'e'd nipped backwards aht of the Walk just in time to miss a real fourpenny one from the tree."

"Where's all this getting us, Bristo?"

"Give us a chance, Pe—" Bristo began to expostulate, then altered it to: "I was workin' up to that, sir. Yer see, soon as Mr. Jackson 'ears the crash, 'e opens the side door, and in the light from it—there bein' no fence nah to stop it—Miss Frost catches sight of the new rector's Chink servant doublin' away smartly along the Walk with what Miss Frost took to be a carvin'-knife in 'is wicked yeller 'and."

"Cut out the Fu-Manchu stuff."

"I 'ad a quiet word with Mr. Jackson and 'e said it was a carvin'-knife too. 'E saw the Chink with it, but didn't give it a second thought, bein' more took up with 'is fallen tree and smashed-up fence than with crazy foreigners."

"What did Dr. Farringdon do?"

"Miss Frost said 'e stood there for a tick, obviously wonderin' what steps to take, then 'e saw the bus comin' an' scarpered up the street to catch it. Well, that's as fer as the evidence goes, but there ain't 'alf some tales goin' rahnd, you'd never credit. Not only that, neether. They've got 'old o' the story abaht the walkin'-stick and it bein' fahnd in the rectory, an' if Gault's name wasn't mud before, it is nah—and in a big way. They're even sayin 'e set the Chink on to the doctor chap 'cause 'e wants Miss Micheldever fer 'isself."

"Any views yourself?"

"I wouldn't put it past 'im," Bristo answered sombrely. "An' with foreigners in the 'ouse, no knowin' what besides."

He seemed not prepared to explain or enlarge upon this Delphic utterance, so Bradfield sent him back to Yateham and went himself to the Lulverton War Memorial Hospital.

Dr. Dick Farringdon joined him in the waiting-room. He had come straight from the theatre and still wore his white operating-gown. His manner was abstracted, but he did his best not to show annoyance at this unwelcome interruption.

"What can I do for you, inspector?"

Bradfield explained his mission, then asked:

"Can you give me your side of the story, sir?"

"They're exaggerating, you know—making something out of nothing, in my opinion. I didn't see anybody at all—and certainly nobody tried to knife me. I was walking along to the bus-stop and heard my name called—a man's voice, I took it to be. Just as I was stepping into the alley to see who it was wanted me, a tree came down, smashing the fence and making me jump back. Then my bus arrived, so I went along and caught it. Do you say he was carrying a carving-knife?"

"Yes, according to two witnesses."

"Some people have sharp eyes, haven't they? Well, that's all I can tell you, inspector."

"Thank you, Dr. Farringdon. I won't keep you any longer."

Bradfield came out of the hospital and got back into the driving-seat of the Wolseley in a thoughtful and rather worried frame of mind. The day had begun well, yet it had brought him no nearer to the truth, and this new element—the supposed attempt on the life of Dr. Farringdon—served only to complicate matters. He had to confess to himself that he was getting out of his depth.

He started the engine and drove slowly down to the gates, wondering what to do next—and where to go. Then, on an impulse, he swung the car to the right and made for Southmouth-by-the-Sea.

It was only three miles by the main road. The day was dull and cold. The gale had abated, but everywhere were signs of the damage it had caused, and the English Channel was in a spiteful mood. Bradfield, however, had no sight of the sea that morning, for his objective lay more inland.

Holmedene, in Northern Avenue, Southmouth, was a foursquare, two-storeyed residence of pleasant aspect. Here lived, in semi-retirement, Bradfield's former chief, Detective-Inspector Harry Charlton, who greeted him at the front door with every sign of pleasure and took him into the comfortably furnished lounge, where logs flamed and crackled in the brick fireplace.

"Well, Peter," said Charlton as they took easy chairs, "this is a nice surprise."

He was in the late fifties, his grey hair brushed back from his forehead. His eyes, too, were grey—and if he looked ten years older than he had looked eighteen months before and had lost some of his physical fire, he was still of impressive appearance, his brain as keen as ever.

Bradfield inquired about his health.

"Much better. Jabbing myself with insulin gets a bit tiresome, and that hound Lorimer has deprived me of most of the simple indulgences of life, but things aren't too bad on the whole."

"Splendid."

"Apart from smoking, what I miss chiefly are the professional problems of yesteryear. Crosswords are a poor alternative, so naturally I'm very pleased when you bring your little perplexities to me."

"Who said I was?" demanded Bradfield, taken by surprise.

"Peter," said Charlton with a reproachful shake of his head, "you underestimate my intelligence. Although it's nearly one o'clock and you might have dropped in for a free lunch, I don't imagine you'd interrupt your day's work for a chin-wag with an old crock like me."

He settled himself back more comfortably in his chair.

"Now start at the beginning and tell me all."

Bradfield complied, giving a concise but detailed description of his investigations and the various persons involved. Charlton listened with only an occasional interruption, and, when Bradfield had finished, remarked:

"My congratulations."

"On what?" asked Bradfield, who saw little cause for felicitation or praise.

"Why, on your good fortune. It's not every D.I. who's lucky enough to have such a case. Most intriguing. Young Micheldever sounds a pretty poisonous parasite, but I think we can rule him out right away." He chuckled deeply. "I wish I could have seen Sammy Trench's face when he heard the jury's verdict!"

"He was livid. He nearly cut the inquisition to ribbons with the nib when he signed it."

"I'm not so sure he shouldn't have adjourned the inquest till Micheldever could appear. Still, that's his affair."

"How does the note on the cigarette-packet strike you?"

"Pretty conclusive evidence that Micheldever didn't

do the murder. He'd only one way of knowing what was written on it—and that was memory. The handwriting was the same in both cases, I take it?"

"Yes, after making allowances for the fact that he was pie-eyed when he wrote the first one, which is a bit wobbly. I made him stand up when he wrote the second one, to make conditions similar. The two notes aren't identical, of course."

"Which strengthens his case. If they'd been word for word, one would have scented trickery. There seems no doubt that he suddenly had a genuine recollection of something he had up to then forgotten completely, and wrote it down as accurately as he could remember it. The three points are there in each: first, he met Price; second, Price gave him five pounds; and third, he was going to write and thank him for it. The chances against guessing those three points and getting them written down in the same order are about a million to one. Then there's the pound sign—"

"Yes. He suggested I had a word with Sir Timothy Chatthume. Presumably it's an old failing of Micheldever's. Whether it is or not, it appears in both notes. From now on, I'm going to work on the hypothesis that Price gave Micheldever a five-pound note of his own free will. That Micheldever was grateful seems a little out of keeping with his generally shabby character, but we must give him credit for it; and if he was proposing to write and thank Price, it's not likely he knew anything about the murder."

"Decidedly not. His part in the proceedings was, I'd say, quite accidental—and very simple. He bought the bottle of beer at the White Lion, took it down into Dark Hollow, drank it on the footbridge, left the empty bottle there, met

Price somewhere between the mill and the stile, extracted a fiver out of him for old times' sake, met his sister at the stile, then reeled off to the Seven Stars. Meanwhile, Price had reached the mill footbridge, where he met—"

"Who?"

"Whom is more dignified, but the question remains."

They went on to consider the implications of the hat under the door.

"The natural assumption," said Charlton, "is that the murderer was in the millhouse when the girl and Dr. Farringdon noticed the hat sticking out, but I shouldn't lose sight of the possibility, Peter, that the hat had been carefully placed in that position to give the impression that the murderer was still inside with the corpse, whereas he might have been miles away by that time. The unlatched window upstairs could also have been prearranged. Was Farringdon positive that he heard someone up there?"

"Far from it. All he would say at the inquest was that he had thought so at the time. A thing that really puzzles me is the walking-stick. How the devil did it get into the box in the rectory garage?"

"You've no proof that it actually did. I know Mr. Nobby Clarke of old. He's a talented liar and an expert trickster. There's only his word for it that the stick was among the articles he bought from the Chinese housekeeper. He might have picked it up anywhere. If anyone in the rectory wanted to hide it away, was the safest place for it a box of oddments liable to be removed at any moment? Tell me again what led up to the sale."

"Before Gault—the rector—left with Yi Liu-ying for the inquest, he instructed Mrs. Yi to sell the box of junk to any hawker who came that way. It so happened that one did—Nobby Clarke."

"Then it was not unlikely that Yi—what was it?"

"Yi Liu-ying."

"It's not unlikely that Yi Liu-ying knew nothing about these instructions."

"Something else connects up with that. Yi Liu-ying was there when I questioned Gault about the walking-stick. I was strolling away with it after our chat, when Yi Liu-ying darted after me and said they would like to keep it because it was a precious relic of a dead master and friend."

"Then perhaps Yi Liu-ying can explain how it got in the box. A talk with Yi Liu-ying, kind but firm, might yield useful results. But don't forget what Bret Harte wrote on the subject. Now tell me some more about young Sir Timothy Chatthume. He interests me—and his fan-dancing fiancée."

"There's something definitely peculiar about those two. They were up to something on the night of the murder, but I can't find out what. They both admit they met Price at about a quarter to nine and that the conversation wasn't friendly. I told you about the previous to-do in the Empire. Chatthume's version of the Sunday night meeting was that Price called Sabina Danbury a woman without shame, harking back—so Chatthume said—to the Salome dance at the Empire. Sabina's version was that Price objected to their boating on a Sunday. The two stories don't tally."

"There could be a connection, though, Peter. It might have depended on the conditions under which they were boating. If I remember rightly, it was one of the warmest nights of the year."

Bradfield gave a long, low whistle.

"You've hit it! Gosh, what a scandal if it had all come

out! The headlines in the Sunday papers!" His voice dropped as he added. "And what a motive."

"Don't be too hasty in jumping to conclusions. I think that if this were my case I would look for the motive farther afield than Yateham. It's only a suggestion, Peter, and you can do what you like about it, but if I were you I'd go along to the headquarters of the Downshire Missions in Asia—they're in Holland Road, about three minutes by car from here—and make a few inquiries about the mission at Haolaofen during the time Gault and Price— and young Micheldever—were there. You may find out something interesting."

This seemed reasonably good advice, though Bradfield had hoped for something better from his old chief, so after lunch with Charlton and his wife, he drove along to Holland Road, in which stood Palmer House, named after Francis Palmer, one of the most eminent of missionaries, who had laboured long under the D.M.A. and in 1900 had been murdered and eaten by the Battas of Sumatra.

Though it was Saturday afternoon, Palmer House was open and, while the aged commissionaire plodded up the stairs with his card, Bradfield had time to examine the alabaster bust of Francis Palmer in the entrance hall, on the base of which was recorded the manner of his death—and time, too, to decide that, though it struck one as comical at first, with mind-pictures retained since boyhood of fully dressed clerical gentlemen in vast cooking-pots, such a fate was far from laughable when one really thought about it.

He was still pondering on this, when the Reverend Bruce Gault came down the stairs and went out into Holland Road without appearing to notice his presence in the hall.

Shortly afterwards, the commissionaire called down over the iron banisters, inviting him to step upstairs; and in a room with "FOREIGN SECRETARY" on the frosted-glass panel of its door, Bradfield was closeted for the next quarter of an hour with that helpful official. When he emerged and came down the stairs, the grim smile on his face suggested that those fifteen minutes had not been spent in vain.

As he passed the bust of Francis Palmer, the sad thought flashed into his mind that even today there were white men no less barbarous than the Battas of Sumatra at the turn of the century.

He drove straight to Chatthume Place, where Sir Timothy received him in the office. Bradfield came straight to the point.

"I have three questions to ask you, sir."

"Then let's have number one," smiled Timothy. "Oh, and by the way, I'm sorry I flew off the handle on the phone last Monday. You were only doing your job."

"That's all right, sir—and I'm still doing it."

"A warning for me not to be naughty again, eh?"

"I hope you won't, sir. My first question is about Mr. Micheldever. I think you've known him a long time?"

"We went to the same prep school."

"I asked him this morning whether it was his habit to put the figures before the pound sign when writing down sums of money, and he referred me to you."

"Extraordinary question! Yes, it's true enough, though he ought to have grown out of it by now. He could never see why, if you did it for the shillings and pence, you shouldn't do it for the pounds also. I spoke to him jokingly about it some weeks back, when I engaged him as bailiff."

"Thank you, sir. My second question is—er—more personal."

Timothy's lean features hardened slightly.

"Shoot—if you must."

"I'm going to be frank with you, Sir Timothy. The police are not satisfied with the accounts given by you and Miss Danbury of your meeting with Mr. Price last Monday evening. Will you please tell me what actually happened?"

"Inspector, the last thing I want to do is prevent you from finding out who murdered poor old Price—and it wasn't Harold Micheldever, whatever the evidence against him. He couldn't murder pussy. But this question of yours has nothing whatever to do with it. I'm ready to answer it, but I'd like your assurance first that you'll keep it under your hat."

"That can't be done, sir. I can say this, though: if it's not found necessary to use it in evidence, it'll be treated as strictly confidential."

"Well, then... No, it's too damned silly."

"Let me make it easier for you. Your story to me was that Mr. Price called Miss Danbury a shameless woman, and that this referred to her performance at the Empire; her story was that he objected to Sunday boating."

He paused for a moment, then went on, brazenly pirating Charlton's idea:

"I suspect that it was not so much the boating he objected to as the way it was done."

Sir Timothy looked embarrassed, then grinned awkwardly.

"Why should I tell you if you know already? Yes, that was it. Old Price caught us at the wrong moment and, being a prude of the first magnitude, swore he'd report us to the police."

"And didn't."

"Not as far as I know. He was murdered before he got a chance." Suddenly he saw the significance of this. "Good Lord, you don't think—"

"My third question, sir, is just this: Did you know Mr. Price before he returned to this country from China—that is, while he was a missionary at Haolaofen in the province of Honan?"

"Heavens, no! I've never been to China. The first time I ever saw Price was when he interrupted the show at the Empire."

Bradfield rose to his feet.

"Thank you, Sir Timothy," he said with a polite smile.

"You've told me exactly what I wanted to know."

Chapter Twenty-two

THE SABBATH BREAKERS

SUNDAY promised to be brighter, though it was still cold.

Mrs. Smart was, as usual, early at Medlar Cottage, and, as usual, full of local gossip.

"The things they be sayin', m'm," she said to Mrs. Micheldever, who was preparing breakfast, as she took off her coat and hat and hung them on the kitchen door. "Shameful they be. If there do be any comfort, it's that no one in Yateham thinks Master 'Arold 'ad any 'and in it."

Which was quite true. For all his faults and weaknesses, Harold was Yateham born and bred, and the village folk were ready to stand up for "th' orld rector's laad" against all comers.

Mrs. Smart went on to tell in great detail the things that had become common knowledge in the village during the last few days: of the walking-stick and the abortive attack on Dick Farringdon; and of—though this seemed to be entirely conjectural, or, at the most, based on the flimsiest of evidence—Dafydd Price's attempts to blackmail Bruce Gault.

"But that's ridiculous, Emily!" protested Mrs. Micheldever. "Clergymen would never dream of doing such things to each other."

"Oi do but tell ee what they be sayin', m'm. It were Mrs. Wilkins at the post office as started it. Week avore last, Mr. Price were in there buyin' stamps, an' 'im told 'er as 'im'd just been up at the rectory. 'Im paid for the stamps with a pound note, an' Mrs. Wilkins do say as when 'im pulled it out of 'is pocket clumsy loike, others coom ayoot as well an' fell all over the floor. 'Er said as a joke whoile 'im were pickin' 'em up as these bain't the toimes for throwin' money abaoot."

"There's nothing in that, Emily."

"Wait till Oi tell ee what 'im said by way o' reploy, m'm. 'Im said with a naasty laugh as there were plenty more where that coom fraam."

"I'm sure it was quite an innocent remark," said Mrs. Micheldever.

But she was not indeed so certain, and wasted no time in going up to the bedroom, where her husband was getting dressed. In a low tone, for Janet was in the next room, she told him all she had just heard from Mrs. Smart. He received it as she herself had received it, using even more forcible terms.

"Utterly absurd, my dear," he said, tucking the neck of his black stock under his collar. "I refuse to believe it."

"Andrew," she said, gently chiding, "you are ready to believe that Harold did that dreadful murder, but not that anyone else did. If that Chinese servant could attack Dr. Farringdon with a carving-knife, couldn't he also have murdered poor Mr. Price?"

"Hmmm," said Mr. Micheldever, taking his jacket from the back of a chair. "I must confess I would dearly like to think so. It seems more natural that those not of our own race should commit such acts of violence. My own view is that aliens should not be employed in domestic service in this country."

Seeing that he was undecided about his next action, Mrs. Micheldever took the jacket from him and helped him on with it.

"Thank you, my dear. I recall Lady Chatthume's horror during the war when she discovered that the young female from Austria, whom she had given a home, had a large portrait of Adolf Hitler on the wall over her bed. One cannot trust them. It may well be that Mr. Gault has his reasons for employing Mr. and Mrs. Yi.... Yes, I am quite sure he has his reasons."

Struck by his change of tone, Mrs. Micheldever asked what he meant.

"It would be unfair to voice my suspicions. Let it suffice that I do not consider Mr. Gault a—ah—suitable person to be rector of St. Anselm's. The parish has suffered sad deterioration during his incumbency. I beg of you, Mary, not to repeat this."

They went down to breakfast. Janet soon joined them at the table. She was pale and listless, as if she had not slept very well, and, as she picked up her knife and fork, her mother noticed the absence of the ring from the third finger of her left hand.

She made no comment, but Janet, who was not one to evade an awkward issue, said:

"I know we're all thinking more of Harold than other things, and praying that he'll come through this awful ordeal. In spite of that, I ought to tell you that last night I broke off my engagement with Dick."

In the past, Mr. Micheldever had been not a little bewildered by Janet's succession of men friends, so he received this news with but mild interest, saying:

"Indeed?"

Mrs. Micheldever was much more concerned.

"Janet, dear, do you think you're doing the right thing? Dr. Farringdon seems such a nice young man. I was looking forward to having him as a son-in-law."

"He's a dear, Mummy, and he took it like a sportsman. For years I've been trying to find the right man and I did sincerely think it was Dick, and that's why I got engaged to him. Yesterday I made up my mind quite definitely that, though he's very sweet, he's not the right man, so ..."

She shrugged her shoulders and continued with her breakfast. Her parents did the same until Mr. Micheldever said:

"Are you accompanying us to All Saints this morning?"

Before Janet could answer, Mrs. Micheldever said:

"But didn't you promise Mr. Gault that you would attend at St. Anselm's?"

"I did give him such an assurance. Nevertheless, I feel I am justified in changing my plans."

"Well, Daddy," said Janet, "you can do as you like, but I'm going to St. Anselm's. I think it's rotten not to keep your word."

"Janet," chided Mrs. Micheldever, "Daddy is doing what he considers right."

"No, he isn't. He's just being stupid and childish."

Mr. Micheldever's thin nostrils twitched.

"I am being neither," he said acidly. "We can show our disapproval of Mr. Gault only by stopping away from St. Anselm's. Had he not come to Yateham, we should have been spared the heavy cloud of sorrow and suspense that now hangs over us."

"Daddy, you're too absurd. You must learn to be more sensible, because, you see, I'm going to marry Bruce Gault."

"Janet!" cried her mother, deeply shocked.

"If he'll have me."

That morning, with breaks in the clouds allowing the sun from time to time to warm the red and yellow leaves on trees and ground into even richer hues, Bruce Gault conducted his last service in Yateham Parish Church. Few, however, of the regular tiny congregation realized this at the time.

And the church was packed.

This unforeseen development was noted by some with alarm; there was, they were convinced, mischief afoot. Some time before the service was due to begin, there came into the village from all around, men and women who had never before been inside St. Anselm's. Whether they had come of their own accord, drawn by curiosity, or had been regimented, did not emerge, either then or afterwards, yet it was a fact that not a few among this grimly silent congregation had brought brown paper packages with them to the church.

Grimly silent . . . They knelt, they stood, they sat as the service proceeded, but only here and there were voices—small brave voices—raised for the responses. The Confession, the Lord's Prayer and the Creed were almost inaudible, and only a handful of worshippers joined with the choir in the hymns and psalms.

Yet Bruce Gault went through it all, not the automaton Janet had seen on her previous visit, but a new man, inspired, aglow with a zeal and fire that so exalted her that more than once she nearly cried aloud for joy. Was this the other man of whom he had spoken to her? His voice, so harsh before, had mellowed, and in the Second Lesson for the day, the fourteenth of September, it rose in its strength to the same crescendo of personal appeal as inspired St. Paul when he wrote it.

". . Giving no offence in any thing, that the ministry be not blamed:

"'But in all things approving ourselves as the ministers of God, in much patience, in afflictions, in necessities, in distresses,

"'In stripes, in imprisonments, in tumults, in labours, in watchings, in fastings;

"'By pureness, by knowledge, by longsuffering, by kindness, by the Holy Ghost, by love unfeigned,

"' By the word of truth, by the power of God, by the armour of righteousness on the right hand and on the left,

"'By honour and dishonour, by evil report and good report: as deceivers, and yet true....'"

For the sermon he took as his text the twenty-fourth verse of the one hundred and eighteenth Psalm: "This is the day which the Lord hath made; we will rejoice and be glad in it." It was a magnificent oration and Janet sat enthralled, oblivious of everything else, even of the large, roughly-dressed man who sat next to her, his hands playing with the untidy parcel on his lap as he softly whistled a popular tune of the day, "Blue Tango," through his teeth.

As the service drew to a close, a restless rustle of excitement became more and more evident in all parts of the little church, and almost before the benediction had been pronounced, they were leaving their pews and crowding into the aisles.

Bruce Gault watched them go till only Janet remained, still seated. He went to her and she rose to her feet.

"That was splendid," she breathed, coming close to him. "I was so proud of you. Don't say anything now, but I want you to know that I love you very much. Look."

She pulled off her glove and extended her ringless left hand.

"I earnestly thank God for that," he said. "Now please do something for me. Leave this church immediately and go straight home."

"Why?"

"Those toughs mean to make trouble. They're waiting for me outside." He gave a low chuckle. "It's rather like being back in Red China, only not quite so terrifying. Now do as I ask, please, and leave here at once."

He left her and went into the vestry to remove his surplice. When he came back, she was still where he left her.

"I asked you to go," he said gently. "You're not safe while you're with me. Please go."

"Bruce, dear, I know where my place is from now onward, and that's by your side. Let's face them together, shall we?"

"No, you wait in here until the excitement's over."

Too swiftly for her to overtake him he strode to the door and went out through the porch. As he came out into the open, a voice shouted.

"Murderer!"

There was instant turmoil, with more shouting and wild accusations, and from left and right came missiles proper to such a rabble: decaying vegetables, rotten eggs, garbage of all kinds. Swiftly Bruce Gault was soiled from head to foot, but he did not flinch, keeping a straight course to the lych-gate. Before he reached it, Janet caught him up and slid her arm into his. This did not deter the attackers, who kept up the bombardment, and there was much raucous laughter when a tomato caught Janet on the cheek and burst.

"Oh, dear, no," said Gault softly.

Moving with a rapidity that took this assailant by surprise, he went up to him and, with a beautifully neat upper-cut, sent him reeling backwards into the hedge.

This angered the mob. Thrusting Janet aside, they closed in on Gault, one of them with a rope, and soon pinioned him.

"Take him to the mill!" came the shouted order.

They jostled him through the lych-gate and along Church Lane towards the stile. Janet tried to follow, but hands prevented her—the friendly hands of old Tom Smart.

"Naw, Miss Janet. Ee'd best not go. Oi'll taake ee 'ome. That'll be best place fer ee."

Janet tried to shake off his kindly grip on her arm.

"Tom, please let me go! He needs me! They'll kill him!"

"They'll naw do thaat, Miss Janet," said Tom soothingly. "Just their 'oigh spirits, loike. Coom on wi' ee."

She allowed herself to be led away in the opposite direction to that taken by the crowd. As they turned from Church Lane into the High Street, they saw Dick Farringdon.

"Dick," said Janet urgently, "please help us! A gang of hooligans have tied up the rector and taken him to the mill. I don't know what they're going to do with him. Can you do something to stop them?"

"I'll try," he said and ran off, calling over his shoulder: "You phone the police."

But word of these disturbances travels quickly and the police already knew. Bradfield and others were on their way from Lulverton.

At Dark Hollow mill, the ringleaders had stopped the

wheel by opening the sluice-gate of the spill-way, had spread-eagled Gault by lashing his wrists and ankles to two of the great spokes of the wheel, and had restarted it by closing the sluice-gate. As the wheel turned with gathering speed, Gault was upside-down once in every revolution, and then his head was under water.

When the wheel brought him upright again, each time there were cries of:

"Murderer!"

"Confess!"

"Who killed Price?"

"Murderer!"

Tight-lipped, he took his punishment without words or flinching.

"Confess!"

"You'll stay there till you do!"

"You murdering—, confess!"

Gault's head was beginning to swim, and soon he might lose consciousness. Then above the hubbub and accusing shouts rose a voice that drowned all the rest.

"Stop, you damned, blasted fools! You'll drown him! He didn't kill Price! I did! Stop the thing, for God's sake! I killed Price, I tell you!"

Those crowded below looked up to the man yelling down at them from the top of the stone steps. It was Dr. Dick Farringdon.

Inspector Bradfield came up behind him and took him by the arm. Hartley opened the sluice-gate and the wheel slowed down. Uniformed police constables, with truncheons drawn, closed in on the disturbers of the Sabbath.

Chapter Twenty-three

EMERSON HAS THE LAST WORD

"TAN-PAI *t'an-pai*—that's how the Chinese put it," said Bruce Gault.

"What does it mean?" Janet asked.

"Literally, 'Open clean' repeated for emphasis, a way they have in China. In other words: 'Come clean! Open up! Confess!'"

He laughed shortly.

"I never thought the lads of the village would do the same to me in sleepy Yateham as the People's Commissars did to me in Haolaofen—try to force me to admit to something I hadn't done."

It was the Sunday evening and they were in Medlar Cottage. Mr. Micheldever, now full of sympathy and gratitude, had offered to take the evening service at St. Anselm's, and was at that moment preaching on the not inappropriate text: "And Gallio cared for none of those things."

Janet said in a voice that shook a little:

"It was a dreadful shock to hear that Dick did the murder. I couldn't believe it at first."

"I haven't been able to say it before, but I can say it now. Farringdon has good looks, intelligence and not a few virtues, but there's a bad streak in him. You can imagine how I felt when I heard you were engaged. I warned him to keep away from you, but could not come to you and tell you the truth about him. I'm glad he had the courage to break off the engagement."

"He didn't—I did. I knew there was only one man for Janet Micheldever—the wicked ogre of St. Anselm's."

"Wicked ogre's right. I'll try to reform. And why not? Everything's different now."

"Prove it," said Janet firmly.

He did his best.

"It's funny kissing a man with a beard," she said at length.

"Not too unpleasant, I hope? It makes me look like some sinister Spanish grandee, but it was rather forced upon me. My face is—well, a bit of a mess. The Reds weren't very kind to me."

She gave a little cry of distress.

"Did Dick...? Was he...?"

"I'm afraid he was partly responsible. He couldn't have really known what the consequences might be. I'd better tell you how he came into it. Not long after your brother left us and went to Nanking, Farringdon joined us at Haolaofen. He, too, had a beard in those days, as many ex-Navy men do. He was with us for some months as what is known in missionary circles as 'medical.' Then the Communists came in, and the three of us—he, Dafydd Price and I—were virtually prisoners. An old Chinese Christian in another village some distance away was taken gravely ill, and when we heard about it, I got permission for Farringdon to visit him and see whether he could do anything for him. Farringdon went off under an armed guard—a soldier—and took with him one of our Chinese servants, Yi Cheng, the father of Yi Liu-ying. Instead of coming back to us at Haolaofen, Farringdon clubbed the soldier to death with the man's own rifle, then shot Yi Cheng through the head. He made his escape to territory still in the hands of the Nationalists under Chiang Kai-shek. This made things very—awkward for Dafydd and myself; the Chinese Communists don't readily forgive little tricks of that kind."

"How terrible!"

They sat together without speaking for some moments before Janet asked:

"Did Yi Liu-ying really try to kill Dick on Friday evening?"

"I'm certain he did, but he won't admit it. I'd had a long chat with him earlier in the evening, urging him not to do anything rash. A waste of breath. All he wanted to do was revenge himself on Farringdon for killing his father."

And for seducing his sister, but Bruce Gault preferred that Janet should not know about Hsi-lo.

"The Chinese are curious people," he went on. "Do you know that Yi Liu-ying actually saw Farringdon attack Dafydd with the beer-bottle?"

"No!"

"Yes, he did. He told me so on Friday evening."

"Why didn't he inform the police?"

"As I said, the Chinese are curious people. Their minds don't work in the same way as ours do. Yi Liu-ying admitted to me quite openly—"

He broke off.

"Do go on."

"What I was going to say would pain you. It concerns your brother."

"Say it. I want to hear everything."

"Well, Yi had a grievance against your brother. As soon

as he heard that he was wanted by the police in connection with the murder, he decided to keep his mouth shut."

"What a horrible idea!"

"Farringdon was Yi's own personal prey. He didn't want the processes of the law to deprive him of his private vengeance. The way he looked at it was that if he disposed of Farringdon and the law disposed of your brother, honour would be satisfied. Loss of face means a great deal to the Chinese. . . . I'm sorry to put this all so brutally, dear, but you wanted to know."

He continued after a pause.

"A thing that might have got some of us into serious trouble with the police was poor Dafydd's walking-stick. That was Yi's doing. When Dafydd left the rectory that evening, Yi followed him. Why? I don't know. He's extremely vague. I do recall that Dafydd and I had been talking together in my study about Haolaofen. He told me some unpleasant facts that I did not know before, and I've a suspicion that Yi eavesdropped, then went after Dafydd to get some more information out of my hearing. According to Yi, Dafydd came face to face with Farringdon on the bridge, where Farringdon was waiting for you."

Another little cry came from Janet.

"Though he'd shaved off his beard, he was immediately recognized by Dafydd, who said he was going to expose him publicly. The bottle left by your brother was standing on the top rail. In a burst of desperation or anger, Farringdon picked it up and struck Dafydd on the head with it. Dafydd fell. Yi saw all this from the footpath leading to the bridge. Then the old man who looked after the mill came along with a lantern. Farringdon carried the unconscious Dafydd down the steps into the yard, leaving the stick lying on the floor of the bridge. Yi had a deep interest in that stick; he and the other Christians at Haolaofen had presented it to Dafydd. If Dafydd had no further use for it, Yi was going to have it, so he brought it away with him and hid it in the garage of the rectory—not in the box of oddments, but somewhere else in the garage. The hawker undoubtedly stole it."

"You know," said Janet, "I just can't credit that all that really happened. It could only have been a few minutes after the scene on the footbridge that I reached it myself. Dick wasn't there, so I walked on and met him. He arrived rather breathless and apologized for being late."

"A trick, I fear. Yi missed that part. The old man couldn't have noticed the stick lying on the bridge. When he had gone down the steps with his lamp and bucket, Yi crept on to the bridge, picked up the stick and withdrew to his previous position. The old man came away from the millhouse, leaving the door unlocked. Yi saw Farringdon carry Price in and close the door behind him. As he waited to see what happened, you came along, across the yard and up the steps. We heard at the inquest about the open window upstairs. I imagine that Farringdon must have heard you coming, escaped through the window and, after a suitable lapse of time, came back again to the mill, giving you the impression that this was his first appearance. In case he'd left any traces upstairs, he went up once more in your presence. That's the whole explanation, I think."

He rose to his feet and paced the room, which did not seem large enough for the purpose.

"Now we'll talk of ourselves, shall we?" he suggested. "First a quite important question: Will you be my wife?"

"Of course I will, dear, but do you think you could behave a little less like an admiral on the quarter-deck?"

He came and sat down by her side.

"Let me tell you," he said very seriously, "what marriage with me will entail. Yateham suffocates me. I can stand it no longer. If I have a mission in life—and I feel I have—it's not among my own people. I've been too long away from England ever to settle down in it until I'm too old to do anything else. The people irritate me—make me impatient—an uncouth boor. I'm wasting my time here. The bishop knows my views. Even though Yateham may now accept me, I've no wish to be accepted. Yesterday afternoon, I agreed to go to Burma under the Downshire Missions in Asia. I thought I should be going alone."

"Not now."

"Then you'll come with me?"

"I'll live with you anywhere in the world—except Yateham." And, in due season, now man and wife, they sailed.

There must be a closing sentence to every narrative. This one can well be left to that young giant, Detective-Constable Emerson. He had been listening to Bradfield's informal report on the case to Charlton, at the close of which Bradfield said:

"I got a signed statement from Yi Liu-ying, and Farringdon refuses to plead anything but guilty, though he says he didn't intend to murder Price in the first instance, but hit him with the bottle to put an end to his noisy accusations. He admits that he deliberately murdered Price by drowning him in the sump.'

Emerson's summing up was a long time coming, but it came at last:

"And after he'd done it, sarge, you gave him a lift home."

THE END